LAND OF SMOKE AND NIGHTMARES

DAWN J BRAITHWAITE

For the lovers of darkness and magic, of petrichor and moths, of foggy days and full moons.

Sylphea

Swan Port
Pale Coast
Light Gulf
Whispering Bay
Mirror Light Lake
Dawn Strand
High Court
Light Spire Forrest
Illumia
Selene Wood
Fale Falls
Timber View
Gold Peak
Trade Cross
Rinnellon Beach
Sand Stone Port
Thorn Fort
Alcara
Glass Desert
Cailloch
Faespire
Hound Vein Pass
Eel Den
Frost Caves
Grimmerell
Under Court
Barrow Clay
Brine Bay
Rage Hollow
Devswillow Wood
Shadowmire
Night Point

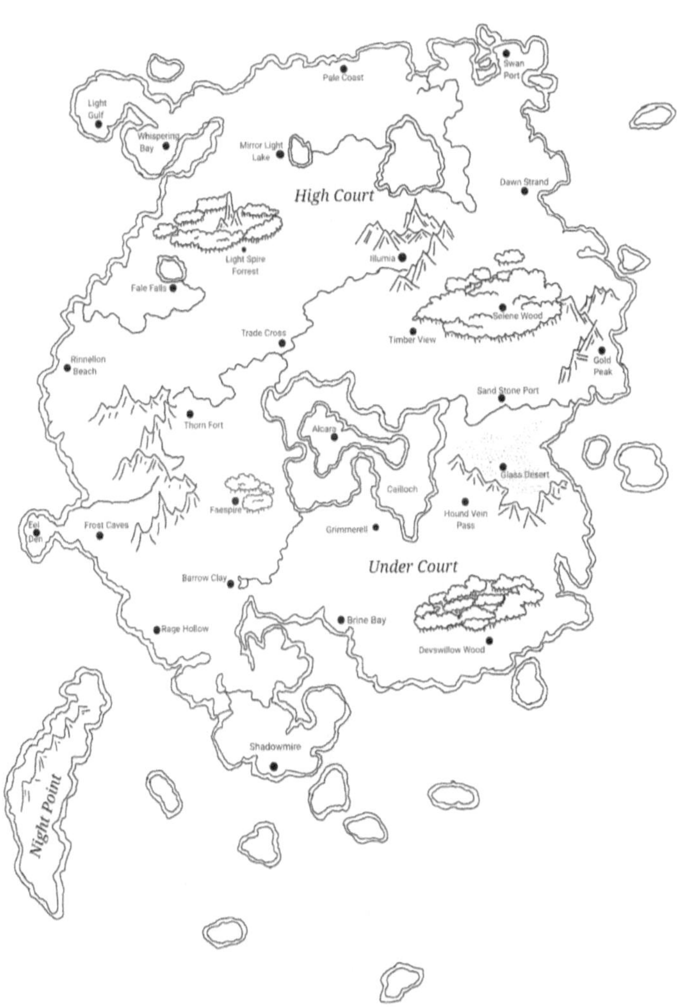

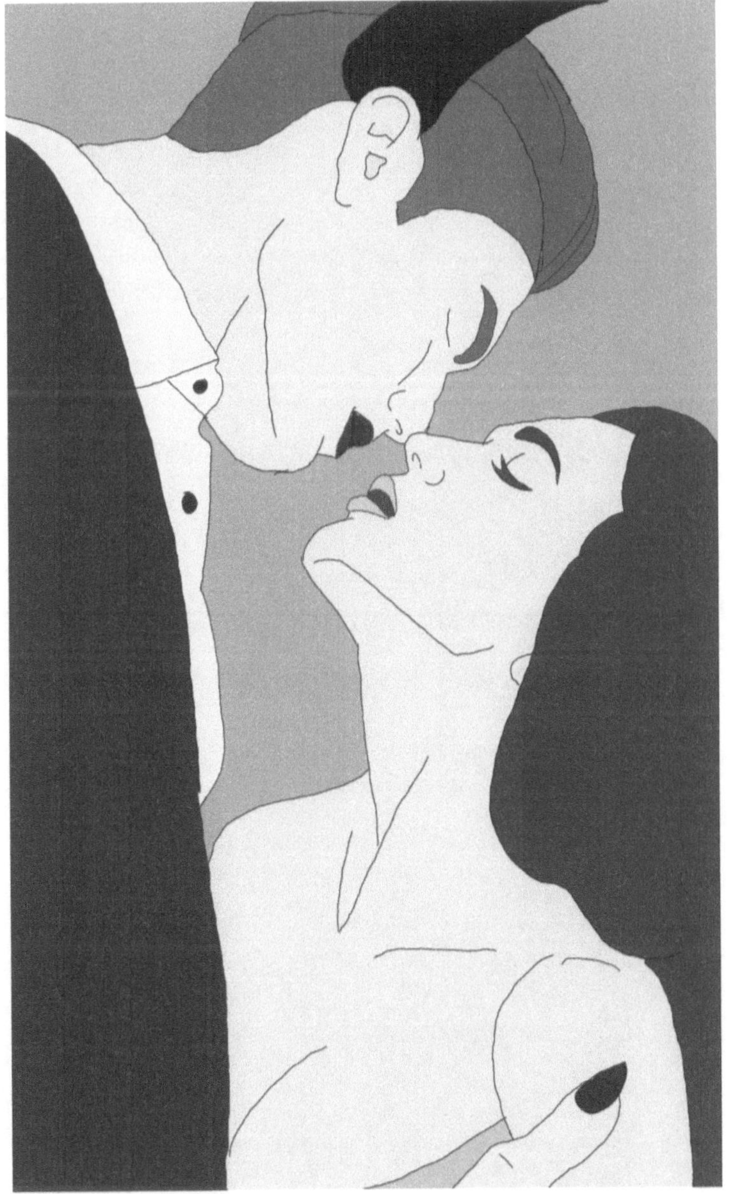

PROLOGUE

When you're in love, truly and deeply in love, it feels like nothing bad can ever happen. But that's what love is, isn't it? The great deceiver. We all forget the bad when wrapped in the thrall of love. We forget until something comes along to remind us. Something or someone.

CHAPTER

ONE

Imara

The damp evening air rushed in the carriage window, wrapping around the bridal figure leaning out of it to cool her flushed skin. She delighted in the icy sensation with every pore. Excitement, and too much wine, left Imara overheated after the reception. The prospect of her honeymoon had her stomach fluttering, her temperature continuing to rise despite the chill. She couldn't resist poking her head out of the carriage for a few moments of fresh air. For the thrill of cold air against her warm flesh. Pleasure was her only goal that night, and she intended to enjoy even the smallest of taste of it.

Her new husband's firm grip on her hand was the only thing keeping her from leaning even further out the window to bathe more of her skin in the moonlit mists. Lorn, her anchor and love. "Come back in here, Mrs. Cawthorne," he tugged Imara's arm with tenderness, pulling her back in the carriage, and closer against him. The water droplets clinging to her hair shook loose as she crashed against him. In moments, her drunken giggles were swallowed away by Lorn's mouth on hers. Deep, rough kisses that threatened to implode Imara's soul. If they didn't reach their destination soon, Imara imagined she'd burst into desirous flame.

They were breathless and hungry for more when their lips parted. Imara couldn't help the blush that crept over her cheeks under the heated stare of his amber-glass eyes. Even after many years of courting and waiting, Lorn could liquefy her knees with a single look. She couldn't believe she was going to spend the rest of her life with him.

Getting to the altar took too long in Imara's opinion. She had been ready to wed him the moment he popped the question after their short courtship over four years earlier. Their engagement dragged out across those years in Lorn's desire to provide a better life for her. "You deserve more than a carpenter can give you, Imara," he argued when he announced he'd enlisted in the army, an announcement met with protestations. Imara's insecurities ate at her at the thought of Lorn being away for who knew how long. Life taught her that time and distance were the best way to forget about people. So many lost interest in people as their world view expanded across time. She would have been over the moon for any life he offered to share with her, but Lorn wanted more, "A soldier earns twice what I do as a carpenter's apprentice. Let me give you a home you deserve."

"But, I only need you. You will be home enough." Imara's rebuttal didn't work. Lorn shipped out in the next week, beginning weeks and months of counted days until she would find herself wrapped in his arms again. To bask in his brilliant smile shining down on her and his love filled eyes looking only at her for the rest of their days.

The time apart stretched into years that were long and hard, held together by whispering pages laced with kisses and parfume. Words of love sent across continents. Prayers of desire between two souls meant to be together, glued with sweet tears. Finally, after a thousand lonely days, Lorn returned home. They survived the distance, despite the hardship of time and naysaying outsiders.

Lorn and Imara's reunion was chaste and short, their wedding thrown together in impatient haste. They wanted their lives to begin together immediately.

The wedding took place in a small stone church near Lorn's childhood home, a few miles outside of Ocean Fare. His parents, Gwenna and Draven, arranged the whole affair where every detail was sheer perfection. Pine pews, laden with garlands of daisies, daffodils, and blue ribbons, flanked the cobbled aisle leading to the altar. Imara wanted to pinch herself every second as she marched toward the man she loved more than anything. She wanted to run into his arms instead of keeping time with the piano. Her heart soared as she slipped her moonlight hand into his own midnight one.

From there the ceremony became a blur to Imara. It was made of fluttering wings and eager kisses. A too long reception followed their vows in the church yard, beneath the boughs of an old yew and an endless blanket of sky. The afternoon passed in hours of merriment and feasting until the fireflies began to drift from their daytime homes to add their gentle glow to the coming night. The whole time, Imara longed to whisk away and be alone with Lorn. Have him in every way, at long last. She was more than ready to be his, to consummate their long awaited marriage. Perhaps then her worthless fears would drift away.

Imara never quite felt she deserved a man like Lorn, like she wasn't good enough for him. He was the kind of man that any passerby could see destiny had great plans for. Tall and hand-some with wise eyes filled with determination. He grew up in a good home that valued hard work and loyalty. Gwenna and Draven were the adoring and attentive parents Imara had dreamt of having her whole life. They gave Lorn and his little sister, Nareen, everything they needed and more. Their parents instilled in them the belief they could achieve whatever they set their minds to, and more. They never questioned where they belonged in the world; never had to worry they weren't worthy of anything or anyone.

Imara had never been afforded that simple luxury. No one ever expected her to rise from the proverbial gutter in which she'd been born.

Her mother, Tilly, was a beauty from a poor family in the run-down outer reaches of Ocean Fare. Her raven-wing hair and rose kissed snowy skin accentuated her eyes, bluer than the brightest sapphire. She was sweet and naive, but prone to flights of fancy, her troubled mind struggled to separate reality from dream. Tilly was only fifteen when she became pregnant with Imara. She never revealed who the father was, only insisted she'd been having an affair with an angel. A man, gold and glittering with gilded wings who would sneak in her room at night. The angel seduced her, giving her sweet ecstasy night after night, until he vanished without warning.

Year after year, without fail, she insisted her story was true. Tilly repeated it to anyone that would hear it, and her family sent her away to Bott's, a home for troubled girls. Imara was born and raised in that place. She was constantly reminded of how insignificant she was, of her bastard status and her crazy mother. Everyone else looked down their noses at the poor little girl destined to repeat her mother's mistakes. Tilly fed her daughter stories about being born from her passionate love affair with a celestial being. Imara was her little Angel.

When Imara was small, before the ladies at Bott's tarnished her sweet innocence, she believed every fantastic word Tilly told her. What little girl didn't want to believe they were special? Especially when they lived as she did, looked down on with pity and disgust by the world around her. As Imara aged, and Tilly's mind spiraled further into her delusions, she saw the light. The negative things Agnes and the others told her behind her mother's back began to sink in. Imara built armor around her heart then, became tougher from their harsh criticisms. Became more rebellious. She came to think that even having inherited her mother's beauteous features, she wasn't special, and never would be, no matter how often Imara wished for it. Because of that, there was no reason to try to be perfect.

When Imara was ten, Bott's got a piano, and the girl got the first taste of her own magic. She found the one thing that made her feel as special as her mother told her she was. Agnes didn't let anyone touch the instrument besides herself. No one was worthy, or capable of doing it justice. Still, listening to the stern woman's fingers glide over the ivories filled Imara with enough peace that she didn't mind.

Soon, Imara found herself humming along to the music, then singing. She found her voice and fell deeper in love. She had real talent, Imara and music were made for each other.

Singing became her life raft, and she clung to it as tight as her mother's stories when she was small. Overnight, she had something that Agnes and the others deemed praise worthy, though that praise was often underhanded. "You'd be more likable if you spent less time mouthing off and more time putting your voice into something more beneficial, like praising our Lord with that remarkable gift he gave you," Agnes would quip, her face pinched with distaste.

"I'm not concerned with being liked," Imara replied, though it was far from the truth. Deep down, she wanted the cantankerous woman to like her, to treat her with the same respect everyone else got. She craved love.

That voice of Imara's, so pure and sweet, was angelic. It became her greatest blessing. After all, her voice was what led her to Lorn. That never would have happened if the ladies at Bott's liked her. If they liked her, they never would have kicked her out.

At sixteen, Imara was forced from the only home she ever knew. They believed there was no reason for her to remain at Bott's since she came of age to survive on her own. She had no impairments that warranted her staying. Tilly begged and screamed for them to let her daughter stay. Her pleas fell on deaf ears. Agnes escorted Imara from the home with only thin clothes on her back and a haughty prayer said over her head.

Alone on the streets, Imara spent weeks tear streaked and struggling on the streets. She often thwarted unwanted advances from strange men to save her. As the world froze over, desperation threatened to weaken her resolve and fear darkened her heart. She knew she would die in those gutters, nameless and unloved, if something didn't change.

Then her salvation came calling.

As she often did, Imara sang to herself on a piss soaked street corner one snowy evening when a man approached her. He was lanky, tall, and wore clothes that looked fine at first glance, but had noticeable wear on the second. "You have a lovely voice," he crooned from across the corner, then pulled on the cigarette delicately balanced between his fingers.

Imara's hand shifted to the piece of glass she hid in her skirt pocket for protection. She yanked it free of its makeshift holster and pointed it straight at the stranger. "Leave me alone." That shard saved Imara from more lecherous men than she could count.

His hands flew up. "I just want to help. I can offer you a place off the streets, for a price." Imara thought she knew what he meant. Men hardly offered charity that wasn't lust in disguise.

"I'm not selling my body, not for anything." The scenario had played out countless times before. Men offered young women the safety of a roof and the security of three meals a day, only to ask them to sacrifice themselves for it. No money needed, the only acceptable payment was in flesh. Imara hung on to a thread of dignity that wouldn't allow her to cross that line. She saw other girls give in to the temptation of warmer living, only to end up passed around, abused, and worse. She didn't want to be like them. Never mind the chances of getting saddled with a child because of it. That was the last thing Imara wanted was to become her mother. Alone with a child that the world looked down on. She wouldn't be the cause of a child's suffering.

"What about your voice?" he stepped closer, the shadows on his face receded to reveal kind brown eyes filled with intrigue set in an angular face. "Allow me to introduce myself. My name is Gio Sconza, showman extraordinaire." He removed his hat with a flourished bow, revealing a head of thick bronze hair.

Sconza. The name floating on the streets late at night. Imara heard tales of the nightclub with the same name whispered in the dark. Men and women flocked there nightly to be transported by the entertainment there. The place had quite the reputation, and that reputation was nothing short of remarkable. A den of decadent debauchery that rivaled any sordid noble affair, where fantasy came to life on stage through all kinds of unbelievable acts.

"How do I know this isn't a trick?"

Gio Sconza held a slender, long-fingered hand out in invitation, "You're going to have to trust me." At first, Imara had her suspicions about his true intentions for her. Besides the nightly shows, Sconza's was famous for having the most delectable and diverse flesh peddlers cavorting in the crowds. Yet, there was something in the man's eyes, a fierce sincerity that swayed her to believe his words. He only wanted her voice.

"I'm Imara," she said as she gripped his offered hand, changing her fortune. It was there, in Sconza's nightclub, that Imara finally found a place she felt accepted. A home where it was okay to adore the outcasts of the world, if only for an hour or two.

It didn't take long for Sconza to transform Imara from an urchin into a songbird. He put her on stage in between acts, at first. A palate cleansing performer after audacious feats. She couldn't believe an insignificant girl like herself belonged on that stage with the daring fire eaters or colorful dancers dressed in next to naught. She had nothing to offer other than a song.

Her first night, Imara felt made more of butterflies than flesh. Never in her life had she performed before so many people, let alone on a stage. With timid steps she left the cramped backstage in a simple woolen dress with plaid skirts borrowed from another performer. Nerves cracked her voice as she started to sing in soft tones. The crowd jeered in response. All those feelings of being small, of being nothing, began flooding back.

Sconza stormed on to the stage snarling at the disrespect they'd shown his newest attraction. The audience simmered as he calmed her. He kissed her brow, an encouraging gesture of care. "Close your eyes, Imara. Breathe and fly. Show them."

Somehow that small thing, that small intimate action, erased every fear in Imara's heart, and she began again. The unsettled crowd fell silent after the first notes and stayed that way the entire song, erupting in applause after. Imara's confidence only grew from there.

As requests for her performances grew, the number of acts

she performed each night did too, until Imara was a headliner. Sconza's premier chanteuse, his Starling. Even though she'd shot to nightclub stardom, she was far from famous, or well off. Imara didn't care. The adulation was enough for her to thrive on. Or so she believed.

Then one fateful night, as Imara sang her heart out on stage, she saw Lorn for the first time. He intrigued her from the get go, his eyes vibrant against his deep umber skin and powerful physique. The moment her eyes locked on his, she wanted something more than songs. When he appeared at her tiny dressing room door after the show, Imara knew life would never be the same. Her voice played for him alone, since.

He didn't care about the less than conventional upbringing, her crazy mother, or her job in entertainment. He saw her as worthy of his goodness, despite it all. She couldn't comprehend how she'd gotten so lucky. She'd never understand it.

"Are you ready for our honeymoon?" Lorn purred as the carriage slowed, breaking Imara from her past. His heated gaze melted Imara from her core, unleashing a tsunami of nervous excitement and sending chills of anticipation through her body. Soon, Lorn would have her in every way. She would have him.

Not giving in to their desires had been torture since his return. Lorn was patient enough to listen to her reluctant refusals every time they came close to crossing that intimate line. Every time Imara halted the course, leaving them both panting with wanting, their bodies aching with desire. Her deep insecurities kept Imara from giving herself over fully until they married. No matter how much Lorn loved her, she couldn't shake the small voice that said he'd change his mind if they didn't wait. She feared he'd leave her with child. Imara couldn't let a child of a man she loved so much be a bastard. A harsh lesson learned from Tilly; children were the ones that suffered when men left women behind.

Imara's lips found his in a wordless answer. She was more than ready to be completely his.

The carriage door opened, the loaned footman interrupting their moment. Lorn didn't pull away, though. They had nothing to be ashamed of. Lorn and Imara were bonded together as husband and wife, beginning their honeymoon at long last. The footman could wait. He wasn't needed anywhere for the time being.

Minutes passed before the pair came apart and left the warmth of the carriage. Near the carriage sat a log cabin, with a mossy roof dripping with vines of magenta bougainvillea and climbing ivy. Peeking around the southern corner were sprays of white climbing hydrangea. The windows were framed by cerulean shutters that matched the door, flanked by decorative shrubs and adorned with a wreath of wild flowers. The cool, crisp air, pregnant with salt and brine; along with the sound of crashing waves, turned the scene magical.

"It's beautiful," Imara gasped, standing on tiptoe to kiss her husband's stubbled cheek.

"General Price was kind enough to loan it to us for a week," the stars in his eyes sparkled as he revealed the surprise. Lorn's commanding officer had been more than generous towards the young couple, offering Lorn the use of his seaside cabin and carriage. He even helped Lorn's parents pay for the small wedding, since Imara had no dowry to speak of. With all his help, she couldn't think of anyone better to walk her down the aisle other than Gio Sconza, who declined even an invitation to the wedding. The brawny soldier wept at the offer, and during the wedding march.

Imara and Lorn walked hand in hand to the door. "I can't wait," she sighed. She squealed as those whispered words became an invitation for him to sweep his new bride into his arms as he opened the blue door before them, once again devouring her mouth with his.

The interior of the cabin held a single room, cramped with all the luxuries of any home. Central to the cabin sat a large fireplace, already blazing with a welcoming fire. A pot of something simmered on the iron crane dipped within the flames. The inglenook surrounding the fireplace hosted a striped settee piled with pillows and a woolen blanket, and a plush red armchair. To the right of the sitting area was an oak table with four engraved chairs to match, a fat loaf of bread and a pitcher of water lay in the center, surrounded by simple wild flower bouquets. There were shelves stacked with dried and canned goods on the other side of the table. Next to those, barrels holding fruits and vegetables. A door set into the floor indicated the presence of a root cellar.

There was a large bed on the other side of the room. Piles of plush pillows and blankets sat on it. To finish up the room, a side table topped with a ceramic pitcher and basin, a standing mirror, and a folding screen.

As Lorn delicately lowered Imara's feet to the floor, she spun around, taking in the space. The intimate cabin was perfect for a week of solitude with the man she loved. Her wedded partner. Her husband. General Price had set up this beautiful getaway with so much care. "I love it, Husband," the word sent warm chills through Imara, a torrent of butterflies made of sunshine. They were her favorite words that she ever said.

Lorn pulled Imara close, a seductive smile lifting the corner of his mouth, "I love you, Wife." A sweet kiss punctuated his statement.

Burdened steps shuffled against the hardwood floor. The newlyweds turned to see the footman and driver hauling in their trunks, setting them down with pronounced thuds near the bed. The footman approached them, wiping his hands against his trousers before pulling an envelope from the inside pocket of his jacket. "Lieutenant Cawthorne, the General asked me to deliver this upon your arrival here," he handed the package to Lorn.

"Thank you."

"If there's nothing else, we will take our leave. Enjoy your week, and congratulations," the footman bowed out, a twinkle in his eye, leaving them to begin their private celebrations.

Lorn turned the envelope over in his hands, curiosity furrowing his heavy eyebrows. "What do you think it is?" Imara asked.

"I don't know," he said and tore into the envelope, and a thin slip of paper fluttered from between the folds of the letter inside. He read as he stooped to pick up the fallen slip, his face morphing to a look of surprise. "He wants to promote me to Captain when I return next week, and has included a bonus with the offer. A bond worth 100 gold coin," he passed the slip to Imara in disbelief.

Lorn and Imara both knew there was no bonus for his promotion. General Price looked on Lorn like a son. He'd bonded with him with ease when her husband first enlisted, saw the potential in him to rise through the ranks. He did too. Under the General's guidance, he'd made First Lieutenant in record time. That was the real reason behind General Price's attempt to disguise another, beyond magnanimous gift. With the gift, their new lives together had an excellent, secure start.

The General's kindness brought tears to Imara's eyes. "That man, making me cry on my wedding day," she joked. Lorn kissed the errant tear away.

It struck the young chanteuse that they were alone, at last. Her heart picked up as a coy smile lifted the corner of her mouth. "We're married," she sighed, content and happy. Many people doubted the marriage would happen. Not because they doubted Lorn's love and loyalty. They doubted hers. An entertainer is no wife. *You know what kind of people she's surrounded by.* Those were the words whispered in Lorn's ears more times than he counted over their long engagement. It broke Imara's heart when he admitted to her what his comrades had been saying. That he never let those doubts get to him, that he brushed off every fake scenario they painted for him, made her love him all the more.

She had been more than happy to prove them wrong, too. Lorn was always meant to be hers.

"Yes, we are. And to think it all started with a song," Lorn hummed the song she sang the night their eyes first locked on one another. He stumbled through the tune, off-key and missing chunks of the melody.

She laughed. "Good thing I didn't marry you for your musical skills." Without missing a beat, Imara hummed over him, helping him find the tune until he gave up completely and she took over. He listened rapt and smiled, wide, beautiful and full of pride, as she transitioned to outright singing the song. Their song.

With perfect unison
   I would be queen
   Shook with magic
   If only he loved me
   Someone beautiful and true
   Suffering from grace

Lorn took his wife's hand, spinning her, and pulled her into him. With one hand pressed firmly on her abdomen, he held Imara close, her back pressed against him. Together they swayed gently to the song she sang, their bodies pressed together as though they were one.

I AM MEANT for queendom
A longing worse than a spell
A heart needs to want
Promises of time unending
Words of former sweetly said

HIS LIPS FOUND purchase at Imara's ear, trailing along her neck, her brain stumbled, losing the song momentarily. The path his mouth traveled burned beautifully against her skin.

EVERY BREATH VANISHES
Beat by beat
In the shivers of passion
His magic is cast
A force stronger than any
Making me his forever queen

SHE STUMBLED AGAIN when he moved to the other side, his hand joining the sweet torture and leaving trails of fire where they touched; along her shoulders, collarbone, and down the back of her neck where they found the silk wrapped buttons of the wedding dress. His fingers fumbled with the closures. He shook with the same excitement that was taking over her body. The song faltered in Imara's throat, dying completely as Lorn gently guided the gown down her arms and body until it pooled at her feet, leaving her standing there in only a thin, cream chemise.

Lorn's attentions stopped, provoking her to turn in time to see him removing his formal jacket and toss it to the floor. His crisp white button-down shirt soon followed. Delicately, Imara placed her hands on his perfect umber chest, sculpted by years of carpentry and military training. She marveled at his supple skin, the light patch of dark curls resting at the top of his pectorals. He was all hers.

She curled against his chest, warmed by his woodsy musk, and sighed just before looking up into his amber eyes, which danced with overjoyed desire. In a flash, his mouth claimed hers and his hands crumpled the delicate fabric of the chemise as he wrapped them around Imara; pulling her in so close no space could be found between them. The kiss, deep and passionate, was full of promises about the night to come. Heat pooled low in Imara's belly, raged for her husband to take her.

A whimper of protest escaped from her as his mouth moved from hers, only to disappear in an ecstatic gasp when Lorn's mouth began trailing along her jaw, down the lines of her throat and over the tops of her breasts. His hands slowly gathered the silken chemise, inching the fabric up over Imara's hips at a tortuous pace. Roughened fingers grazed over the exposed flesh there, eliciting a throaty breath to escape from her. In her growing passion, Imara nuzzled against Lorn's neck, her mouth whispering against his throat. The desires they'd denied themselves came knocking, ready to be unleashed. Lorn's every touch consumed Imara, lighting a new blaze that she would not extinguish. Not this time. Never again.

A sudden pounding thundered across the cabin walls, the door and windows vibrated from the noise interrupting their love. Lorn, his training kicking into gear, shifted into a protective stance as it continued. Glass and wood shattered, letting in dark black smoke that filled every corner of the cabin until nothing could be seen through it.

Dark laughter and disembodied chittering echoed off the cabin walls, neither quite human nor animal. Monstrous. What emerged as the shadows receded into themselves was worse. Figures made of the darkest shadow Imara had ever seen encircled the newlyweds, their eyes glowing red. Ten of them. Sinister gleaming weapons shone in their amorphous hands. The hate they emanated palpated the air. A coldness crept into Imara's heart despite the pulse pounding in her ears.

"Lorn," she stuttered, "what are they?"

"I don't know. Stay behind me, Imara. I'll protect you," he kept one arm wrapped protectively around her, moving his wife with him as he circled to see each of the supernatural intruders.

In a flash, their cirrus bodies shot towards them, more menacing in their unformed state. Their movements were unpredictable without solid bodies to track, and they came at the pair, swerving away at the last minute as if to taunt. Every time, Lorn punched at them only to find no purchase. At the rate they swerved at him, he was bound to tire sooner rather than later. If that happened… Imara didn't want to think about those consequences.

The shadows dodged and swirled around the cabin. All the while, Lorn tried his best to track their movements. His best bet, monitoring the silver weapons they wielded, his tracking paying off as a shadow brandishing a short, gleaming athame came in closer than the others. Instead of punching at it, Lorn grabbed for the hilt of the weapon, and managed to make contact. The creature let loose an ear-piercing shriek as it dropped the athame and retreated.

Lorn scrambled for the weapon. His effort rewarded with something to defend against the beasts with.

As if Lorn's small victory granted them permission, the smoky creatures intensified their attack. With unearthly screeches, they exploded to fill the room once more with darkness like no other. Unseen hands ripped Imara from her husband's protection, her screams swallowed by theirs.

"Imara!" Lorn called to the darkness just before grunting in pain. He howled with each invisible hit, his useless sciamachy against them growing weaker and weaker. Imara cried, thrashing against her captors and her eyes straining to see anything through the darkness gilling the room.

A sudden silence gripped her senses, a dreadful silence that held nothing good, she was sure of it. Soon after, the darkness began to fade and morph back into the bright eyed monsters. The natural light of the space, though dim, felt blinding after being encased in pure darkness. When Imara's eyes adjusted, she screamed.

The beautiful cabin destroyed and marred by the presence of those smoky creatures, every one of them brandishing weapons smeared crimson in their billowing appendages. In the center of the cabin Lorn lay motionless, soundless. His body was broken and bleeding, covered in wounds.

Imara couldn't breathe against the erratic stuttering of her heart, that drowned in a nightmarish scream of her own. Desperation surged within her and drove her to fight wildly against her captor one final time. Whether it was her struggling or that the beast let her go, she didn't know, but the moment its grip loosened she broke free and stumbled forward until she crashed to the floor next to Lorn. Warm blood slid beneath her hands and soaked into the chemise as she threw herself over his body. "Lorn, no. Lorn, wake up. Lorn, please. I love you, don't leave me." Her pleas were unanswered.

Phantasmic fingers wrapped around her arms again, dragging her back to her feet, howling against the tears that freely flowed. No matter how hard Imara struggled, there was no breaking free. There was no time to. Their clouds enveloped her into nothing.

CHAPTER

TWO

Imara

In the blink of an eye, the creatures tore Imara worlds away from Lorn and spit her out somewhere new. The scene at the cabin was a too close nightmare left behind for General Price's hired hands to discover when they returned for the Cawthorne's.

They pushed her from their grasp as soon as their clouded means of travel dissipated, sending her tumbling to the cold, dark marble floor, shot through with bolts of gold and polished to a mirror-like gleam. Imara looked at her reflection on the floor. The large curls Gwenna and Nareen spent hours placing in her hair were flat and mussed, matted with struggle. Her makeup was smudged, with streaks of black running alongside the tears that stained Imara's cheeks. The cream chemise she wore was torn and dyed deep crimson where her husband's blood soaked into it.

A fresh batch of terror laced grief coursed through her, unleashing more tears. Lorn was dead. Dead for protecting Imara from those nightmares intent on separating them.

20

She tore her eyes from the ragged image staring back at her and looked around. The space she found herself in was tenebrous and opulent. Everything appeared in shades of gray and black, some hints of oxblood red and aubergine in the decor. The high windows, glazed in gray smoked glass, gave no indication of the world beyond. The gloomy atmosphere felt heavy. It was grotesque and gorgeous in its oppressive coldness.

Movement shifted her attention. The menacing smoke monsters morphed, their amorphous bodies becoming solid. Their glowing eyes dimmed to orbs of yellows, oranges, and reds. Some of them had horns, any number of them protruding from their heads. Others had tusks or spikes. A couple had scales rather than skin. Imara thought she spied a tail or two. All wore scars that marred their strange flesh, painting them as fierce and lethal warriors. Their true forms revealed, while still not entirely human, were not as horrifying as the smoke monsters they had been. Seeing them in their true form, Imara knew that if this wasn't a nightmare, she was in real danger.

A glimpse of their bloodstained weapons, no longer brandished but held prone in clawed hands, sent her reeling back to the cabin and seeing Lorn's lifeless body. She shrunk further into despair, her heart breaking all over again. A heartbreak she'd never get over. The love of her life had been stolen mere hours after swearing his life to her.

The creatures all watched Imara with careful scrutiny, their unnatural eyes evaluating her. Appraising her as though she was something to eat. Their silent watch was as unnerving as it was mystifying. Not one of them approached Imara or offered any reason for the ambush at the cabin. They only stood in silence, waiting. Questions grew in Imara's mind.

Something about the way they watched her caused a change in her sadness. A spear of anger sliced through the grief, a fresh scar on her soul. A strange anger that only silenced the sobs, but did nothing for the tears leaking down her cheeks. "What do you want?" Imara unleashed an inhuman screech as these things looked down at her, her cry was high and warped with terrified grief.

Not one deigned to answer her, only shifting their weight and passing unreadable glances to one another. The inaction only infuriated Imara. She struggled to her feet and stood tall in the center of the ring they formed. The need for answers stiffened her spine. "What do you want?" She repeated, her voice shaking. Still, they said nothing. The defensive creature Imara became on the street before Sconza found her, came back to her. She circled, sizing them up, deciding which of them would have the answers, which of them she could pull answers from.

She froze when her eyes fell on one that fit the bill. A behemoth the color of decayed flesh with orange eyes. It was bald, save for the dozens of small horns jutting from its scalp. A scar wider than a finger split its face diagonally from the left eyebrow to chin. But it wasn't its colossal size or frightening appearance that made it Imara's target. It was the way it held its body, tall and proud; it had more air of authority than the others. Picking a fight with that one would send a message.

Imara charged at the beast, seething venomously, "What do you want?" Standing toe to toe with the beast, her insides quaked. Had she been in the right mind, she wouldn't have gone anywhere near it. She wasn't. Her anguish soaked brain needed to unleash on something. Imara glared up into its blank, orange eyes and narrowed her gaze. Like a viper, she struck, her hand meeting its face.

Nothing.

She slapped it again, and again, and again; each time demanding an answer. Its refusal to answer sent her further and further into her rage. With every hit, Imara's accompanying screeches morphed back into sobs. Soon, her attack devolved, and her hands pounded against its chest, culminating in shoving at the creature to get any sort of response. Her angry insanity deepened when it still didn't respond. Desperation drove her to more drastic actions.

Without thinking, Imara reached for the bloodstained weapon hanging from its hand. Either it didn't resist, or it didn't have time to, but she managed to disarm the beast. It wasn't until she held the weapon pointed at its throat that she realized it was the same athame Lorn had taken during his fight. "Tell me," she panted. "Tell me why, or I swear I won't hesitate to ram this into your neck." Imara didn't know if she could do it, no matter how much she wanted to. Still, the monster said nothing. It didn't even blink. Imara's threats didn't phase these monsters. She believed nothing would. Frustrated at the stalemate, she flung the athame to the floor with a scream before burying her head in her hands. It clattered across the room with echoes of metal meeting stone.

The air in the room shifted and the creatures snapped to attention. Peeking through her fingers, Imara witnessed the change in them. They lost the relaxation in their forms and they looked nervous. Whatever entered the room to cause their shift had them terrified. Imara didn't think she wanted to know what horror these monsters could fear.

She pivoted around to see what or who had these things on edge. Standing in front of a pair of sparkling obsidian doors that stretched from floor to ceiling stood a figure. More man than the shadows that abducted her, he exuded power; dark and haunting power. He had to be almost seven feet tall. Wearing only a pair of dark pants and a sleeveless robe made of night sky, his skin rippled with lean muscle. Long, sharp, shiny black horns rose from his crown of matching wavy hair. He had a god-like face, perfection in sharp angles paired with glimmering obsidian eyes. His full mouth lifted at the corner with a pleased and wicked smirk. He was exquisitely terrifying.

The sight of the man turned Imara's blood to ice. She couldn't move or breathe, or even blink. The absolute fear he instilled, gorgonized Imara. "Well, well," his rich, dark voice reverberated against the wall, "seems there's more fire hidden in that delicate form of yours, Starling. Impressive." He lifted a hand, decorated with black nails, rings, and banded leather wound around his wrists, and as he did, the athame rose from the floor and floated to his outreached hand.

His steps echoed like thunder, more evidence of the power in him, as he strode across the room, straight towards Imara. She wanted to flee, or cower, yet she couldn't move, as if enthralled in some trap by his presence. Every step he took galvanized the fear growing in her chest, filling Imara with enough dread to set her stomach in knots and leave her throat coated in bile.

Imara had to crane her neck to look at him when he stopped, towering over her. She swallowed hard against the lump forming in her throat. Up close, his fearsome beauty increased tenfold, sending her heart into overdrive, transfiguring it into a caged charm of hummingbirds; wings beating in desperation against their prison of bones to escape this predator. His large hand lifted, reaching for her. She cringed from his touch, afraid of what he might do; of how he might hurt her. Avoiding it was a wasted effort, though. His fingers, warm and strong, cupped her chin, "Do not ever fear my hurting you, my Starling; my chosen."

My chosen. Those two words clamored in Imara's head, hammers against steel. They were as close to a clue to why she'd endured such torment on a night that should have been nothing but pure bliss. Pure love. Instead, she found herself a widow because this monstrous man thought she was his. Rage simmered beneath fear and broke the spell on Imara's body, and she stepped back from his grasp, narrowing her eyes in a venomous glare.

The corner of his mouth lifted again, a light chuckle of amusement accompanying it. His lightless eyes danced with delight, raking over her body. An impossible shadow crossed his face when his eyes passed over her arm. Imara followed his gaze. There on her arm, a large, hand shaped bruise bloomed.

"Who harmed her?" his voice became almost too big for the space to contain, angry and full of catastrophic power. The man glared at the monsters that answered to him, a look that promised death. They shifted nervously. No one wanted to take credit. Taking credit for this mark meant having to face all of his wrath. "Have you no tongues, no honor in your vaporous souls? If you will not step forward, I am left with no choice but to glean the answer for myself."

He reached for Imara, his voice once more quiet. "May I, Starling?" He indicated to the mark on her arm. Instinct told her to hide the appendage from him. She wanted nothing to do with this beastly man, and definitely didn't want him touching her, no matter what his intentions were. He met her refusal with a snarl as he grabbed for her anyway, catching Imara's wrist when she tried to shift away again.

Imara fought against his gentle yet firm grip. "Let me go," her voice squeaked, though she knew it was useless. His strength outmatched hers, and likely outmatched any man's.

"I won't hurt you," he calmed, trying to soothe Imara with a gentle approach. It was useless to struggle, and she gave up the fight, letting her arm go slack in his hand. With a surprising, delicate touch, he flattened his hand over the bruise. He drew in a deep breath and closed his eyes, only for a moment before letting go. The moment he did, Imara cradled her arm against her body, as if to protect it. As his eyes opened, they burned with a dark fire. He turned to his right and targeted the creature there. It was smaller than the others, with enormous arms and hands that looked too big for its body. Tusks protruded from the sides of its mouth, set against scaled, sand colored skin. Its yellow eyes darted nervously, unable to look at its approaching master.

"I ordered you not to harm the girl," he snarled. The rumble reached his broad chest, making it all that more intimidating.

"Sorry, my Lord, it was an accident. She struggled," the beast whimpered, a wounded animal that sensed its end.

"That's no excuse," a threat lingered in the low tone he took. A flash of silver followed his words, leaving the sight of the athame's handle protruding out of the creature's skull. Its yellow eyes dulled and it slunk to the ground, oozing strange colored blood on the floor. "And you," he turned his attention to the beast Imara threatened. "You were promised a death. One much deserved. In one night, you allowed two humans to disarm you."

Without uttering a word, he called the athame back to his hand. It left the fallen monster's skull with a sickening squelch and left a dripping, teal trail of its blood as the weapon carved a path through the air.

The horned one the athame belonged to didn't quiver before its master. Instead, it remained stoic, showing no signs of fear; not even when the blade sliced through the flesh of its neck. The large behemoth was a good soldier and accepted death without fear.

"Orders are meant to be followed to the letter. Weapons held onto." The man looked to her, stern as a parent scolding a child, "Promises kept."

The remaining monsters replied in unison, "Yes, Lord Mallan."

Mallan. An ominous name to go with the terrifying man. If

she were to get answers from anyone, they had to come from him; and she wanted answers. "Mallan," his name blurted from Imara with a summoned boldness.

He turned his attention to his chosen, lifting his chin pridefully, "My name is a song on your lips, Starling," he kept using her name from Sconza's. How he knew it, she didn't know. That irritated her, as she was certain she had never seen Mallan in the club. Someone as unique looking as him would have caused more than a stir at the venue.

"I didn't say it to flatter." She squared her shoulders, fighting the nerves that made her want to run and hide. After his display of authority, the last thing Imara wanted to show was weakness. It was plain to see, fortitude and respect were the languages he listened to.

"I didn't assume, only expressed how lovely it was to hear."

"Why am I here? Why did these monsters slaughter my husband and bring me here?" Tears welled in her eyes, despite her best efforts to keep them away, spilling down Imara's cheeks yet again at the mention of Lorn. She willed them away with a deep breath, resolved to be strong. To show Mallan she would not be swayed or bought. She was not his.

"Because you are my chosen. We are destined."

"I was destined for Lorn. You stole him from me," Imara spat.

"Lorn?" he chuckled. "I saved you from real heartbreak. How long do you think your beloved would have stayed with you? How long before he realized he mistook you as worthy? With me, you will be eternally worshipped. No one would dare treat you like nothing ever again."

The words hit home, plucked at every strand of insecurity Imara ever felt; their vibrations waking the child in her that had been mistreated by the rest of the world. He knew exactly what to say to win her, or so he thought. Despite never feeling worthy of Lorn, he'd more than proven Imara's intrusive thoughts weren't reality. She shook off the feeling. "You don't get to say his name. You don't get to defile the love he had for me. Take me back!"

"Where would you go? I don't think you realize going back would not be good for you."

"Nobody would accuse me of murdering Lorn. Nobody."

"Starling," he clicked his tongue, "you don't honestly think anyone would believe a tale of monsters killing him, do you?" Her eyes widened at the hint he gave, "They'll lock you up, just like your mother."

Imara's thoughts narrowed with breakneck speed as his words settled. He was right. No one would believe monsters made of smoke murdered Lorn and abducted her from General Price's cabin. They would lock her up for that alone, even if they didn't accuse her of Lorn's murder. It was the one thing Imara fought so hard to avoid doing; becoming her mother. Imara let the one last fat tear escape her sapphire eyes, then snapped her head up to look him in his. "I hate you. You've ruined me."

"It doesn't have to be that way. You can stay with me, free from judgement. Safe."

"Your shrouded niceties won't win my heart. I cannot love you. I never will. I'll never submit willingly to you."

He reached out, then pulled back before touching her, the look of pure hate on Imara's face making him think twice. "You misunderstand. I would be delighted for our destinies to come to fruition, but I will not force you to love me. I am just offering you a place to live where you can be free. I will not have you unless you choose it; and if you truly want to return home, as you call it, I will oblige." Mallan kept plucking the harp strings of Imara's fragile mental state. This monster of a man, if he was even a man, seemed to know all of her darkest fears. He had the right words to make Imara question what she wanted; to go home and returned to Lorn's family. She wanted to bury her husband.

What he proposed, as unimaginable as it sounded, was perfect to keep Imara from ending up like her mother. That had always been what she feared most. The life Tilly had was no life at all. Even with as much as she loathed the idea of staying wherever Mallan had dragged her, Imara didn't want that life more. Shuddering with old and new emotions, the young widow blinked away her tears and gave in. "I'll stay," Mallan cracked a wide smile, revealing gleaming white teeth with sharp canines, but Imara didn't let him feel the victory for long. "On the condition that I reserve the right to ask to be returned if I change my mind. In no way does my choice mean I will ever be yours. Choose someone else."

Mallan blinked, lowering his head in a bow, "Whatever you desire, Starling."

Imara

Once Imara agreed to stay, Mallan showed her to the suite that would become her temporary home. A tense silence topped the uneasy accord they'd come to. Imara promised to stay. He'd leave her alone and take her home if she asked. That's exactly what she planned to do, ask to be returned once she felt it safe to do so.

Two weeks. That was all Imara planned on taking Mallan up on his offer. After that, she figured plenty of time would have passed since General Price's men found Lorn's body, and discovered she went missing. The plan was to concoct a believable tale from the truth, leaving out the appearance of her abductors and that they traveled by smoke. She just knew her new family, and the General, would see to it she was cared for. Then she'd find a new way to live. Perhaps she'd even return to Sconza's, the only place that made her feel complete before meeting Lorn had been singing on that stage.

Mallan led Imara from the room, exiting through the oppressive doors into a hall with black and white damask patterned walls adorned with fine art depicting forested scenes with mystifying creatures more terrible than the phantasms that abducted her. The dark marble floor shone beneath white tables topped with vases filled with dark bouquets; flowers in deep purples, reds, and blacks. A chandelier hung above the center of the hall, the crystals dripping from the golden branches sent light dancing through the room.

They crossed the hall to a foyer with twin grand staircases of marble lined with a rich velvety carpet in charcoal gray that picked up the silvery tones of the marble. Imara followed Mallan in silence up two levels of stairs, drinking in the opulent decorations along the way, and coming to a sitting area carpeted with the same gray from the stairs. A floor to ceiling window sat opposite the stairs. The smoked glass once again gave away nothing but night outside. Two overtly high-backed chairs in a rich mahogany nearly the color of blood faced one another, upholstered in plush black material that sparkled with the sterling studs set in them. Perpendicular to the chairs were long couches of the same material. In the corners were statues and tables with plants matched diagonally with their counterparts. Behind each couch were double doors, both ornate and glimmering in the firelight from the sconces that flanked them.

Imara shied away from Mallan's gesture to lead her to the heavy doors on the left side of the room. No matter what he'd said, she didn't trust him. He was the reason her world had upended and the reason her heart shattered beyond repair. The rejected gesture led him to step ahead, making it unclear to Imara if she'd offended him.

"This shall be your suite here at Shadowmire," he declared, as he pushed the doors open to reveal a suite that was twice the size of General Price's cabin. Imara had never seen such a large space meant for only one person.

The suite seemed a world apart from what she'd seen in the

estate already, the most notable and immediate difference being the warmth that emanated from the stone and glass pillar in the center of the space. Flames danced in the three-hundred-and-sixty degree tempered glass section of the fireplace, their seductive dance hypnotic. Imara wanted to plant herself firmly before it and soak up every ounce of heat it offered. She had to force herself to tear away from her need to do just that, and take in the rest of the room Mallan gave her.

The far wall was broken up by a large floor to ceiling peaked window inlaid with decorative silver thorny vines. A decorative folding screen jutted out from the far end of that window, its dark wooden panels intricately carved with swirling clouds. Above the screen, the top edge of an arched door could be seen.

A large four-poster bed flanked by smaller peaked windows sat on the wall to the left of the room. On the opposite end of the room, a small table with two chairs could be seen in front of yet another silver inlaid window. Various tables, in varying heights, dotted the room and were topped with exotic, dark flora in ornate vases.

Imara had never been in such a luxuriously dressed room. A small part of her wanted to dive onto the bed and revel in its opulence, a fact that made her heart twist even more than it already was. It scolded that small part of her, reminding that girl that once longed for a different life of the truth of how she came there. The beauty before her dimmed, tarnished by what had been done to her. By what she had lost. The gilded room became little more than a prison in her eyes. Another one of Mallan's disguised evils.

Mallan left without a word, without a sound, and Imara found herself alone. The anger holding her together had no purpose in his absence. There was no one to lash out on, to distract from the fathomless grief beneath the surface. She fell apart. Her body gave and fell to the shining floor as though she were a marionette whose strings had been severed. The delicate scaffolding holding her broken heart together collapsed, unleashing a swift tide of sadness. Imara let herself be pulled under by the rush of emotion so suffocating, so filled with torrential pain, it filled every piece of her with heavy emptiness. It was the kind of sadness that seemed to eat everything in its wake.

The feeling consumed her until nothing existed outside her broken heart, exhausted her beyond repair.

Dreams, dark and terrible recreations of the events before, haunted Imara's unconscious mind. Despite the horrors in them, she didn't want to wake. Waking up meant facing the even worse reality that they were real. Accepting that she hadn't merely dreamt of sentient shadows attacking her and Lorn, murdering Lorn, and stealing her away in the night. The monsters those shadows shifted into afterwards became tangible in a strange world where they served their master. Mallan, a name like bile on Imara's tongue, the man who orchestrated it all in the waking world. Facing that these events were real, meant Lorn was truly gone. That Imara would never see his strong and beautiful face again.

She dreamt of her wedding, in all its beauty. Every detail perfectly replayed in her sleeping mind. Until the preacher announced it was time to kiss the bride. As Lorn leaned in for the kiss, the second creature Mallan killed appeared over his shoulder and rammed his athame through Lorn's neck. The wedding erupted into chaos as the rest of the shadow men appeared, slaughtering the guests. Mallan then appeared in a puff of smoke and sauntered to the altar, that annoying smirk on his face. He took Imara's hands in his and came in for the kiss Lorn did not get. When the kiss broke, they stood before an assembly of his monsters, who were drenched in the blood of everyone in attendance.

Imara lay with her eyes closed, willing the dream to stay, for Lorn to be by her side when she finally faced the new day. Though her other senses wouldn't let her forget he was truly gone. The sharp tang of old blood clung to the surrounding air. The stiff, ruined chemise she wore was hard and itched against her delicate skin. It was enough to send silent tears pooling in the corners of her eyes.

The silence of the room broke when the door opened and closed, followed by shuffling feet. More than one person, or creature, entered the suite. None of the steps belonged to Mallan, that much was clear. He could be deceptively light on his feet, moved with the shadows. Imara tensed, closing her eyes even tighter. She didn't want to know who or what entered. The smoke-men were more than enough to curb her curiosity about who else lurked in this place.

After a few minutes, the shuffling of feet stopped. The door opened and closed again, then silence greeted Imara once more. Her body relaxed, but her unease grew. The intrusion solidly ended any fantasy she had about everything being a dream. There was no choice but to wake.

The moment her eyes opened, she regretted it even more. Her eyes burned like a desert. Every ounce of moisture in them had drained away in grief. She couldn't focus through the hazy film of dryness that blurred everything she looked at. The sensation only amplified the emptiness rooted in her core and branching through every vein, and made her head throb.

"Water, Mistress?" Imara jumped at the unexpected feminine voice at her bedside. She blinked hard, forcing her vision to clear.

A girl stood to the left of the bed. Short in stature, with chestnut hair and sharp green eyes, she exuded a forced sweetness; nice because her job demanded it. The girl held a glass of water in one hand and a cloth in the other. "Water?" she repeated, smiling to reveal gleaming sharp incisors set in her teeth. She wasn't as human as she first appeared. A closer inspection revealed missed details, or overlooked because Imara wanted her to be human. Her skin wasn't quite flesh tone, but a pearlescent orange, barely pigmented enough to see, and her ears came to slight points.

"On the cloth, please." The girl did as Imara asked, pouring some water from the glass on the cloth and handing it to her, and placing the glass on the side table. Not missing a beat, Imara pressed the dampened cloth over her eyes. The damp compress immediately soothed her scratchy dryness. "Thank you," she paused, not knowing what to call the girl. Imara removed the cool cloth and looked at her again.

"Fern," she offered with another smile. Imara returned her smile hesitantly, pressing the compress back against her eyes to hide the discomfort her slight otherworldliness caused. "Is there anything we can help you with, Mistress?"

There hadn't seemed to be anyone other than Fern and herself in the suite, leaving Imara confused and a little wary. Perhaps there was some invisible creature lurking somewhere in the room. It was an uncomfortable idea. She hadn't been worried about being spied on until then. "I'm sorry," Imara dropped the cloth in her lap and stared at the maid with wide eyes, "We?"

"My sisters and myself. We are linked, so whatever you need from wherever in the estate only one of us needs telling and the one most capable will provide." Fern's explanation fascinated Imara. To think as one, to know as one, held all sorts of potential, both positive and detrimental, and it didn't make Imara feel any better. Only one maid had to be near and the others would all know what happened; there would be no secrets with any of them. "Do you need anything else?" she asked again, eager to be of service.

Imara wondered if Fern's eagerness came only from the need to do a good job, or if there was some true care behind it. The maid certainly had a kinder demeanor than the monsters and their shared master. Mallan, the true enemy. There was no reason she could think of to answer with stubborn silence. Though Imara just wanted to be alone, she couldn't bring herself to brush the maid off. "No, thank you, Fern," she sighed heavily.

Fern nodded and dipped into a shallow curtsey. "Very well. There is food set out at your table, and when you have need of it, the facilities are through the door behind the folding screen," she pointed over to the other side of the room before turning to leave.

As Fern turned to leave, Imara realized there was something she wanted from the maid, her and all her sisters. "Fern," at the sound of her name, she paused her retreat and turned back.

"Yes, Mistress?"

"In the future, I don't want anyone in here if I'm sleeping, and I'd appreciate knocking before anyone comes in."

"What if you are not in, Mistress?"

"That's fine. I would just rather be left alone as much as possible." Imara was determined to stay in the suite, secluded away from Mallan and his monsters until she asked to be returned to Ocean Fare. Until then, she would be alone between those four walls, counting the days until reuniting with Lorn's family. Until she could try to pick up the pieced of her life.

"Yes, Mistress," she curtsied again and left.

Emptiness grew in being alone, allowing invasive, dark, depressing thoughts to form in Imara's mind. They sunk their claws into her and dragged her back into the folds of the over-sized bed she didn't remember getting into. Had Fern, or one of her sisters, or a group of them, carried her from the floor? The extreme highs and devastating lows of the day before left Imara too emotionally exhausted to be bothered by the unwanted encroachment of her personal space. Instead, she buried herself under the heavy blankets to hide from this strange world with no intention of coming out for anyone.

Withering away as Lorn would in the earth seemed the thing to do.

Lorn. As Imara's thoughts drifted to him, the rings wrapped around her finger grew heavy. They too grieved for their partner, attached to the hand of a man taken too soon. Taken before their lives together could begin. There were so many regrets tied to those golden circles, so many years lost and things that should have been. Most of all, Imara regretted their decision to wait until they were married to truly be together.

Drawing her hands in to her chest, Imara toyed with the rings, spinning them around her finger melancholily. Every turn of the cool bands became daggers twisting at the thing keeping her alive. It hurt so much. No pain had ever met it, nor would any pain ever.

Soon, the darkness under the blanket morphed into visions of Lorn's beautiful smile; his gentle and fierce eyes, flecked with gold and moss, illuminated the small world she cocooned herself in. Even there, in her imagination, his eyes saw her.

He'd always seen Imara, there was no questioning that. Beyond the bastard station and the glamorous song bird performing for dozens of men every night. Imara. The girl in-between those two things. To him, she wasn't a wretch or a trollop. She was Imara. His Imara, and he made sure to remind her of that with every breath and word ever sent.

As if his good spirit guided her away from the dark thoughts of his death, better memories flooded Imara's mind. Namely, the moment he first slipped a thin band of gold topped with a dainty gemstone onto her finger.

That night, Imara performed as usual, headlining after a string of performances. Lorn hadn't been in the audience, which laced her song with sadness. He'd promised and didn't show. Imara's mind went right to the worst. Something had happened to him. Even worse, he changed his mind about her, listened to the words of those that spoke against her and disappeared without a word.

Her heart was heavy as she bowed and accepted the tossed flowers from the stage floor, then left the stage.

As she made her way through the wings, a terrible caterwauling drifted from the stage. Though the words were unmistakable, there was nothing recognizable in the sound. Curious, Imara spun on heel and dashed back to the stage, halting just beyond where the curtains separated the two worlds. What she saw loosed a laugh from her saddened heart, which eased at the sight of the unexpected performer.

At center stage stood Lorn, looking right at Imara rather than out to the audience, who booed and tossed shot glasses filled with cheap libations at his terrible singing, showering him in an alcoholic spindrift. The onslaught didn't phase him, didn't pause the wailing song that caught his beloved's attention. He only smiled and stretched a hand out to her in a silent call to join him.

The moment she slid her hand into his, he dropped to one knee and stopped his song. The audience's boos turned to cheers. Imara's heart exploded, a vibrant warmth shooting across every inch of her skin. She had to blink away the amazed tears the gesture caused. In that moment, she didn't think she could get any happier, and then the actual words came out of his mouth. "Be my wife?" Imara's heart burst, too full of love to contain it, her happiness leaping beyond the boundaries of the stars.

Lorn had barely uttered the question before Imara gave her answer. "Yes," she sobbed happily, nodding her head as if the word alone wasn't clear enough. He leapt up, gathering her in his arms, and kissed his fiancé as if his life depended on it, deep and soul shattering. The audience whooped and hollered at their display.

Sconza's vibrant atmosphere seemed to shine brighter as Imara took in the club, amazed by Lorn's surprise and the amount of love that poured from the audience and other performers. Yet, when her eyes fell on Gio's lanky frame, there was little love there. His long face was etched with anger, his eyes full of fire and hate targeted on Lorn.

Days later, Imara approached her boss, "Aren't you happy for me?"

"Of course, my Starling," he sighed, cupping her chin. "Your happiness means everything to me."

"Then why were you so angry when Lorn proposed?"

"I just wish he'd cleared it with me first. I had no idea he planned to commandeer my stage, and I'm no fan of surprises in my club."

Tears Imara didn't know she had left whispered down her face. If only time could rewind, freezing that night would have been her destination. She could have spent the rest of her life with Lorn on that stage, safe, happy, and free. Together. Forever living somewhere between night and dawn, seconds passing like years. That was what life with him would have been like. Sleepless nights filled with love, tender and passionate with their bodies on fire as kisses became their only sustenance. Maybe there would have been children, beautiful children with Lorn's midnight complexion, bouncing dark curls, and, maybe, her cerulean eyes full of the magic that created them. Love. Real and enduring, and living beyond their parents to keep that legacy of love alive for generations to come.

Imara could see it all, what could have been.

The security of the blanket above her became suffocating as that future fizzled with her loss. It tore at the wounds Mallan and his monsters created, and deepened the already unfathomable pain in her heart. Something hotter than mere grief simmered and oozed from those emotional wounds, cauterizing the edges to keep them open forever. What she felt was an infinite heat, a million times more dangerous than a simple anger.

Throwing the blankets off, an unearthly scream shattered the leaden silence of the suite, sorrowful and feral. What was supposed to be Imara's future unleashed a monster of its own. A monster that wanted to tear down the gleaming walls of Mallan's home, and crumble every exquisite detail into the ash he deserved to live in. She wanted to leave him with nothing to cherish, just as he had done to her.

Imara trembled with the urge to destroy and surveyed the room, her mouth lifting in a cynical smirk when her eyes fell on the table next to the bed. The glass left by Fern gleamed in the low firelight, a fine sheen of condensation gathered on the rim. It was perfectly innocent, and perfect to start with.

Without another thought, Imara's hand closed around the cool glass and chucked it as far as she could. The glass landed with a satisfying crunch against the marble floor, breaking into thousands of shimmering shards. A perfect allegory of her heart, broken beyond repair. Seeing those bits of glass scattered across the floor, drenched in the water that once held by them, unleashed a satisfying rush that fed the anger taking over. Like lightning, it surged across muscles and through veins to fuel her rampage. Leaping out of bed, she sprinted across the suite toward the dinette topped with the tray of food left by the maid. Pieces of glass jabbed into Imara's feet as she went, but she didn't care. She barely felt the pain. Compared to the anguish that raged through her, the shards embedded in her feet were nothing. All her focus was on her need to ruin the beauty surrounding her.

She grabbed blindly at the offerings, hurling them sporadically at nothing and everything at once. The china shattering, the decadent foods squelching; those sounds fed the euphoric and rage filled trance Imara fell into. Her rage multiplied, becoming as insatiable as her grief with every move made. When her hand wrapped around a gleaming knife, a wickedness morphed her smile.

Imara dashed back across to the bed, knife in hand, and her mind separated from her body, locking her away from a true understanding of what she was doing. Though she was aware of the madness coursing through her wreaked havoc, her actions were so at the mercy of her fury that they didn't sink in. Before one act of destruction ended, another began and blended into a dance she'd never quite remember. Time was lost, or perhaps didn't exist, as she uprooted plants from their vases, smashed small statues against the floor, and tore pieces of art from the walls.

Soon enough, her rage ebbed, leaving Imara standing in the center of the chaos she created. She drank in the gorgeous ruin of the suite, somehow brought by her own hands, with smug satisfaction. Anyone looking on the mess would believe it was the work of some vengeful God, not a lowly human girl.

Smoke hung thick in the air, spilling from the fireplace. The glass once keeping flames at bay lay shattered, a stone vase dangled from the lip of its base. Remnants of something melted in the fire and filled the space with an acrid air. Blood and water decorated the gleaming floors beneath the debris of Imara's tirade. A watercolor painting of chaos. Broken dishes, shattered glasses, and piles of food were everywhere, topped with strips of fabric and goose feathers that seemed more artfully places than the random destruction it was.

It was a symphony, an aria, to Imara. As she stood there, feet stinging and lungs heaving, Imara's grief ate away at the remaining anger. She found she couldn't look at the product of her ire. It was just another reminder of what she lost.

She turned, rushing to the doors, intent on banging on them until someone set her free. As she shook the handles, it surprised her to find them unlocked. Mallan hadn't seen fit to lock her up like the prisoner she felt like.

Flinging the doors open, Imara stepped out of the suite. A chill settled over her shoulders, the warmth of the fireplace dissipating into the cold estate, bringing with it the smoke and smell of whatever burned inside it. The icy floor stung against the wounds on her feet, some still packed with glass, and every muscle screamed. Imara felt numb and too exhausted to go any further than the sitting area there. Nor did she want to. Not knowing what horrors lay outside the walls of Mallan's home was enough to keep her from attempting to run. Instead, Imara curled up on one of the long black couches, a wounded kitten, and let her weariness take her into a dark and dreamless slumber.

CHAPTER

FOUR

Mallan

Mallan chuckled to himself, lounging in his office as he listened to the ruckus coming from floors above. Imara's fire never failed to impress him. Nor did it surprise him, not truly. It was such an appealing aspect of her. Set against the frailty of being mortal and her beauty, that fire added so much depth and intrigue. Made Imara so much more than a pretty songbird.

His fae ears picked up every crash and shatter that came from Imara's suite. Each sound lifted the corners of his mouth more. Even if she hadn't been his destiny, loving her would have came easy. Her spirit matched his, challenged his own. One thing he knew for sure, things would remain interesting now that she was there.

Smoke drifted in the air, and Mallan shook his head. Yes, Imara would keep things interesting. He would gladly let her destroy everything, burn his estate to the ground just so he could witness that passion that fueled her every action. Rebuilding was nothing to him compared to having what he

43

wanted most so close. Besides, he had other homes throughout the Under Court he could transfer to.

The destruction above quieted, and Mallan once again smirked. His Starling must have tired out. She was only human, after all. That would change soon enough, when she came to her senses and chose him. Long had he fantasized about the day Imara agreed to be his, take his blood and venom to shed her mortality for the life of a fae and live alongside him for centuries to come. For when she stood against his enemies with him to conquer them and take Sylphea away, bring it all under the rule of the Under Court. All his plans would come to fruition then, and he'd have it all.

Mallan itched to sneak to Imara's suite and witness what she'd done, but he had things to do before he could even consider abandoning his office for the comfort of his own. The unfortunate loss of his goblin guard captain left him no choice but to appoint another. It was his own fault, he supposed, promoting Hersk to the role when he beat the previous captain during the winter trials. The goblin was far from ready to take the reins, immature and easily distracted, but he bested his opponent fair and square to win the role. His failure told Mallan things needed a shaking up, and old ways needed changing. The trials would no longer be open to all guards, only to the most deserving.

In the meantime, he needed an interim captain. The winter trials were too far off to wait for a new victor. It was the only reason he called the old captain, Braxar, to meet with him. Still, regret nagged at Mallan's mind the later that the goblin was for their meeting.

Without the distraction of Imara's tantrum tantalizing his ears, Mallan's patience wore thin. He drummed his blackened, sharp nails on the desk, each one striking in its own small dent created by years of doing the same thing. Braxar would get his role back, Mallan had no choice in the matter, but he'd do it less of a goblin than he was before. That would ensure the goblin wouldn't tarry in the future, and force him to work harder to keep the title of captain when the trials came. That was the price Braxar would pay for testing his master's patience.

Heavy breaths and a lumbering gait approached the office.

"Come in, Braxar," Mallan ordered before the goblin could even knock. The goblin shuffled in, letting the door click closed behind him, and stood before Mallan's desk with his eyes locked on the floor. "Eyes on me, captain," Mallan ordered.

Braxar's head snapped up to meet his master's gaze, a flicker of surprise dared to cross his face. "Captain?" He stammered. "You're giving me my post back?"

Mallan narrowed his gaze at Braxar's audacity to question him. "Should I not? It's mine to appoint how I see fit." He stood from his chair and rounded the desk, sizing up the goblin before him. Once a bulking and proud specimen in his prime, Mallan had watched as Braxar crumbled after his defeat and became the weakened and disheartened goblin before him. He would need motivation to fight for his title come the trials.

"Thank you, Lord Mallan," he tipped his head in respect, his slitted orange eyes meeting Mallan's as he righted himself.

"Don't thank me yet. You know as well as I that you aren't fit to be captain. The title is yours only because it was before Hersk took it from you. You are undisciplined, irresponsible. Lessons need to be learned." Mallan crouched eye level to the goblin and growled, "Place your hand on the desk."

The goblin swallowed thickly, and his eyes darted around the office. There was no salvation, no negotiating promises with his master, so he did as he was told. Mallan watched as his newly appointed captain's hand trembled on its path to his desk. There, against the polished wood, the meaty, mottle skinned appendage lay prepared to take whatever punishment he meant for it.

Mallan called his weapon to him in a cloud of thick smoke, an axe of dark steel, the blade long rusted with blood, and tipped with a sharp spike. He spun the deadly weapon in his palm, recalling every swing he'd made with it, all the blood shed for his queen and court. The corner of his mouth lifted at the memories.

He gave no warning before leveling the axe and ramming the spiked tip into Braxar's left eye. The goblin choked back a scream as he took his hand from the desk to cradle his ruined eye.

"Hand back on the desk!" Mallan bellowed, and the goblin obeyed once again, his bloody hand slid against the furniture. "That was for being late. Learn to keep your eye on the time." He gave Braxar no time to prepare or settle himself before his next lesson and, in one swift action, guided his axe to sever the goblin's hand. Blood sprayed out from the wound and splattered on both of them when Mallan removed the blade and left a deep gash on the desk's surface. "That is to motivate you to work for your title. You don't have a chance in Hell to keep it if you don't."

"Thank you, Lord Mallan," Braxar sniveled, knowing his master wouldn't accept anything less for the lessons bestowed on him.

"Now leave me, tend to your wounds." The order fell cold from Mallan's lips, he had no expectation that Braxar would work hard enough to remain captain after the winter trials. Nor did he care. Goblins were easy to replace and eager to gain favor. With the changes he planned for the upcoming trials, there was more at stake than Braxar keeping his title. His life would be forfeited if he failed.

Braxar reached for his severed hand as he bowed to leave,

only to have Mallan stop him. His smoke whisked the appendage away and deposited it in the fires burning in the kitchen, all while giving the goblin a warning growl, "Not yours anymore." He wasn't about to give Braxar the opportunity to have the hand reattached.

Without another word, Braxar turned to leave Mallan's office, but he didn't beat his master's exit. Mallan smoked away, too impatient to wait any longer to take his leave. To finally witness Imara's handiwork.

He reappeared just inside her suite, her orders be damned. Shadowmire was his home, he made the rules. Despite the remaining ire from his meeting with Braxar, he couldn't help the chuckle that escaped his throat as he surveyed the room. Mallan found it hard to believe that someone so fragile, so soft, could bring about the amount of destruction she did.

Glass and blood littered the floor, and smoke filled the air. Food splattered on the walls. When he looked at the bed, his chest tightened. Imara wasn't there, all he saw were the shredded bedding. It took all of a few moments for him to register that it made sense that Imara vacated the suite. Her human body couldn't handle the smoke that poured from the fireplace. Still, he had to find her. It wasn't safe for her to wander, especially if she was foolish enough to leave the estate. He wouldn't put such a move past her.

Mallan rushed from the suite, dread trickling into his veins, and halted in his tracks the moment he did. On one of the long couches, curled up and shivering, slept his Starling. She looked so innocent, so pure despite the anguish etched her features still. He tiptoed up to her, careful not to make any noise and wake her. Mallan released a heavy breath that slowed the adrenaline in his veins. She was safe in Shadowmire.

Relieved, he smoked away to the servants' quarters with two jobs for the maids: to clean up the mess in his office and the one in Imara's suite. He smoked back moments later and turned his attention to fixing what the maids couldn't clean. With a wave of his hand, he snuffed out the flames and the lingering smoke cleared. Another wave and the debris littering the floor, all the smashed glass and stone, mended themselves and drifted back to where they belonged. The rest he left for the maids and returned to the sitting area as they filtered past him into the suite.

He sat on the couch opposite Imara and waited. Watched the girl as she slept while the maids busied themselves tidying the suite and replacing the bedding. The temptation to invade her mind, see the intimate secrets her dreams held, gripped him. He knew he would give in someday when he needed to, but it wasn't time yet.

THIRTY MINUTES LATER, the maids filed out of the suite, alerting Mallan it was ready for Imara once again. He stood from the couch and looked over his Starling, pondering the puzzle she presented. He longed to lift her from her choice of bed and hold her in his arms, but he swore not to touch her without her permission. That order likely applied to his smoke as well, but it was the only reasonable way to get her back to her suite. If he woke her, she'd likely run; and he wasn't about to let any of his goblins lay a finger on her again. They'd done enough damage. He'd risk her fire, her wrath, for a minute of contact.

Carefully, Mallan called his smoke and wrapped Imara in the vaporous tendrils. He shuddered at the sensation of her soft skin against them, the scent of her filling is every sense. His smoke caressed her body as it gently lifted her, hovering her mere inches away from his arms and chest. Imara groaned softly, curling in closer as if snuggling into him, and her features softened. Mallan guided Imara's sleeping form, with reverence, to her bed, loving the closeness and wishing he could touch her with more than his smoke. But he gave his word.

Once he tucked her securely in the bed, Mallan took one more moment to watch her. He savored the serenity that laced her features, knowing they'd give way to anger when she woke to find herself back in her room, in her bed, with everything perfectly in place.

FIVE

Imara

Even before she opened her eyes, Imara knew she wasn't in the sitting room anymore. Warmth caressed her skin beneath a soft blanket. At first, her mind convinced her that her tantrum had been nothing more than a dream, a fantasy of power and anguish. The familiar carved posts of the bed greeted her, and there was no tang of blood nor a hint of smoke lingering in the air. It was her body, aching and tired, that reminded her it had been real.

That meant only one thing.

Someone had, yet again, moved Imara while she slept. Only this time, it felt worse than a mere violation of personal space. A low grumble escaped as she sat up to find the suite had, by some miracle or magic, been repaired. One would never tell it had been in shambles hours ago. It looked as perfect as it had before her tirade. Pristine, down to the half empty glass of water on the table next to the bed.

Imara prickled. This world, Mallan, had stolen yet another

thing from her. There would be no satisfaction gained in destroying the beautiful space.

Her rage, her opus of wrath, all erased before she could enjoy it, before she got to witness Mallan seeing what she'd done. Her message, that accepting this place would never happen, lost. The sweet little song bird he thought Imara was, didn't exist. She'd become a feral creature made by his hand that he would never tame.

Whatever fantasy of being with Imara he held in his mind would never happen.

A gentle rapping at the door drew Imara from the bed. She threw the blanket off, finding her feet bandaged. Someone had tended to her injuries as well. Still tender, her feet felt as though they were still filled with glass as she hobbled to the door. A maid waited there, she was almost identical to Fern. The only difference between them; her skin was pale iridescent pink. In her hands she held a tray heavy with tea service. "Hello, Mistress, I'm Briar."

"I don't want it," Imara motioned to the tea in her hands.

"Should I leave it on the table for you?"

"No," the time for niceties was done. Imara's curt response didn't phase Briar, nor did it stop her from making her way inside and leaving the tray at the table anyway. Listening wasn't high on this one's skills, Imara thought. That or she had orders from higher up that weren't to be ignored, which was much more likely the case. The vicious way Mallan slaughtered that shadow man for disobeying orders flashed in Imara's memory, sending a chill deep into her bones.

Briar eyed Imara as she turned from her task, stopping at each bloodstain that clung to her hands, her chemise, her legs. "Perhaps I could draw you a bath? Or ready the shower?"

Her assessment brought an acute awareness to Imara about

the state she was in. Nausea welled in her stomach, traumatic memories came screeching with it. All Imara could think of was how much she needed the horror erased from her skin.

Briar intuitively read the panic growing in the girl before her before she could answer. "Follow me, Mistress."

The maid led Imara past the folding partition and ushered her into the washroom beyond. Yet again, Imara was taken aback by the astounding beauty Mallan's home held. Beauty surrounded by monsters. As they entered, there was a vanity with a marble basin, a gilded mirror adorned with golden feathers and snakes hanging above it. A large bathtub took up the center of the room, made of the same marble the vanity basin was. The tub, large enough for at least two people, was shallow at one end where a stone and gold beast's head hung high above, jutting from the wall. As it stretched on, the tub deepened into something near deep enough to swim in.

As Imara marveled at the bathroom, Briar began filling the tub, as she turned the knobs at the head of the bath, hot water began pouring from the mouth of the beast above it. Though she hadn't seen the maid add anything to the water, amber and cedar began wafting from the steam. It was inviting and comforting. A slice of normal in this strange place, and Imara found herself looking forward to letting the water wash over her to erase her husband's blood.

She waited for Briar to leave the room before stripping the crusted chemise from her body, gently removing the bandages from her stinging feet, and submerging into the welcoming water at the deep end of the bath. Running her fingers through her hair, Imara worked out the tangles and pulled the remaining pins and sprigs of flowers from her hair. Her heart twisted with every removed remnant of brief wedded bliss. The water enveloped her, seeping deep into Imara's pores and offering some relaxation. For the first time since the shadows appeared at General Price's cabin, breathing came a little easier.

Whether the warmth or the aromatic steam, or both, were the key, the festering anger chipped away from her heart. The shield it created left Imara vulnerable to the ocean of anguish beating against the walls of her chest waiting to flood into every molecule of her body. As the sadness crashed through those barriers, she broke. The last bit of grit she held onto washed away, leaving Imara to crumble. Face in hands, she sobbed endlessly, staying there until long after the water turned icy.

She could have stayed there forever, emptying her heart into the bath until Imara became one with it. Melted away. If Briar hadn't returned with a robe and urged Imara from the frigid, filmy water, she would have.

The bath left every part of Imara numb, feeling nothing, not even the chilled air against her damp skin. Not the plush of the thick burgundy robe as Briar slid it over her arms, or the jostle of it being tightened around her waist. The wounds on her feet didn't seem to even be there. She barely heard Briar excuse herself, or the sound of the maid padding from the bath and through the suite.

An unknown amount of time passed before Imara remembered she could move of her own volition. As she plodded through the bathroom, a glimpse in the gilded mirror stopped Imara in her tracks. Withdrawn eyes rimmed in pink and framed by dark circles stared back at her from the glass. She was unrecognizable. It was as though this place, these strangers, had transformed her into one of its creatures. Imara turned from her reflection, a smaller slice of her heart left there as the emptiness multiplied, she couldn't look at what she became in such a short amount of time.

Her mind heavy, and her body weary, she made her way back to the enormous bed. Her island sanctuary in a sea of darkness. The only place left where normal existed if only in sleep, if only on the rare occasion where this nightmare world didn't invade there. That sliver of a promise to see her love, to feel his ghostly arms about her, called to Imara, *come to me. Come, hide away in fantasy and disappear from the world.*

That promise faded the second she rounded the partition. Mallan lounged at the end of the oversized bed, elbow propped on bent knee and his temple resting against his fist. He oozed a confidence no mortal could; dark, mysterious, and other-worldly. Once again, his vile beauty struck Imara as out of place. He was a prince among monsters, Lord of Nightmares, and he looked at Imara like she was his prize.

"Starling," he shifted upright before settling in the same position, "how are you finding your suite?" A dig at the attempted destruction Imara hoped to rile him with. She lacked the energy to even respond, despite the flicker of anger the reminder caused. The gleam in his dark eyes and the smirk playing on his lips suggested he noticed the slight change. "I do love your fire, even when you try to hold it in, it's beautiful," he pushed off the bed, closing the space between us. "It's nice to see."

Dwarfing Imara, he gazed down, careful not to touch her. He meant to keep his word, he wouldn't touch his chosen unless she allowed it. Imara was prepared to make him wait forever, and stepped around him without response. Words were wasteful, pointless to use against the man. Nothing would change his mind about what he wanted, no matter how much she protested and screamed. Aside from that, Imara had nothing she wanted to say to the man that ruined her life.

Mallan turned, watching Imara climb into the bed intent on

burrowing beneath the covers and only emerging when the time came to return to Ocean Fare. "Not enough left to try then," his chuckle ran Imara through, a blade twisting in her already hemorrhaging wounds. She shot him an icy glare, "Maybe not," he rubbed the corner of his smirk with a thumb.

He leaned against the post of the bed, meeting Imara's glare with one of amusement. A stalemate of wills built between them, but Imara's defiance didn't last under his heated stare. Glaring at the man only increased her awareness of the predicament at hand, and fat tears rolled from her eyes. Her attempt to hide those tears by looking at her lap was useless.

"Oh, my Starling," he softened, "I am infinitely sorry you're hurting." The bed shifted as he perched on the edge. "Yet, you will see, in time, this, being here, is for the best. What has happened is for the best. That life, that marriage, were fantasies. You are meant for more than a mere mortal man who'd never fully appreciate you. Who didn't understand you. He would have grown to resent you and the attention you would have garnered as your talents grew, and then turn on you."

His apology fell flat. Lorn never would have. Never.

"You're wrong," Imara seethed, her head snapping up to meet his eyes.

"There are two things you should know about me, Imara," the sound of her actual name on his lips threatened to choke her. "I don't mince words, and I am rarely wrong."

Imara squared her chin, her spite reforged by Mallan's truths and accusations. Heat once more exploded through the fog of grief, quick and burning. "You're wrong," she affirmed, her hand reaching for the water glass on the table next to her. The thought barely formed in her head as she chucked the glass at Mallan, sending water flying when it connected the side of his head, leaving a small cut. Dark blood seeped from the wound.

He met the assault without physical reaction, though his eyes burned for a split second. "Fire," he chuckled with dark hunger as he stood, wiping the blood from his brow.

"Get out."

"Of course, Starling," he bowed and disappeared in a cloud of smoke.

Riled by Mallan's words, and unnerved with the knowledge he didn't need to use the door, and most likely never would, to enter her suite, Imara fell back on the pillows. A cocktail of emotions sang in her blood. There had been little calm since Mallan forced her on this unpredictable ride. Constantly being torn between rage and sorrow was exhausting. She wasn't sure how long she could keep reeling without losing her mind. She had to find some sense of serenity, some comfort to keep her sane.

Something General Price had once said drifted in her thoughts, "Knowing what you're up against is the first step in overcoming it." Sage advice from the second kindest man Imara had ever known. So far, the answers to her questions had been poorly given. Little revealed, and with skewed opinion. The vague responses had only added to how drained Imara felt.

She knew then what she needed in order to keep calm. She had to learn more about Mallan and this place his monsters dragged her to.

A gentle rapping came at the door, interrupting Imara's thoughts. She didn't want to see anyone, but some part of her wanted to protect the maid she knew stood waiting for permission to enter from Mallan's ire. "Come in." The maids, from what little experience Imara had with them, seemed kind and honest. They were eager to please. Likable, despite their slight unnaturalness.

Two maids, Briar and Fern, entered at the command. They barely acknowledged Imara's presence as they set to work in the suite. Briar hurried to the bathroom to clean up and Fern attended to the broken glass and water from her little tantrum.

Imara watched the pale green maid work, listened to the sweet humming she entertained herself with as she did. Fern gingerly picked the shard of glass from the duvet in time to her song, placing them in a small bucket tucked under her slender arm.

"What are you humming?" Imara asked, drawing Fern's attention to her.

"It's a lullaby from my home, in Faespire."

Faespire, the name tumbled in Imara's brain, the most revealing answer anyone had given her. The name conjured up images of tales found in books about tiny beings with crystalline wings. "Faespire? As in faeries?"

"Yes, or rather fae. Did you not know you're in the Under Court, in the fae realm?" she asked, her large eyes blinking in wonder. Imara shook her head in response. "Aren't you familiar with fae, you must at least know about us and our world?"

Imara shook her head again, "No. I've heard fairytales and stories of magical creatures, but they're all fantasy. At least I thought they were, everyone does."

"Oh!" she exclaimed, then continued cleaning up the glass shards scattered about the foot of the bed.

"Fern," she paused her task and looked at Imara with bright, earnest eyes and a smile. "Can I ask you something?"

"Of course, Mistress. We maids are here to help you with whatever you need."

"Tell me about Mallan."

Fern's face turned somber, "We may not speak of him to you. The master wishes you to get to know him one on one. From him." The response was strange. It also explained the serious nature Fern took on at her request, Imara had seen first had what Mallan did to those who disobeyed. As if she didn't want to disappoint Imara either, Fern continued, "But if you're interested in learning more about Sylphea and the courts, there are books I could show you in the library."

Imara was interested, the more she learned about where she was, the better. Perhaps, she thought, the knowledge might even help her try to escape. The only problem was, she didn't want to risk running into Mallan or his monsters by leaving the suite. "I'd like to learn more, I just... I'm not comfortable leaving the room, yet."

Fern nodded, her eyes dipping with concern, "I understand. I suppose this place could be quite jarring to those unfamiliar with it. I will have some informative and historical books collected from the library and delivered to you then."

"Thank you, Fern. I'd appreciate that."

Imara worried her lip as she watched the maid finish up her task and thought about her revelation. She was in the fae realm, the Under Court. Fae. Imara had grown up with stories spun by her mother about fae and angels, but she'd tired of those tales quickly. Imara didn't have time for the world her mother's mind lived in once she realized they were all just stories. From a young age, she knew she wanted to be set in reality if she was going to have a chance at a normal life one day.

As unbelievable as it seemed that fae existed, Imara accepted it as truth. If fae existed, perhaps, just perhaps, Tilly's story of her parentage held a fraction of truth too. She'd seen far too many horrible things, fantastical things, to deny it.

IT DIDN'T TAKE LONG for Fern to send a book from the library with yet another maid. Thorn was a copy of her other sisters with different coloring; blue eyed with sky blue skin. She delivered the promised tome with another tray of tea and other offerings that Imara would ignore. The book, however, Imara had no intention of letting sit untouched.

The book, thick and hefty, was bound in cream-colored leather with brass details, but no title or information about it on the outside. It reminded Imara of a bible the ladies at Bott's kept in the foyer, and dragged out anytime they felt the need to lecture on sinful behaviors. The matron, Agnes, was particularly cruel and often used the tome to punish as well as lecture the girls for perceived crimes. Anything from making them hold the heavy book for hours on end without wavering, closing delicate fingers between the pages, or even swatting rear ends with it, her use of the bible was awful. All it did was teach them all to hate her and that book.

Imara accepted the book from Thorn and shuffled back to bed, eager to crack it open and begin her research. She found herself entranced the second she opened up the first page, revealing an enchanting illumination of three beautiful women.

They were fae queens, according to the crowns adorning their heads and the pointed ears some of them displayed. The tallest of the three stood in the middle, her copper hair topped with a rose crown with spires of golden light stretching up from them. To her left, a slight female with cedar skin and a halo of short dark curls, her pointed ears easily seen, and a silver crown lined with tendrils of smoke. A simple circlet in an iridescent blue metal that caught the raven hues of her long, ebony hair, adorned the third's head. Her figure was fuller than the others, with envious curves. Of the three, she was the most serene, a sharp contrast to the fire in the other two's sharp eyes.

The book wove a spell over Imara as she read through, following a tale of the three queens; Cyrene of the Light, Ondine of the Shadows, and Alette of the Seas, and their harmonious beginnings as rulers of Sylphea. The realm hadn't yet been closed off from the mortal world, the fae and humans of Morrea were free to roam across the borders, their worlds symbiotic; relying on each other for survival. As time passed, the relationship between the two races shifted as the mortals grew to envy the fae and coveted what they had. In response, the fae felt they deserved more than the humans, that they should have more power in their dynamics than them.

The queens Cyrene and Alette, in a move to protect their people from the jealous hate that grew in Morrea, voted to withdraw Sylphea from the rest of the world. Ondine, Queen of the Shadows, did not want to abandon the human world. Her kind, the fae that dwelled in darkness and dealt in darker magic, had become addicted to the pain and suffering fed to them, the adulation of being worshiped and given tributes of wealth. With a majority vote, the borders were closed and barriers erected to hide the fae realm, deter-rents that kept outsiders from reaching their shores.

A rift formed between Cyrene and Alette and their shadow sister, with the most tension between the Queen of the light and Ondine, the latter uncovering the former's plan to take the most power for herself. Not to be outdone, and prone to jealousy, Ondine began her own bid to become the sole ruler of Sylphea.

Alette was the only one who desired to keep the power split equally between the three of them. Stuck in the middle of the struggle for power, her sister queens, unable to hear or see reason, the Queen of the Seas grew heart weary, and feared the war brewing between the others. She knew her power was not near as great as Cyrene or Ondine's, and because neither would concede to share or to the other, Alette did the only thing she could think of to keep herself free from having to choose between the two. Though it broke her heart to abandon her domain, abandon the fae that dwelled in the waters of Sylphea, she disappeared, never to be seen or heard from again.

Soon Cyrene and Ondine's differences led to the Great War Alette knew was inevitable. The war lasted centuries, control of their armies passing to their descendant's descendants as their times to fade came. Their fight lasted until Ondine's armies, led by the General Mallan, were defeated. Cyrene's descendant, Khryton. The Lord of the Light banished Mallan to the Wastes, the regions of Sylphea where the most loathsome and where the foulest creatures dwelled.

CHAPTER
SIX

Imara

Weeks passed, and Imara had learned little more about Sylphea and nothing about Mallan, aside from what she already knew. There certainly wasn't enough information in her mind to orchestrate an escape. But, in her mind, enough time had passed since her abduction to be returned to Ocean Fare and tell her harrowing tale. It was time to try to move on with her life.

"Send me home." Imara burst in to Mallan's office as he gave orders to some of his shadowy monsters. Their chatter abruptly ended with her presence, the air heavy with tension. Imara sensed she'd interrupted an important discussion. About what, she didn't care. All she wanted was to go home.

"Leave us," Mallan ordered his monstrous underlings in a booming voice and they dispersed from the room in a chaotic clattering of weapons and boots. He walked around the table and sat on the edge before her. The usual swagger in his eyes was replaced by something Imara hadn't seen there before:

concern. She suspected his concern was solely for himself. He didn't want her to leave, and there she was asking to do just that.

"We had an agreement," Imara reminded him. "You said you would send me home when I asked to go. I'm asking."

"I was hoping you wouldn't."

"Hope in one hand, shit in the other. See which one fills up first," she glowered, crossing her arms across her chest.

Mallan smirked for a brief second, amused by Imara's feisty response, before growing serious again, "I care about you too much to let you go."

"Just because you think you love me doesn't mean I love you. Doesn't mean I ever will. I'm not yours, Mallan. You can't go around claiming women expecting them to just go along with what you decree."

"You misunderstand, Starling. My care for you is strong enough to put your happiness above my own. I'd gladly let you go if I thought it was safe to. I simply don't want to be the one to break your heart."

Imara scoffed, "You did that already when your monsters killed my husband."

"I reiterate, I gave them no such orders. I can't be blamed if their instincts to defend themselves hurt you that way. They were only told to collect you. We are destined."

"Stop saying that. Stop trying to justify kidnapping and murder because they fit your agenda. Send me home."

"I won't do that to you," he took Imara's hand in his, touching her for the first time since her arrival. His touch was firm and delicate, warm, exposing a tenderness in the fae lord Imara hadn't known could exist.

"You promised!" She yanked her hand from his, as though afraid, not that he'd hurt her, but that he wasn't as much of a monster as he seemed to be.

"That was before my suspicions were confirmed," his quieted voice was emphasized by the dipping of his head.

"What do you mean?" worry shrank Imara's resolve. What had Mallan gleaned since they made their accord that made him change his mind, she wondered. If there was anything Imara knew about him, it was that he ensured promises were kept. He wouldn't break one on a whim.

"I knew this was coming, you asking me to keep my word, wanting to go home. As a precaution, I had a few of my men do some recon, get a feel for the atmosphere of the family you want to return to. I only wanted to make sure they had a place for you in their hearts still. What my men found is not promising."

The question froze in Imara's throat, afraid of the answer coming.

"They accuse you, Imara. The things they say are hurtful enough that I'm afraid they wouldn't believe you if you told them the truth, that you were taken against your will."

"I don't believe you. Lorn's family loves me."

"How sure are you that their love was not for their son's sake?" Mallan swirled his hand in the air, a mirror appeared next to him, held up by the magic that summoned it. Across the glass played images of Gwenna, Nareen, Draven, General Price, and other soldiers under his command gathered in the Cawthorne home.

"*I'm afraid there's still no sign of Imara anywhere, Draven,*" *General Price said somberly.*

"*I just don't understand,*" *Gwenna sobbed,* "*why would she do this? We thought she loved him.*"

"*So did I. It's possible she did, that something else made her do what she did,*" *the General looked to the others in the room, almost ashamed of the words he was about to speak.* "*I can't be the only one thinking it. That she suffers some mental illness passed down from her mother. I can't see her doing this on purpose, like some scheme."*

"But what if it wasn't her," Nareen interjected. "What if it was bandits, and they took her?"

"Not likely in such a remote place," General Price commented. "My cabin isn't easy to get to. Bandits want quick and easy."

"We should have known better to allow the match," Draven cursed.

The scene faded away, gutting Imara. Mallan's words rang true. *I'm hardly ever wrong.* She had hoped with all her soul that he was wrong, that his prediction she had nowhere to go proved false. If she went back, Imara knew she'd end up somewhere like Bott's or worse. Unless she went somewhere else she knew would be safe, it already was for so many that had nowhere else to go. "Sconza's," Imara sniffled, fighting the tears trying to come, "I'll go to Gio. He'll understand, he'll protect me."

Mallan's sharp features dropped, he had more bad news.

"What is it?" Imara's voice trembled, not knowing if she could handle yet another blow.

"Sconza's is gone."

"What do you mean, it's gone?" She held onto a thin hope that the club had merely shut down, as it had been threatened with so many times in the past.

Mallan *said nothing, only turning his head as the mirror flared to life again. In the glass, the street where Sconza's should have been. All that stood in that spot, all that remained of the infamous night-club, was a smoldering pile of wood and brick. Bouquets of flowers and bottles of liquor made up a small shrine amongst the rubble. Sconza's was gone, burned to nothing.*

Imara's heart twisted and her stomach sank with a sour feeling that it wasn't the worst of it. "Is everyone okay, at least?"

"I'm afraid not. The performers, servers, all the employees made it out. But, Master Sconza, he hasn't been seen since the blaze."

The demise of Sconza's, that vibrant breath of life that thrilled the nights of Ocean Fare, along with the presumed death of Gio himself, drove the final nail in the coffin of Imara's hope. She had nowhere to go. No safe-haven from being stuck between insane or criminal other than right where she stood, a place she didn't want to be surrounded by beings Imara didn't trust. Like it or not, the Under Court was home.

Imara's stomach churned as the lights seemed to dim around her and the world spun. Before she could pass out, Mallan wrapped her in his arms, enveloping her in his strength so she could crumble. She didn't care about the closeness, or that he'd touched her without permission. Nothing mattered, there was nothing left to fight for. He held her close, attempted to soothe Imara, but it didn't work. The numbness grabbing at her senses ran too deep for anything to console her.

When Mallan scooped Imara up as though she were a feather, her mind wanted to protest. She didn't need his help. Didn't want it. But her body, weak from neglect and distraught from the totals of her losses, didn't have the energy. Rather than whisking her to her suite in a cloud of smoke, he carried her from his office and up the two flights of stairs to her suite.

The doors to her room opened up with a silent command from Mallan and closed behind them the same. In one gentle, swift motion, he lay Imara in her bed, tucking the surrounding blanket snugly. It felt familiar, as though he'd done it before. Imara realized he was likely the one that had put her in bed before, that he hadn't kept his distance as he promised. The thought didn't last long, though, and was gone before it could be considered, fleeting away into apathy like everything else did. Then he was gone.

Imara didn't sleep or move. She only stared into oblivion, the world around her blurring into the slow tears she had no control over. Her eyes didn't even have to close for horrible and dark dreams to fill her subconscious.

❧

"IMARA," a cold hand brushed against her neck. She wanted nothing to do with whoever it was, with anyone. She craved solitude, wanted to disappear into nothing. The world would make sense then. This one certainly didn't. Feeling so empty, so blank, wasn't natural. If she were gone, the emptiness would go away too.

"Mrs. Cawthorne, would you look at me?" warmer hands gripped her shoulders lovingly, a familiarity in the touch and the voice unmistakable. For the first time in hours, endless hours of being numb and weeks of rage, Imara felt something other than grief and anger. That spark of hope that voice created set her chin to quivering and swelled her heart.

Those hands guided Imara to face their bearer, and her world stopped. Imara sobbed, happy and disbelieving. Had her grief snapped her mind? But when she reached for him, and he pressed his beautiful face into her palm, he was there. "Is this real?" she asked. "Please tell me this is real."

"This is very real, my love. I'm here. I came for you," his amber eyes glistened, rimmed with silvery tears that matched hers.

"How? I, I saw you. I saw your body. You were dead."

"Does it matter? I'm here now. Come home with me, be with me." Lorn picked Imara up from the bed, wrapping her in his arms, his scent enveloping her senses. Her heart sighed as Imara leaned against him, home at last. This was where she belonged.

As he carried Imara from the suite and through the adjoining sitting area, she became lost in staring at the miracle that was her husband. She didn't notice Fern as they passed the maid on the stairs and hardly heard the tray she carried clattering on the floor. Soon, a series of high-pitched screams shook the walls of Shadowmire. Imara ignored those as well.

Whatever had set the maids off, Imara didn't care. She had Lorn back, and that was all that mattered.

Nothing genuinely registered in Imara's brain until a cool breeze whipped her hair. She was outside for the first time in what felt like ages. She had been freed from the gilded cage that was the opulent suite Mallan gave her, and Lorn was taking her home. He could explain everything to his family and General Price. Just him being there would exonerate Imara, saving her twice over.

A feral roar cut the quiet air, and a cacophony of ravens cawed in response. The noise sent fear cascading into Lorn's eyes, and his brilliant smile faltered for the first time since taking Imara in his arms. "Drop her," Mallan's voice ordered once the distant birds settled, and all was once again quiet. Lorn turned to face Imara's kidnapper.

Mallan's face was fury and fire, his fangs exposed in a frozen snarl and a promise of death simmered in his obsidian eyes. "I'd take more care with your words, Mallan," Lorn taunted with a distorted voice.

Imara's eyes widened at the sudden change in her husband, something wasn't right. When she took her eyes off Mallan to look at her beloved, her heart dropped. No longer was she nestled in the safety of Lorn's arms, but in the skeletal arms of some emaciated creature that reeked of decay and dirt. The creature's face, if it could be called that, had soulless sockets where eyes should have been, no nose, and a gaping maw of needle-like teeth.

"I might be inclined to follow your order to the letter, Lord Mallan. A dangerous one standing here at the edge of this sweet little garden you made just for her," the creature hissed through a sardonic grin. Its words drew Imara's attention to her surroundings.

They stood on the precipice of a rooftop, adorned with a vibrant garden of exotic fauna. Ravens circled high in the air silently, as if waiting for a word of action to be called. Below, another garden of sorts waited to see if the creature would hold true to its threat. The fall itself wouldn't kill Imara, it wasn't high enough to do more than mangle, but the rocks, large and small, with jagged points jutting into the air, were daggers that meant certain death if he did.

Instinct kicked in, and Imara flailed against the creature's hold in an effort to free herself. Save herself from the drop it had no problem committing and delighting in. The creature only chuckled at her struggle and turned to hold her further over the edge. Just as Imara opened her lips to make a desperate plea, the arms holding her loosened and Imara fell through the air, her screams frozen in her throat.

Though she was terrified of the pain rushing toward her, there was an ironic sense of peace as Imara fell. Her death would rip her from this world, from Mallan and all his horrors, and reunite her with Lorn. Their love could continue in death.

Before she made impact, a cloud of smoke wrapped its fingers around her body and deposited Imara back on the gravelled path of the rooftop garden. Mere feet away, Mallan held the creature by its throat, its clawed, bony fingers gripping desperately to free itself from his grasp.

"You play a dangerous game, Wraith," Mallan bit. "Coming into my home and trying to steal what is mine."

"I had no choice," the wraith rasped. "Her pain called me from across your court, so sweet and irresistible. She'd have fed me with her fear and anguish for weeks before succumbing to that final death." Even in the frightening fae's clutches, the wraith continued to taunt Mallan. It was like it had no fear, only hunger and truth.

Horror ripped through Imara. How long would she have been in its clutches before she realized the face it wore was a honey trap? She imagined being in its company for weeks, like it promised she would have been, thinking it was Lorn, dying a happy, slow death. It was a chilling realization that had Imara trying and failing to fight the bile rising in her throat.

"She is mine," Mallan growled, throwing the wraith into a nearby bed of flowers. In a flash of black, he was on the creature again, holding the wraith's head in both of his own clawed hands. He twisted. The frail bones in the wraith's neck crunched with a sickening pop, and it went still. Mallan wasn't done with it yet, his anger demanded more. With only his hands, he ripped its head from the wraith's body, splattering blood across his face and onto the garden path alike.

Casually, he tossed the severed head behind Imara. "Mount this at the gates," he ordered someone there. It was only then that Imara realized they weren't alone on that rooftop. A handful of his monsters and a few maids were there, too. "Let the wretch's head be a warning to those that would bring Imara any sort of pain, to those who would dare try to steal her from me." As a final blow, Mallan kicked the wraith's headless body off the edge of the roof. Even from above, its body hitting the rocks below came with a grotesque squelch.

Mallan's formidable shadow crept over Imara moments before he squatted to her level. She was afraid to look at him. The sheer magnitude of his wrath made him absolutely terrifying to her, even though it hadn't been turned on her. Even though he'd used it to stop the wraith and save her.

"Are you hurt?" For the second time she was aware of,

Mallan's hands lay on her skin without permission, delicately lifting her chin so her gaze met his. His eyes still burned with dark fury, though his voice dipped into something more human. "Did the wraith hurt you?" he asked again when Imara didn't respond.

Physically, she was fine, other than neglectful weakness and the tremble taking over her. But her head was spinning as it finished coming out of the enchantment the wraith placed there, its death severing the spell. A new trauma wove into the tapestry of grief Imara worked through. The wraith had meant to kill her, and she had almost died. If it hadn't been for Mallan's interference, his protection, she would have.

Though she welcomed it only moments ago, she wasn't ready to die. Lorn wouldn't want her to leave the mortal coil too soon, even if it meant being together again.

"No," Imara stammered after reining in her thoughts, but failed to conceal the fear in her voice. She wasn't fine. Not at all, and didn't think she would be for a long time.

As if he knew her mind, Mallan's brow furrowed with concern. "My Starling," he hushed, reaching for her hand. Those words branded deep in Imara's soul, and reminded her how she'd gotten in that position n the first place. His deluded claim on her, which he declared to the wraith twice over.

"I'm not yours," Imara met Mallan's eyes with a fire she hadn't felt in days, maybe longer. Time had blended seamlessly over the weeks as anguish transformed her to a wallowing, empty shell. The wraith's mistake had one silver lining to it. It affirmed that she didn't want death. It taught Imara that she couldn't disappear into herself and survive that place. A hard lesson learned for sure. "Just because you saved me from that thing," she spat, "doesn't change my own promises."

The gravel slipped under Imara's feet as she stood, a satisfying crunch that resonated through her. A defiant sound that matched a re-found resilience that Imara had lost in times of happiness. It became new armor against the darkness, against slipping away into oblivion where she could be manipulated again and again. Without another word, Imara turned and headed to go back into the estate.

"Imara," at the sound of her name she turned, ready to pounce at whatever was said. Mallan's proud form slouched, appearing vulnerable for the first time since meeting him. He whispered low, "I'm sorry."

"You don't get to be sorry for something you're ultimately to blame for," Imara bit over her shoulder. She didn't bother to look back again as she made her way inside.

SEVEN

Mallan

"Fucking wraith," Mallan spat on the ground near the gates as he tore his sight from the still oozing head adorning one post. Its black blood ran down the iron slowly, gathering on the dusty gravel.

Mallan had enough on his plate without the headache it presented. He'd been well within his rights to defend Shadowmire and Imara from the intruder, still there'd be new tensions with the wraiths because of it. Mallan didn't need two battles looming on the horizon. With any luck, the self-appointed Wraith King would see reason.

A message had been sent west to the wraith lands of Night Point within the hour after the rooftop incident. Mallan had to act fast to keep the peace between them. If he wanted to keep the wraiths on his side for the coming battle with Lord Khryton. There was no threat of them joining the wretch, he loathed them more than Mallan, but to have them fighting with him instead of not would change the game nearly as much as having Imara.

Mallan expected the Wraith King's arrival at any moment, the only reason he stood outside his gates. He may have wanted the wraiths with him in the coming fight, but he didn't trust one to be in his home at the moment. Imara's pain and grief were too fresh, too tempting to the soulless creatures, as the attack on her earlier proved. Meeting at the gates just gave a good opportunity for the king to see which of his kind was to blame, Mallan was interested in seeing his reaction. To see what lies the wraith would spin, if any.

Mallan rolled his shoulders, the attack on Imara had wound him up. It affected him in a way he hadn't expected. His feelings grew for her, deepened with every moment. He had to temper them, or else they'd derail the end goal. After, after he had what he wanted, he could let them rampage. Give in to the desire laden tension.

There was a shift in the air, Mallan's breath becoming frozen clouds. He turned to greet the Wraith King.

"Lord Mallan," she bowed, her stringy ash colored hair dipped to skirt the ground. When she rose, she offered him a sharp smile from her rotting mouth. The Wraith King settled the gaze of her one eye, half blinded by decay, upon the impaled head above them. "Why do you summon me for this stranger?"

"He's a wraith."

"I don't know this wraith, all are accounted for that have not been exiled. For that, you're lucky."

Mallan growled, "Is that a threat?"

"Take it as you will, my Lord. Had that wretch been a loyal, the unprovoked murder would cause waves that even you can't handle."

"He trespassed, tried to kidnap and murder someone dear to me," his roar shook the gates of Shadowmire.

The Wraith King's knees buckled as she skittered back, her hands held up in front of her face. "There's no foul between us then, I would have done the same were the roles reversed. That wraith is an exile and I care not what you do to the rogues. No one does. Though if he was one of Torlid's, you may have an issue on your hands."

Mallan's lip curled. "Wraiths are defecting to join that spoiled, halfling bastard?" Torlid was ruthless, and every move he made was to help his father, that golden asshole Khryton. He eyed the corpse, it was far too wasted to be anything other than rogue. Torlid had to be smart enough to keep his wraiths well fed to ensure their loyalty.

"His empty promises of recognition by the High Court have lured some away. Nothing to sweat about," she dismissed the reported defectors casually. "They don't have the numbers to make a difference when it comes to blows."

Mallan studied the head he'd had placed on his gates, the blood now congealing and already attracting creatures looking for a meal. Flies buzzed around its eyes, the ravens of Shadowmire circled high in the air, giving wide birth to the condor in their midst. The message the wraith's head sent wouldn't last without protection. A tendril of smoke emanated from his hand to encircle the warning and soaking deep into the skin.

"Still, it must make you nervous that some have chosen someone other than you to serve. It would do you well to align your wraiths with the Under Court."

"You have sweet words and lies for us too?" the Wraith King taunted with a hiss.

"No. No strings, just a strong hand to scratch your backs in return." Mallan made no promises. The wraiths would be vindictive if double crossed. What he wouldn't pay to see the efforts of those that joined Torlid when Lord Khryton's promises proved hollow. The carnage would be glorious.

"I'll consider it. Though it wouldn't hurt to sweeten the

pot," she slid up to Mallan, placing her skeletal hands on his chest. "Something to seal the alliance."

He removed her hands from him. "That is off the table, Wraith King. My destined is the person the rogue wraith attacked." Disappointment flashed over the Wraith King's decaying eye, and Mallan knew he had to offer something. "I can offer sacrifices, a thousand virginal nymphs."

The Wraith King smirked. There was nothing sweeter to a wraith than the succulence of a virgin's fear. "That's even sweeter. Send them to me in a fortnight and you'll have your army of wraiths."

Mallan offered a half bow in thanks, not because he saw her as an equal. A little stroke to her ego couldn't hurt his case. "I'll have it done."

The wraith vanished, standing a little taller. Mallan felt pleased with himself, he'd gotten the Wraith King to agree to siding with the Under Court. All that was left to do was win Imara over, then things would truly be perfect. For the time being, his goblins had some hunting to do. The wraiths needed their sacrifices, and a fortnight was barely enough time to get them.

CHAPTER

EIGHT

Imara

Imara fermented in her renewed iron spine as she prepared for bed, rather than simply crawling into it to hide from her woes. She took extra time in the routine, each task done with intent and care. The decision was made to stay in Sylphea, in Mallan's court and home, probably forever. She'd be damned though, if she let it defeat her again. Imara would thrive for Lorn, as he would have wanted her to. Thrive on her terms just to spite her host.

After a long bath, she sat at the vanity and noticed, truly noticed with her now open eyes, how gaunt she'd become. The sight jarred her to her core. She was a ghost of her former self, paler than usual and much thinner than she had been on her wedding day. Would anyone have even recognized her if she had been successful in getting Mallan to return her home?

The vanity before her held an array of bottles and small silver canisters of ointments, lotions and balms. Her hands traced over the containers, pulling especially interesting ones from the selection to sniff and sample. Imara ultimately chose the contents of a long-necked glass bottle with an amethyst jeweled stopper as her tonic of choice. Amber scented oil, with notes of bergamot, clary sage, and lavender, poured from the bottle as she tipped it over an open palm. The oil spread over her dried out skin, absorbing flawlessly and leaving no greasy film behind. She even ran a small amount through her raven locks, brushing it through with her fingers to bring some life back to those neglected tresses.

The simple routine did little to improve her appearance, but Imara felt definitively more human when she finished. Recovery would take time.

Somewhat refreshed, Imara returned to the main area of her suite, finding the trio of maids tidying the space and refreshing the linens. Briar busied herself behind the partition, adding fine clothes and dresses to the large mahogany wardrobe there. Fern and Thorn worked together, putting the finishing touches on the freshly done up bed.

Thorn paused when she noticed Imara's approach. "Look at you, Mistress. You look to be feeling better," she remarked.

"Could use a bit of food," Fern added, noting the leaning of Imara's figure with a bit of criticism.

Imara flushed with embarrassment at the maid's remark. She'd left the daily offerings of food and drink mostly untouched, only sipping at the teas and water brought to her.

"I'm sorry," she said, ashamed of how she'd behaved over the weeks.

"No reason to feel bad about that, Mistress," Briar chimed in from behind the screen where she worked.

"Grief is a strange bedfellow indeed," Fern continued. "It affects us all differently, takes it time with some and rushed through others."

"Since you're feeling a little better now, things will change. Perhaps you will see things aren't so bad here," Briar added.

"Yes, things aren't so bad in Shadowmire. There are far worse hosts than Mallan." Thorn finished the maids' point as she fluffed a pillow.

Imara doubted their words. She may have accepted her fate, that her place was there, but she didn't expect to grow to love it. Or Mallan. She was firm on keeping the fae at arm's length, not giving in to what he wanted. "I'd appreciate some food now," she conceded. Imara's appetite still hadn't returned, despite the gnawing at her stomach, but it had been far too long since she properly nourished her body. It showed. "Nothing too heavy, please."

"Of course, Mistress," Fern complied and hurried from the suite in search of something fitting the bill.

"Please, call me Imara," she told the remaining maids after Fern's departure, knowing their hive minds would share the request with the absent maid. "I'm no one's Mistress. Titles are wasted on me," Imara offered with a sheepish smile.

It wasn't long before Fern returned with a tray. Imara followed the soft orange skinned maid to the dinette waiting on the other side of the suite. The tray didn't hold much, a glass of water, some plain bread, and a small bowl of a clear broth with bits of green onion floating in it, a distinct umami aroma wafted from the steaming liquid. Also among the food and drink was a small glass with a dark liquid in it. "What is that?" Imara inquired, hesitant to ingest something so forbidding looking.

"A vitamin tonic. Please be sure to take it, you sorely need it, Imara." Fern replied before excusing herself and the other maids.

Once she was alone, Imara took a sampling sip of the broth before her, pleased with the earthy, salty, sweet flavor, and deciding to wait until after taking the vitamins to have more. She was nervous the dark and viscous looking tonic would be unpleasant and wanted to save something delicious to wash it down with.

The vitamin drink had no scent Imara could discern as she smelled it, giving nothing away about the taste. She took a tentative lick of the contents, surprised to find it had a mild aromatic flavor she couldn't quite place, medicinal but not horrible. Imara downed the rest of the tonic in a swift gulp and turned her attention back to the broth.

She could stomach drinking only half of the soup. Any more than that, she knew she'd be sick, her neglected stomach needed to adjust slowly. That minuscule amount of food was exactly what she needed, however, and settled in her warmly, relaxing her weary body.

Before turning in for the night, Imara took another look at the book Fern sent to her. There was still more she needed to learn about Sylphea, especially the Under Court and Mallan. Rather than picking up where she left off, she flipped through the pages until she found a passage specifically about her host and the forming of the courts.

LORD MALLAN, *Ondine's favorite general and lover, was given her legions and lands when she was defeated by Lord Khryton, Queen Cyrene's heir. He proved unwilling to be tamed by the rightful King of Sylphea, ignored his orders to leave the mortals of Morrea alone in his quest to rule over something. The dark fae reveled in bringing his darkness to them, influencing man into depravity and torturing them with nightmares.*

The atrocities brought by Mallan and his followers threatened the stability of the land, of the mortals Lord Khryton longed to protect like his own kin. Desperate to save mankind, Lord Khryton made a deal with Mallan, he would share the rule of Sylphea with him, split the fae lands, if his adversary would promise that he and his kind would leave the mortals alone.

Mallan agreed on one condition: that Lord Khryton would stay away from Morrea as well. No fae would hold dominion or influence over mortals ever again.

They struck an accord, both parties signing the decree in blood. Lord Khryton, good to his word, divided Sylphea, giving Mallan the continent below Cailloch and crowning him Lord of the Under Court. Lord Khryton kept the larger half of Sylphea above the southern shore of the lake and named it the High Court. The whole of Sylphea now sat under two separate rules, all for the wraith home in Night Point, the southern-most tip of Mallan's lands, and Alcara, the home of the witches who swore no allegiance to either fae.

Once the fae left the mortals lands behind, they cast a spell over them. Man forgot the fae were real, turning them into sweet stories for children.

THE INFORMATION IMARA gleaned was little but succinct. Lord Khryton had banned Lord Mallan from Morrea to protect mortals. She wondered if she ever got the chance to leave the Under Court, if she could manage to escape somehow, if the protector of mortals would deign to help her.

CHAPTER
NINE

Imara

*S*conza's misted into existence. Imara stood on the stage, a husky ballad emanating from her. The song faltered unnaturally in her throat at the surprise Imara spotted in the audience. Lorn sat in his usual spot, a mid row table, aligned with center stage. Best seat in the house, he'd claimed. He looked handsome in his crisp and clean uniform, decorated with the medals he'd earned. A sweating glass of cheap whisky sat on the table next to an illuminated oil lamp. Lorn reached for the glass and took a long swig, keeping his eyes locked on Imara, proud and adoring.

A recreation of the night Lorn returned home, a night Imara remembered vividly. She hadn't been expecting him to return for a few more days. But in his impatient excitement to see her, he'd gotten leave early and rode out ahead of the troop. Sconza hadn't tried to stop her when she leapt from the stage and mastered the maze of tables to throw herself in his arms. He did reprimand her later that night, though. He'd only allowed it because he knew there'd be no stopping her. No stopping love.

The dream diverted from memory as their clothes transformed into their wedding attire. "Imara, my beautiful wife," Lorn's eyes glittered with tears made of stars. "How I miss you."

"Lorn," she sobbed into his chest, "I wish you were here. I'm so lost without you."

"I know, I know, baby girl. But you're stronger than you know, you can survive this interlude of our lives. Just be the woman I know you are, good and thoughtful. Do what is right."

"I don't know what's right anymore, Lorn. This place is so strange, so unnatural. It scares me."

"It's okay to be scared, my love. When one door closes and one you never expected to open, being afraid is expected." He planted a kiss on the top of Imara's head. "I want you to do something for me."

"Anything," Imara looked up into her husband's face. She'd walk through fire for him.

"Thank Mallan for saving your life."

Imara was taken aback by his unusual request. Mallan was the enemy, the reason they weren't together. "Why should I?" she questioned. "He's the reason all of this happened. I can't forgive him."

"Thankfulness and forgiveness are not the same, Imara. I didn't ask for you to forgive him, I'd never implore that of you. That's up to you to decide to do or not. I said to thank him for me. The world wouldn't be right without you in it. Your life is important, more important than mine ever could have been." His ghostly lips found hers, as sweet and wonderful as they ever were. "Promise me, Imara. Please," he said when the kiss broke.

"I promise," she agreed with his wisdom before he kissed her gently one last time.

Pride formed a lump in Imara's throat, one that wouldn't be swallowed away, no matter how hard she tried. The idea of thanking Mallan for anything still felt like defeat to her. But she made a promise, even if it was only a dream and held no credible way to be accounted for, and Imara intended to keep it. The Lorn in her dream was right. It was the right thing to do.

The more she thought about it, the more she realized her behavior had been so much worse than she realized. Imara never would have acted that way, or stood for anyone else to either. Rude and ungrateful. If she didn't right herself, she risked losing herself. She risked becoming someone Lorn never would have loved.

The doors to Mallan's suite, set up directly across from hers, were intimidating, even though they were no different in appearance. Perhaps it was knowing who lay behind them that made them so foreboding. Or maybe it was what Imara needed to do that halted her in her tracks. Whichever it was, her hand trembled as it hesitated to knock on the solid wood.

The gentle rap barely sounded against the door, and Imara almost expected it to go unanswered. She thought it had, as no sound came from inside, no movement could be heard for minutes afterward. As she raised her fist to knock again, the door swung open, revealing Mallan. His sleepy, disheveled appearance knocked the intimidation scale back a few notches. He seemed a little more human, a little less monster. Imara sighed in relief, thinking his more approachable look made her apology a little easier to deliver.

"Starling," he rubbed the sleep from his eyes, "what do I owe this pleasant surprise to?"

"May I come in?" The knot in Imara's throat dropped, settling deep enough to elicit a wave a nausea.

"Of course, you're always welcome." Mallan swung the door wide, gesturing for her to enter; she had to force herself to take that first step across the threshold. It was the first time Imara had seen Mallan's suite. The grandness exceeded that of her own. Darker, lush in decor, and much, much colder. "Please sit," he directed her to a long curved couch made of rich, purple, almost black, velvet with glossy decorative arms and legs. It sat in front of a grand fireplace built into a wall. The dull charred logs in the andiron ignited to life as Imara approached. The warmth of the flames began eating away at the chill immediately.

Imara settled onto the sofa, running her hands over the plush fabric, adoring the soft fabric. The feel of it took her back to the tiny dressing room at Sconza's. The couch there was far smaller, red, and the fabric worn thin in spots and dotted with cigarette burns and makeup stains. Despite the sad state, it was the most comfortable piece of furniture in the place. More than once Imara opted to sleep curled up on it rather than make her way to the apartments where many of the entertainers lived.

Her first kiss with Lorn had been on that sofa. His lips meeting her with soft nervousness, sweet and unsure. That kiss changed her life.

Mallan settled at the other end, one leg lounging across the empty space. Cool arrogance exuded from him as he became more alert. "What has you up at this hour?"

Imara stared at her hands, folded demurely together in her lap; if she looked at him, she knew her resolve would wane. "I wanted to thank you. Apologize. You saved my life. Instead of being grateful, I treated you like a villain."

"There's nothing to apologize for, Starling," he excused her behavior. "You're still grieving, and I am to blame for that."

"No, Mallan. Yes, if you hadn't... If I wasn't here, if I hadn't tried to disappear, the wraith wouldn't have tried to take me. I was rude when you stopped it." Imara took a deep breath, relieved the words had come. "Good should always be acknowledged, no matter the source," she met Mallan's eyes, wanting him to see the sincerity behind her words, even though they were difficult to admit.

Imara wanted nothing more than to hang on to hating Mallan, blaming him for all the bad things that happened and would inevitably happen while with him. But that would be wrong. While the wraith would never have gone after Imara if Mallan hadn't kidnapped her, he didn't tell the wraith to do it. He stopped the wraith. For that, he didn't deserve to be punished. "I'm not forgiving you, by any means, don't confuse that with being thankful. What you've done to me can't be erased by any number of good acts. It'll always haunt me. That being said, I will accept being here and won't vilify everything you do from now on."

"A truce then?" Mallan sat forward, interest waking him further.

"A tentative one, at best."

"I'm happy to hear it. I assume this means you'll stop cloistering yourself away?" he asked, hope shining in his dark eyes. Imara shrugged, she didn't know if she was ready to do that, that she'd feel comfortable living at Shadowmire enough to roam the halls amongst the monsters that made her palms sweat and her heart erratic. Monsters who killed Lorn. "When you're ready then," he acquiesced. "Although I would like to extend an invitation to join me for dinner. A celebration of our accord."

Imara scoffed louder than she meant to. Even though the decision to thank him and move on was hers, it was not cause for celebration in her eyes. Celebrating wasn't on the list of things she felt like doing. After all these weeks, she still only wanted to hide and weep. She wouldn't, though. Imara would fight that urge and live for Lorn.

"A commemoration of our accord," Mallan corrected, noting Imara's reaction. If he was anything, he was perceptive.

"I'll think about it," Imara replied, standing to leave. She'd accomplished all she meant to in visiting Mallan, and had no intention of staying longer than that. "Goodnight, Mallan."

"Goodnight, Imara," escorted her to the doors, parting without another word.

TEN

Imara

About mid-day, Imara sent notice to Mallan that she would accept his invitation for dinner. In response, he sent word that dinner would be formal. As evening approached, the three maids assigned to her appeared at Imara's door with a garment bag and instructions to help her get ready.

Briar hastened away to hang the garment bag in the wardrobe while Fern and Thorn ushered Imara into the bathroom to scrub and polish her body. They massaged a variety of lotions and oils into her skin, then teased, curled, and pulled her hair into a cascading updo. For the final touch, they applied simple, glowing makeup on Imara's face, just enough to enhance her natural beauty. It was strange to be doted on; for someone else to do her makeup and hair. The only other time since her childhood she'd had someone else in charge of her appearance was when Gwenna and Nareen did her hair for the wedding. Even then, it hardly happened in her childhood with

Tilly preoccupied with the world in her head and the ladies of Bott's not caring if Imara looked presentable or not. Most days she ran around with her hair in tangles until she learned how to care for it herself.

Once Imara's hair and makeup were done, the three maids took her to dress. When Briar untied the garment bag, the dress inside stole her breath. The dress Mallan selected for Imara was stunning, the most beautiful garment she'd ever seen. Ever had the opportunity to wear, for that matter. An off the shoulder soft lavender gown, the soft color became incrementally darker from the collarbone down and from the bottom of the full, gauzy, taffeta skirts, becoming a rich royal purple at the fitted bodice. It fit her like a glove.

Imara couldn't help but spin as she checked her appearance in the full-length mirror in the wardrobe door. Despite having looked gaunt and weary just hours before, the woman the maids transformed her into was radiant.

THE MINUTE she left her suite, Imara's nerves were electric, a storm contained in her heart. Following Thorn, she made her way to the banquet hall, and her mind tumbled. She did not know how she was going to sit through this dinner with her host. What sort of conversation did one have with the being who orchestrated your kidnapping? Who, by proxy, murdered your husband? The thought of a cordial meal with him still made Imara feel she was betraying Lorn somehow.

By the time she reached her destination, she wondered if it had been a bad idea to accept the invite. But there was no turning back, because as she approached, the doors swung open of their own volition. The exposed banquet hall proved to be another exquisite room in Shadowmire. Imara doubted there wasn't a room inside the home that wasn't more stunning than the next.

In the center of the room, a long, lacquered table extended for near the whole width of the space. Matching high-back chairs, upholstered in the same deep purple velvet as Mallan's personal couch, flanked the table. Three smoky crystal chandeliers hung, evenly spaced, over the table, their purpose purely decorative as the room was lit by sconces lining the walls, as well as two ornate black and silver candelabras adorning the table. Arrangements of blood-red roses and black orchids adorned the bases of the candleholders.

Mallan, sitting at the far end of the table, stood when Imara entered. He wore a mostly all black, form fitting shirt and pants under a long coat, his toned physique easy to make out beneath his clothes. Pops of lavender embellished the ensemble as a pocket square, shimmering cufflinks, and the satin liner lining of the coat. He cut a dashing figure dressed in his finery, which somehow felt more intimidating than his casual attire and flowing robes.

Imara winced inside at the sight of him. He'd dressed to match her, linking them together as a couple. It was the sort of gesture that would have had her stomach filling with butterflies if he'd be Lorn. On Mallan, it was a mere reminder of his obsession, of his deluded belief that they were destined. It only solidified Imara's thinking that going to dinner had been a mistake.

"You look lovely, Starling. A vision," he moved for Imara, meeting her halfway and offering an arm.

Resisting the urge to reply with a snide remark, she plastered a smile on her face. "Thank you," Imara slid her arm through his and allowed him to escort her to the seat next to his. Every bit the gentleman, he pulled the chair out for her and pushed it in after she sat.

Everything he did was perfect, too perfect. His actions

contrasted the monster, the dark fae Imara knew him to be. The things he'd done that she read about in the book Fern gave her, that the fae he watched over did, were chilling. Mallan was a creature of the night, of things hidden in the shadows that toyed with theming and tortured the soul. A creature long banished from the mortal world. A banishment he broke when he decided he wanted Imara.

Mallan had barely taken his seat when a troop of servants entered the banquet hall in a flurry of china and crystal. An earthy skinned male, even more human-like than the hive minded maids, approached and poured a ruby port into the crystal chalices another had just set before then. Another followed, bringing with him appetizer plates of silver-lined china beautifully plated with servings of soft cheese and figs with a balsamic glaze served over crostini.

Imara's captor and host dug right into the plate before him, his elegant fingers plucking a fig from its nest and placing it in his mouth. He kept his eyes, gleaming with wicked seduction, focused on his guest as he sucked the residual glaze and cheese from his fingertips. The gesture revealed his intentions for the invitation to dine with him. It was an attempt at courtship, a realization that put Imara off her already meager appetite.

"Do you not like it?" Mallan asked, noting Imara's lack of enthusiasm.

"I'm not very hungry," she replied, her hands worrying the napkin in her lap as Imara fought the urge to run from the table and never look back. She wouldn't, though. Imara promised to try, and had no intention of breaking it. Imara had no desire to raise Mallan's ire by breaking the verbal contract. If he enforced those consequences with the same vigor as he did with his monsters, with her, was yet to be seen. She hoped to never learn the answer.

A swift shift crossed Mallan's face and lip curled just enough to be seen. Imara didn't want to test how far he'd let her go in disappointing him. She lifted a crostini, taking a small bit from the amuse-bouche.

The crunchy, sweet, creamy, and tangy combination blended together in harmony over her tongue. It was delicious, decadent even.

With his eyes trained on her, Mallan sighed into his chair, the corners of his mouth lifting behind the hand resting on his chin. That minuscule bite pleased him to no end. His silent study nagged at her mind and brought up questions that she shoved aside when grief held Imara in its steel grasp.

Questions that demanded answers if she was to stay in his home. Part of her feared those answers, feared they'd churn her stomach further. Imara popped the other half of the crostini in her mouth and contemplated if it was worth the risk to her peace of mind for them.

"Something on your mind, Starling?" his use of Imara's stage name, yet again, chaffed her curiosity. She had to know how Mallan knew so much about her, because she certainly didn't buy that he learned it from his agents watching her.

"Why do you call me that?"

"It's who you are, is it not? Sconza's Starling?"

"Not anymore," she bit back the emotion the reminder of her former employer's apparent death caused. Imara would have given anything to have been able to return to his stage rather than remain in the overdressed prison Shadowmire was. Her life would have gone on, and perhaps her heart would have healed in time. Maybe she would have found love again. "I mean, why do you call me Starling? How do you know so much about me, so much more than if you were keeping to the treaty?"

"The treaty?" Mallan sat up, amused interest dancing in his eyes. "Seems you've been doing your research on me. Is it so hard to imagine I did the same for the person destined for me?"

"So you had one of your shadows spy on me?"

"Shadows?"

"The monsters you sent for me," the words lumped in Imara's throat.

"They're goblins, and no, my goblins are too noticeable for espionage, I'm afraid."

"A servant then," having seen the males tonight, proved some could pass as human.

"No."

"The mirror then?" Imara was running out of ideas about how he'd spied on her. "You can't leave the Under Court, let alone Sylphea."

Mallan laughed, biting his lower lip, "Oh can't I? You think I wouldn't be bold enough to break the treaty to seek you out myself?" He admitted he broke the agreement that he was bound to by the High Court. The knowledge pierced Imara's mind, sending a jolt through her. Mallan leaned in close to her ear as a cloud of smoke enveloped him, "I call you My Starling because you are. I found you. I made you." As he spoke, his voice changed, becoming less rich and all too familiar.

Imara's spine stiffened with the ice settling in it, and her head turned just in time to see the smoke dissipate from around him. Instead of Mallan's, she looked right into the eyes on the one and only Gio Sconza. "Like I said, master Sconza hasn't been seen since his club burned."

Imara's vision tunneled. There wasn't anything her former employer hadn't gleaned about her, and hardly any part of her he hadn't seen at some point or another because of some costume fittings or a neglected lock on the dressing room door. Those moments never bothered her. Sconza, who Imara believed was Sconza, had always treated her with the utmost respect. But realizing her whole career as a chanteuse had been an orchestrated illusion for Mallan to get close to her, that changed everything. The violation of being manipulated scorched the memories into blackened husks, just like the nightclub named for the fake man.

"Were you the only one?" Imara asked blankly. "Were the others fae too? Was it all a ruse?"

"No, not all of them. Care to know who?"

"No!" Imara had enough, her heart twisted as she shot out of her seat. Mallan matched her movement, glee sparking over his features. Though he towered over her, she dared to keep her eyes locked on his. Imara imagined shredding him into nothing. Not only was her entire relationship with Gio a sham, some companionships formed with her fellow performers had been too.

"You're stunning when you're angry, Starling," he taunted.

Imara's hand left an angry red mark on his cheek before she stormed out of the banquet hall.

The last place Imara wanted to be was in her suite. It was too close to Mallan's. He wouldn't be there until the wee hours, he never was before then, but still knowing he'd be there made him too close for comfort. She didn't want him to know where she was, checking on her. Instead, she wandered up past the floor the suites were on, venturing further up in the estate than she had before.

One floor up, there was only one door at the end of a short hallway. Imara tried the handle on the door, but it wouldn't give. Locked. Not that it mattered, she thought it too close to Mallan still, and wanted to be as far as possible from him. That meant ascending even higher.

She followed the stairs as high as they went. The small space had a black marbled floor, bolts of gold streaking through it, and a three hundred and sixty degree window that looked out over the land. A lone chandelier of gold sat centered on the ceiling, which stretched up at least another story, to illuminate the space in a soft glow. Nothing else was in there. The room was a blank canvas. To Imara, it was the perfect place to simmer alone and undisturbed.

She settled in the northern corner, her back pressed against the cool glass as Imara looked out over the mist covered world. Imara couldn't see much through the smoke-like fog that swirled past the window, only obscured dots of light flickered across the blanket of night.

The dress offered little protection from the cold that constantly filled in the vast space of Shadowmire not lucky enough to be warmed by a blazing fireplace. She didn't care, though. The cold could seep deep into her bones for all she cared and freeze her from the inside out. It would be a welcome relief against the lava-like anger that rolled through her veins.

Mallan's deception devastated Imara; filled her with a sense of betrayal fueled by an anger like none she'd felt before. Sconza didn't exist, he never did. That bit of news reeled over and over in her mind, a broken wheel. Imara had trusted Gio Sconza far more than most everyone else in her life. More than any other man besides Lorn. She loved him, even. Admittedly, her thoughts had more than once wandered into the what if of romantic encounters with the man, that was until she met her future husband. Her crush on her mentor was extinguished then.

To find out he'd been Mallan all long, with his obsession of making Imara his, only showed that trust was a fragile thing in the delicate lives of mortals. She wondered what sort of unspeakable things had been done in the fae's name during his time pretending to be someone else, when he was supposed to be banished from Morrea.

As she sat there, looking over Mallan's land and replaying his revelation, Imara's eyes grew heavy as her heart felt, and her thoughts stumbled incoherently together as sleep claimed her, with promises of wintry nightmares.

Imara stood on the stage at Sconza's, singing for an audience of one. The man himself. Gentle snow drifted from the rafters, immune to the sweat inducing mirrored lamps lighting the space, and formed small drifts at her feet.

When she finished her ballad, his singular applause filled the room, slow, loud, and hypnotic as he climbed the steps to join Imara in the spotlight. Her fingers slipped into his hand, which morphed from Sconza's lanky digits into Mallan's black nailed appendage, and he lifted it to his mouth. When he kissed Imara's hand, his lips burned against her delicate skin and sent a different kind of heat pooling low in her abdomen. A slow wanting that needed to be fed woke in her blood.

Mallan's lips moved from her hand, to her wrist, to inner elbow and shoulder, and finally trailing along Imara's jawline. He stopped there, pulling away with questioning eyes. Imara answered without a word, caressing his face with a gentle hand. As his lips moved to meet hers, a voice like music called her name from the wings. Her attention pulled, only catching a glimpse of Lorn before he turned to smoke.

Imara woke with gray morning light washing through the large windows, surprised no one had moved her in the night. Not that it meant she hadn't been found. When she first opened her eyes, her lead lay upon a pillow, and a white blanket, warm and softer than rabbit fur, covered her body.

Despite the additions in the night, sleeping on the hard floor left Imara aching and cold, but the raging fire in her had dimmed to embers.

Cooled, and a little smug she'd been left relatively alone, it was time to face whatever waited for her two floors below.

Leaving the pillow where it lay, Imara gathered up the blanket, wrapping it around her shoulders, donning it like a cape. It was with a heavy heart she headed down to her suite, her every step haunted by the dream of Mallan's lips and the guilt that came with it.

CHAPTER

ELEVEN

Imara

Breakfast waited for Imara when she arrived in her suite, almond scones with lemon curd accompanied by a pot of rich floral coffee and containers of cream and sugar. She sat, discarding the blanket, which became useless the moment she entered the room. The crackling fireplace kept Imara's suite warm and welcoming to her aching, cold bones. As she reached for a pastry, a swirl of smoke appeared next to the meal, disappearing as quickly as it came. When it cleared, a single black orchid remained, a folded note tied to its delicate stem, Imara scrawled in a fine script across the front.

She ignored the note. Knowing it was from Mallan, she wanted nothing to do with it, yet. She wasn't ready to address the previous night. Whether it was the shock of his revelation over appetizers, or the unsettling dream she had during the night, Imara was shaken. She needed time to come to grips with it all.

After finishing her meal, Imara gathered up the blanket and placed it on her bed before getting ready for the day. The note and orchid appeared on one of the plush pillows, their appearance halted her. She looked back to the table, almost in disbelief that the gift followed her, and to her surprise a note and flower still sat where she left them. Imara rolled her eyes at the absurdity of Mallan's insistence, then turned on heel and marched to the bathroom. She'd get to reading what he had to say when she was ready.

The notes and flowers continued to appear at random points throughout the day. A pair of orchids appeared on the vanity, along with another note, as Imara pampered her skin after a hot bath to relieve her aching body. She found another up in the tower when she went to retrieve the discarded pillow, finding the items in place of what she sought. When Imara explored the library, not desiring to read, wanting to be out of her suite, a deep red rose was added to the orchids and note.

They kept coming. The flowers doubled every time a note smoked into existence. During lunch. As Imara dared to revisit the rooftop garden outside of the library. At dinner, which she took in her room, still not ready to deal with Mallan. With every attempt, her mood soured even more. At the end of the day, as she prepared to climb into bed, one final and exceptionally large bouquet popped up in the center of the bed. Imara had enough.

Exasperated, she gathered the notes and flowers still scattered about the room, with every one her irritation grew ten fold. The grand, heartfelt gesture Mallan dogged Imara with all day, fell flat. The latest one only made it worse. She didn't want his apologies or presents. He'd manipulated and lied through omission for years. Years. She'd always feel grateful toward the man she thought was saving her from life on the streets, but it wasn't enough to negate everything else.

His apology might have been better received had he not persisted with it all day. If he allowed Imara to come back to the original gift, when she was ready to face it, it might have been different. But he hadn't. He forced the issue and made it all about him without even being there.

Imara was fed up by the time she gathered every flower and slip of paper. Her arms were overflowing with the unwanted presents, and she knew just how to get rid of them.

The blazing fire in the center of the room crackled and popped as it kept the suite warm. The inferno inside was perfect for disposing of the nuisances. Placing the oversized bouquet down next to the fireplace, she used the curved side of a poker to open the glass doors, smiling as the seat washed over her. The flames were perfect for ridding herself of the overbearing apology. They almost seemed to want them as much as she didn't.

Imara stooped to gather the bouquet once more and toss them in to incinerate them, but as she reached for them, a cloud of smoke whisked them away. Furious, she turned about to survey the room for their reappearance. They were nowhere to be seen.

"Good riddance," she mumbled to herself as she headed bedward. At least she didn't have to deal with them anymore, though she couldn't say the same about their sender. She knew she'd have to deal with him sooner or later. Preferably later.

Imara attempted to settle into bed. She tossed and turned, the adrenaline fueled anger keeping her from getting comfortable. Kept her mind too active to calm down. After trying, and failing, to fall asleep after more than an hour, she knew sleep wouldn't come on its own. She needed something to help her rest. Imara pulled the call bell hanging next to her bed and waited for a maid to answer.

A few minutes later, a knock came at the door. "Come in," she called, expecting a maid to enter as they usually did with the verbal permission. Instead, the knock sounded again. The strange repeat made Imara debate not answering it. A new maid would know to enter when she granted it. The problem was, she needed a sleep aid. Imara had to answer. Reluctantly, she tossed aside the blanket and went to answer the door.

The knock repeated just as Imara gripped the handle. Whomever was waiting on the other side was persistent and impatient. Two qualities that gave Imara a good idea who stood there, leaving a knot in her chest. She could have not answered, but it didn't mean the being there would go away.

Imara opened the door just enough to see that her suspicion was correct. Mallan waited just beyond her threshold with the massive bouquet in his arms. Imara slammed the door in his face, growling as she stormed away with heavy enough steps to sting her bare feet.

Half-way to the bed, Mallan blocked her path, appearing before her in a wisp of smoke. His eyes blazed. For the first time since Imara had been forced to Shadowmire, his ire was directed at her. She didn't cower. His fury only made her own burn hotter.

"You lived in the mortal world long enough to know a door slammed in your face is not an invitation to enter. You can leave," she sidestepped his massive frame.

Flowers skittered to the floor, the stems and petals crunching softly under a single heavy footstep. A warm hand wrapped itself around one of Imara's wrists, reversing her retreat and spinning her back to face Mallan.

"Don't touch me," she seethed, yanking her wrist from his grip.

"Don't ignore me," he retorted with a snarl, his lip curling to reveal his sharp canines.

Imara's mind couldn't help but wander back to that dream and how his lips had felt on her skin. She forced the unwanted thoughts from her head as guilt wound its way in. "I'll do as I please when it comes to you. I want to ignore you, I don't want your gifts or apologies. You lied to me."

"Omitted information, not lied."

"Same thing," Imara screeched, lifting on tiptoe to get closer to his face. His arrogance pushed her over the edge, "You're an asshole." She left another handprint on his cheek.

Whether it was the name calling, or the fact Mallan was already burning with anger because of Imara's rejection of his apology, he didn't take the assault on as he had before. In a flash, he was on her, his large hand grasping her throat just enough to be uncomfortable, and his obsidian eyes blazed with wanting madness.

The initial shock of his physical act of dominance elicited a sharp gasp from Imara, fear passing through like a ghost before dissipating. Imara narrowed her eyes and grit her teeth. She was done letting this man control her, "You'd hurt your precious Starling, your destined, Mallan?" she challenged. "Do it then," she pressed her throat tighter against his palm and her heart galloped, both thrilled and frightened. The looming danger had her taunting the fae further, "Take what you want and prove how much of a monster you really are."

Mallan unleashed a husky growl in response as he dipped his head closer and grazed his mouth along her lips. Imara shivered, loving and hating the sensation; the igniting warmth of desire. It broke her. Imara couldn't stop the tears that formed from spilling, or the whimper that escaped her throat.

Mallan released his hold on Imara and stepped away, the fire in him doused by the anguish he caused her. His head hung, regret hunching his tall, proud frame, and making him appear vulnerable. More human. "Please," he whispered, "accept my apology." He smoked away, taking the mess of flowers and notes with him.

Every bit of strength and resolve Imara possessed left with

Mallan, knocking her legs out from under her. She crumbled to the floor, sobbing angrily and letting all of her emotion spill. She was hurt, afraid, and angry at her own weakness. Guilty and disgusted. Imara enjoyed that feeling of control taunting Mallan elicited. She wanted it. She'd wanted Mallan's lips on her own as much as she wanted them in her dream. That ate at her, roiled her stomach with shame.

She missed Lorn.

All of it held her to the floor, washing in her tears until Imara was empty. It could have been minutes, or hours, she didn't know, but she was absolutely spent when she pried herself from the cool marble and slunk back to bed feeling nothing. As she lay down and pulled the heavy blanket around herself, a shield against everything, she spotted a folded note on the bedside table. Plain and humble.

With no energy left for anger, she reached for the note and unleashed a heavy sigh as she unfolded it to reveal the words inside.

Imara

I ache with regret for the pain and hurt my actions and words have put on you. If I could undo it all, I would. I would start over with honesty and transparency. I will open the rest of my days making it up to you. Serving you. Only when you are ready. Until then, I will distance myself and wait for your word.

Mallan

The sincerity of the words on the paper weighed a thousand tons and occupied Imara's every thought for days. She malingered in her suite, contemplating the entirety of her time at Shadowmire. Her entire relationship with Mallan, with Sconza.

What it all broke down to was that Imara had nowhere else to go. From what she'd seen and read, the Under Court at large was no place for a human. She wouldn't dare venture out there on her own. Every bridge back in Ocean Fare had been burned. Mallan's estate was her home for the foreseeable future. The strange tension between herself and her host made for an uncomfortable living situation.

Mallan made it abundantly clear what his intentions were. He wanted no ill will between them, and he wanted her to be his. Everything was in Imara's hands. It was her choice to make Shadowmire a home or a prison. She knew she would wither as a prisoner. Imara also knew she couldn't live walking on eggshells all the time with heavy tension and silent interactions. Living with jumbled emotions in her heart would be torture, as well as make everyone around her miserable.

It was time to move on. Time for forging a peaceable existence with the one Imara swore she wouldn't concede to. Do the one thing she swore she would never do. It was time to forgive Mallan, accept his apology and begin a new. Not for him, for her own sake. That forgiveness, though, was a gritty and jagged slope that threatened to break the bigger promise she'd made to herself. Her promise to never be his. Her recent dreams showed her it wasn't an impossibility. Part of her already craved him, despite her best efforts. Getting close, giving up the unadulterated hate, would only make it worse.

Even though she knew how much she risked, Imara would forgive Mallan.

THERE WERE MOTHS, delicate and frightening, in every corner of Imara's body as she headed down to the banquet hall for dinner. Mallan was hosting a dinner for his regents and other high fae of the Under Court that held influence. They met to discuss business, for taxes to be paid. Imara knew interrupting the monthly gathering was risky, and the best way to make the biggest impression. Interrupting the affair ensured Mallan knew she meant every word she was about to divulge.

The dinner, she also knew, was formal, as were so many of the evening meals at Shadowmire. Some more so than others. Mallan liked the grandness of them, the luxury. Imara needed to dress up, perhaps more than she had for the dinner where she'd learned of his deception. Luckily, Mallan had seen fit to suit her wardrobe with many fine gowns of varying formality. She selected a sky blue strapless dress with a sweetheart neckline. The gauzy skirts gradually turned midnight and were embellished with crystals that twinkled like the night sky. Imara accented the gown with a teardrop diamond on a sterling chain. Since not even the maids knew of her plan, she was left to do her own hair and makeup, opting for some simple lipgloss and to pin her hair back with diamond studded combs. Had she let the maids in on her secret, perhaps she would have been the picture of perfection. Made up to look like a princess. But the look she did herself was simple and elegant enough to be effective.

The goblins at the banquet hall door snapped to attention as Imara approached, surprise lifting their strange eyes. They knew she wasn't supposed to be there. "Dinner is in your suite tonight," one garbled, his jowls wobbling with every word. "Mallan has important guests."

"I thought I had an open invitation to join Mallan whenever it suits me," Imara feigned ignorance. "Are you going to tell him you turned me away simply because he has guests? I'm sure he won't get angry."

Fear flashed across the goblins' eyes. The last thing they wanted was to be punished for barring Imara entrance, and she knew it.

The other goblin standing guard wasn't so sure about Imara's reasoning, "Mallan never confirmed that with us."

"Does he have to clear everything with his henchmen?" Imara arched her brow. "Is it worth the risk of not letting me pass?"

The pair of monstrous creatures whispered heatedly among themselves for several moments. Self preservation won out in the end, and they granted her passage through the doors.

"It's only a matter of time…" Mallan's deep timber halted abruptly when Imara entered the room. Every eye fell on her. The corner of Mallan's mouth lifted with a glint in his eye, she'd intrigued him with her unexpected presence. "Imara," he greeted, and a susurration swept through the gathered myriad of guests, "what are you doing here?"

"I've come for dinner," she replied coyly.

"I'm afraid there's no dinner tonight."

Imara looked around at the plates of food and filled goblets sitting before each of them. "The meal before you all says different-ly," she joked. The gathered fae chuckled at her witty observation.

"What I mean is, dinner is a private affair tonight. Business. Much too dull for…"

"A woman?" Imara cut him off. "A lowly mortal?"

"I was going to say for me even. I'd much rather have your company, no offense to my associates," he acknowledged them to keep them appeased. "But, as I understood, you wanted nothing to do with me." Mallan rubbed his cheek as though he could still feel the sting of Imara's hand.

She bit her lip, "About that…" Mallan's eyes locked on hers, a thread of hope linking them, and a broad smile broke across his face. "In that case," he turned his attention back on his guests, "if you'll excuse me for a moment to two, we will continue our discussion when I return." The room nodded, though Mallan didn't need their permission, there were formalities to follow. He'd do as he wished, anyway.

Mallan crossed the hall, joining Imara. "Shall we?" He offered with a sweeping gesture and a look that said he couldn't wait to hear what she had to say.

Before leaving, Imara gave a nod and curtsey to the fae, accentuated by a saccharine smile. With a hand hovering over the small of her back, so close she could feel the heat of his flesh through her dress, he ushered Imara from the room. The look he gave the goblins standing guard as he passed could have melted them.

"You interrupted a very important meeting," he began the moment they entered his office. "Have we moved on from hating me to trying to destroy me?"

"I have something to say, and I needed to make sure I had your attention."

"You always have my attention, Starling." Mallan, looking concerned at Imara's admission, crossed the office and sat in the chair behind the large desk, resting his feet on top. "What did you want to tell me that couldn't wait?"

"You don't deserve my forgiveness," Imara started.

"Then why the dramatics?" He interrupted. Imara hardly thought her interruption was dramatic.

"If you interrupt me, I might change my mind," she warned, knowing he'd benefit from what she had to say. With a slight eye roll and a waving hand, he cued Imara to continue. "You don't deserve my forgiveness, Mallan. You've upended my life in the worst ways, for your gain. If I had another choice, I'd burn the bridge you've attempted to erect over and over again. Since I don't, since I am forced to be in your life, I won't. For my sake, I'll build it with you, give you the forgiveness anyway so I can move on. Living with this angst isn't what I want. I want peace. So, let's start over, erase our history and start fresh."

"You'd do that for me?"

"No. Aren't you listening? I'm doing this for me. So I can be something other than sad and angry all the time. It's too hard, too confusing."

Mallan dropped his feet from the desk, sat forward, and rested his chin on templed fingers. His brows furrowed as he mulled over what Imara said. Meanwhile, she worried her lip, hoping he'd see the advantage for him in what she wanted. This was his best shot at being in Imara's good graces, even though it wasn't likely she'd ever give in to what he truly wanted. It had to be better than having her hate him.

After a minute of thinking, he stood and came back around the desk where Imara stood waiting for his answer. He towered over her, smirking for a moment before taking one of her hands and placing a soft kiss on the back of it. "My name is Mallan, Lord of the Under Court. It's an honor to have you in my home."

"Imara, Lord Mallan," she dipped her head in a slight curtsey.

"Just call me Mallan, Miss Imara. I hope you enjoy your stay. I must say, I'm looking forward to getting to know you."

"And I, you."

"Now, if you'll excuse me, Starling, I should return to my guests. I promise tomorrow I'll give you a proper tour of my home."

"I'm looking forward to it." The part of Imara clinging to her grief and anger had no interest in learning more about Shadowmire or its master. The other part of her looked forward to it. To moving on and trying to find some happiness as she learned more about her new home.

CHAPTER
TWELVE

Mallan

The regents all turned to the sound of the doors opening and witnessed their Lord's entrance. Mallan couldn't help the grin that graced his usually stoic face.

"Was that the girl?" the Wraith King perched her head on a skeletal fist, and Mallan schooled his features.

"Yes."

"She's the one meant to be your key to the downfall of the High Court? She's human," the regent from the Frozen Caves scoffed, his blue tinged skin paled by the soft warmth that the candles gave off.

"There's more to her than what she appears she is," Mallan seethed in response. He narrowed his dark eyes at each of the regents around the table. He'd have none of them questioning his judgement, let alone Imara.

"I take it from your change in demeanor," Samir, the Living Ghost, noted from behind his obsidian mask, "that you're pleased at the results of her interruption?" The regent from the

Glass Desert's warm eyes glinted with his question as he pulled the thick, fur-lined cloak tighter around his shoulders. The fae of the warm climates didn't tolerate the constant chill of Shadowmire in even the mildest of seasons, let alone as the coldest of them approached.

"We have tentative reason to think so, though she is a fickle creature. I'm sure she'll be threatening me over something again, soon," Mallan chuckled, reliving the memories of every fiery encounter he shared with her these past days. He didn't want those moments where she challenged him to end.

The regents tittered approvingly, dared to show excitement that one day they might have a hand in the control of all of Sylphea. "Perhaps a toast is in order?" the Wraith King hoped.

The Lord of the Under Court tipped his head with a smirk. His regents' moods elevated to match his own, and change was in the air. He called over a servant with a wave of his hand, whispering in his ear before he disappeared to the kitchen with the request. The servant returned shortly after, followed by several others, each carrying two crystal stemless goblets filled with viscous dark red liquid and setting them before the guests.

"Brandied blood!," the Wraith King exclaimed, taking a whiff of the contents. Greed lit her milky eye as she waited impatiently for Mallan to make the toast. He knew well enough a wraith's taste for blood, despite their diet being only that of fear and souls.

Mallan sniffed his glass as well, the heady copper laced with sweet brandy made his head swim with fantasies of how Imara's flesh would feel and blood would taste when he finally claimed her.

Raising the cup in the air, Mallan stood, creating a wave of motion as his regents followed suit. "To the Under Court, long may it prosper," he toasted.

"To your destiny," Samir added before anyone could move

to sip from the crystal. His toast made Mallan smirk once more. It delighted him to no end that his regent included her in the moment. She was, after all, more important than any of them could fathom.

PROGRESS. The taste of brandied blood still lingered on his tongue, sweet and burning. Mallan sighed into the lush cushions of the couch in his suite. Even though his night ended in the company of his regents, his mind couldn't break free of his Starling. Imara was full of surprises. He'd expected a gradual change in her after he'd invaded her dreams, came to her as both himself and the insipid husband she refused to let go of, but he hadn't seen her acquiescing so quickly to those planted seeds. Soon enough, he'd move his plans forward, seduce his Starling and make her his.

He promised her a tour, and he would give her one and then some. A grand gesture to start their fresh slate. It had to be perfect, be one that would reignite her true sparkle. The magnificence she had when all eyes were on her on the stage and her heart soared free. The woman she was before she met that Lorn and the woman she should have been if she hadn't allowed the wrong love to diminish her star. She needed music back in her life.

He stood, crossing the suite to his bed and tugging the call rope. Minutes later, a maid with pastel yellow skin entered his suite. He didn't know her name, he didn't need to know it, to him the servants were disposable and easy to replace.

"Lord Mallan?" she inquired, keeping her eyes locked on the floor. None of the maids dared to look him in his eyes. Her subservience only reminded Mallan of his destined, how different she was from all others in Shadowmire. She stared him down with no issue from the beginning.

"I want a team of maids in the locked room on the floor below the tower. Make it sparkling by morning. I'm gifting it to Imara first thing."

"Yes, Lord Mallan," she bowed deep and scurried away to complete the task given.

Once the maid was gone, Mallan fell to his bed, splaying on his back and stared at the ceiling. Sleep would not come easy, that he knew. Imara had wiped the slate clean and gave him the chance to know her as himself. She forgave him, in a matter of speaking, and that was enough to keep his thoughts spinning toward the day he rid himself of Lord Khryton and ruled all of Sylphea. Dreaming of the day when Imara would say she'd be his, and she'd transform into a dark beauty as ruthless and hungry as he was. Hungry for power. Hungry for him.

Thoughts of that future made his blood race.

THIRTEEN

Imara

Imara's breakfast was served with a note from Mallan asking her to meet him at his suite in an hour. No matter how hard she tried to take her time, to enjoy the lush frittata bursting with bright vegetables and salty ham, she finished faster than she meant to. She felt happier than she had in a long time. That happiness had her looking forward to getting ready.

There was something different in the air, brought on by the lightening of Imara's heart, her soul. Choosing to move on without anger was freeing. She was even excited to see more of Shadowmire.

After breakfast, Imara dressed, picking a soft pink empire waisted dress, and a cropped black jacket with matching pink piping, braided her hair, and set out to meet Mallan, who was already waiting in one of the high-back chairs in the sitting area.

"Am I late?" it surprised Imara to find him there, and she wondered if she'd taken more time than she thought.

"No, not at all," he rose to greet her, assessing her attire as he did. Under his study, she felt like she wasn't wearing a thing. Imara couldn't help but notice how casual he looked in a simple white tunic, the sleeves rolled to his elbows, and black trousers. She couldn't help but think he looked more human that way. If it wasn't for his horns, he'd be unnoticeable in Morrea. "My impatience made me early."

"You didn't wait too long?"

"For you, Starling, I'd wait centuries."

Mallan's flattering words pushed his obsession to the front of Imara's thoughts. They made her want to run, to turn icy and forget the day he had planned. She closed her eyes and steadied the irritation that tried to take over. Keeping her word to Mallan was going to take a lot of patience and work.

"I have a surprise for you before I keep my promises."

"Oh?" Imara opened her eyes, Mallan's voice breaking her meditation.

The corner of his mouth lifted in response as he held a hand out for Imara. Her lips pulled between her teeth, unsure if she wanted to take his offer. Yet, she'd promised herself she'd be better. She had to remind herself of the blank slate she'd offered Mallan. With that, Imara relaxed and slid her hand into his.

"Thank you, Starling," he pressed his lips against the back of her hand. They were warm and soft against Imara's skin, sending a shiver through her that escaped as a barely audible gasp. Her reaction left his eyes shining and left her cheeks stained with blush. He released her hand moments later and led Imara toward the stairs, allowing her to pass him before ascending.

They climbed the low lit stairs, his hand guiding her from the small of her back. Up and up they went to the floor just beneath the glass tower, Imara's nerves grew with every step. Her breath hitched even more when he led them to the locked door there and handed her a heavy golden key shaped like an eighth note.

"Open it," he directed in an eager tone. His excitement was palpable, making Imara wonder what surprise lay behind the door.

With an unsteady hand, Imara slid the key into the lock, which fought against being turned, as if time had tried to keep it sealed. When it finally gave and the cool handle beneath her palm twisted, the fluttering of wings in her abdomen quickened even more.

Imara pushed the door open, revealing a large space completely unlike any other she'd seen in Shadowmire. The curved walls were done up in gold and silver marbled plaster, smoothed to a shine that reflected the soft glow of globes of light that hung from the ceiling on varied length gold chains. No other decorations added to the opulence, not even windows, and there was only one set of furniture.

Sitting in the center of the space sat a golden grand piano, its accompanying bench upholstered plushy in a sparkling gray fabric.

"Welcome to your music room," Mallan crowed in his excitement over the reveal.

Imara stepped into the room as though it were a place of worship, her steps echoing against the walls as she made her way to the piano. "Mallan, it's beautiful," she sighed, her words a prayer of worship to the exquisite space. She ran her fingers along the edges of the instrument as she walked around it, the keys she plucked answered back in perfect tune. Imara took a quick peek inside the bench and found it full of sheet music, some she recognized from Sconza's. "This is the best surprise."

"You like it?"

"I love it." The gift reverberated deep inside Imara's soul. She had no idea if or when music would fill the walls, though.

Music abandoned her after Lorn's death. The music room wouldn't go unused, however. Imara knew that just being near the instrument would bring her more joy and peace. It would be her sanctuary.

"Would you like to?" He gestured to the bench, his dark eyes full of hope.

Imara swallowed against the thickness in her throat. She didn't know how to tell him she didn't have music in her anymore. That she didn't know if she ever would. Instead, she shook her head, "No. There will be plenty of time to spend here in the future. You promised me a tour."

"That I did," Mallan gave a slight nod, the corner of his mouth lifting in a half satisfied smile. There wasn't a lot of Shadowmire Imara hadn't yet seen. The floor below their suites held four identical suites, smaller than the grander ones above them. Each of them decorated with their own themes, all dark and opulent as Mallan's room. Imara's room was the only one not decorated completely in deeper hues. She wondered if it had always been that way, or if it had been done up special for her, like the music room.

On the same floor was the library, which she was already familiar with. The rooftop garden accessible through one of its grand windows, while beautiful, still conjured the frightful memory of the wraith.

Of course, there was the main level, with the banquet hall, Mallan's office, and the ballroom. All of which Imara had seen, leading them to skip the floor altogether and head straight to the lower levels. The servants were housed in the first sub-level, and the goblins in the second. Then, far below the main house, Mallan's dungeon lurked in absolute darkness.

The dank jail level smelled of mildew, every sound echoed against the stone walls. That bottommost level gave Imara chills, her mind going wild with thoughts of what lay in the dark. She never wanted to see it again.

"Thank you for the tour, Mallan," she said, lingering at the bottom of the stairs on the main level.

"It's not done yet, Starling. You still need to see the grounds."

SHADOWMIRE SAT ATOP A HIGH, stepped hill and backed by a cliff overlooking a vast slate ocean, thick fog hugging the surface until the world at large turned gray. That fog, a magical blanket, was a barrier between Sylphea and the rest of the world, a cloak separating the magical world from that of the mortals.

"The fog is called the Terrors, or it once was by mortals because of what happened to most that dared take it on," Mallan explained as they stood at the edge of Shadowmire's land looking over the sea. "It was put there by Queen Alette, before her disappearance, of course, and will remain until she takes it down. Which will never happen, of course. She has no line to claim what was hers, and it's more than likely she's faded as her sister queens have."

"What happens to mortals that cross it?"

"Most mortal ships that enter are never seen again. The men, forever changed and haunted by things only they'd seen but can never quite remember. The sea plays with their minds, alters them, and only them. It doesn't affect fae."

"Have any mortals ever made it through?" Imara shivered at the thought of moving through that fog, happy she hadn't come to Sylphea by sea. "Not through to Sylphea, but turned around and back to where they came from somehow. There's a distinct lack of mortals in fae lands."

Mallan's response sat heavy in her body, made her feel a

second of loneliness before forcing it away. Imara was likely the lone mortal in that stage place. She stared out over the expanse of water south of the Under Court, and couldn't help but wonder if there ever would be others like her. If her presence in Sylphea might change things. She also couldn't help but wonder, if she ever left, ever made her way back to Morrea and Ocean Fare without Mallan's help, would she suffer the same lifelong terrors others had?

"Are you coming?" Mallan's touch on her shoulder pulled her from her thoughts. "There's one more thing here, at your new home, I want to show you."

Home. Thinking of Shadowmire as her home, accepting her place among a world of fae and other creatures, soured her insides. She saw it as another example of how she needed to remind herself that her decision was for the best, and in time those feelings would lessen. She hoped they would. After all, habits and emotions couldn't change overnight.

"Yes," she tore her gaze away from the churning sea and its blanket of clouds with a smile, tried to hide the unease she felt.

"Good." Mallan led her along a wending path. The trail forked, one branch leading back to the estate, and the other down a gentle slope hidden by thorny bushes at the cliff's edge. They took the second path, which led to an outcropping with a large deciduous tree. Every branch held several large ravens, and even more filled the sky nearby.

Next to the tree sat a stone tower, a great oak door at its base, and small arched windows lined the height of it, all the way to the top. An oxidized copper roof topped the pointed structure. The large birds swooped in and out of the windows, flitting between tree and tower as if in a dance.

Mallan whistled low as he approached the towers, stopping with one arm stretched out. The responding cacophony of caws that filled the air could have been heard from miles away. "This is the rookery."

Imara laughed at the sight of the birds flocking to the fae, "Why doesn't it surprise me that you have pet ravens? It's so fitting."

"They're not pets, I assure you. Most of these birds are as wild as they come. Some are trained messengers, but their social nature has attracted their wild friends to live among them, too. It's good for them, helps them stay connected to nature." As he explained, the black birds defied his words, many of them landing on his arm in greeting. A few dared venture closer to deliver light pecks on Mallan's cheek or to steal a few hairs from his head.

"Sure, they aren't pets," Imara teased while watching the ravens continue to greet him and fly away. The way he gently ruffled their feathers or returned their light pecks with light kisses on their beaks spoke volumes about how he felt about them. It also tugged at her heartstrings, just a little, to see him be so tender.

One raven, a piebald bird smaller than the others, approached Mallan in a flurry of white and deep blue black. It landed on his arm, eyeing Imara with curiosity when all the others only had eyes for him. He chittered, cocking his head from side to side, and paced up and down the length of his arm impatiently.

"He wants to say hello," Mallan chuckled. "Go on, Starling, hold your hand out." The bird cawed as if to affirm what he claimed.

The bird's sharp talons set a tremble in her hand as she held it out for him. He made no move to hop from Mallan to Imara, only looked between her hand and face with curiosity. It was like he wanted her closer. She stretched her hand closer, inch by inch and watching the raven's reaction, until Imara's fingers grazed Mallan's skin. Only then did the raven move, a gentle step onto her offered hand and taking care not to put too much pressure on the talons she feared. He continued his climb up her arm, chattering as he went, until he reached her shoulder. Then he settled, puffing his feathers contentedly.

"He likes you."

Imara's nerves settled as the raven made himself comfortable. "He's sweet. Is he one of your messengers?"

"No, and I'd wouldn't call him sweet. I have known him to peck anyone that gets too close to him. I have scars to prove it. It took years for him to trust me. But you..."

"I don't believe it," Imara scoffed.

"No, I mean it," Mallan brushed aside his hair to reveal a circular scar behind his ear. "He's mean."

"Don't listen to him, Corvus. You are a very sweet bird." The raven chittered and ruffled his feathers.

"Corvus?" Mallan arched a brow, mystified by how quickly the bird had taken to Imara, and vice versa.

"Why not?"

"Redundant, but Corvus it is then."

Corvus stayed with Imara, perched on her shoulder until they reached the top of the path, happily cawing in her ear. Imara pretended she understood his language and responded to every chitter. Mallan stayed silent as he hiked behind her, though she could feel his amusement. At the trail-head, Corvus flew away. Imara watched him, a little wistful as his snowy feathers disappeared toward the rookery.

Mallan continued to escort Imara until they reached her suite. "Thank you for the tour," she said as they approached the door. She turned to see Mallan, his face wistful and sad. She always felt taken aback when he showed emotions other than cockiness and wrath.

"I'm sorry, Starling."

"For what?" Mallan's apology confused her. Nothing bad had happened on the tour that made her think he owed her one. To assure him, she added, "The rookery was magical, and the music room... I can't thank you enough."

"You're lonely."

Imara was lonely, mostly. But she wasn't alone, she had people to talk to. "I have the maids," she said. She genuinely liked the maids once she overlooked their fae features and got comfortable with them. They were kind.

"The maids aren't enough. You need a proper friend."

"I have you, aren't we trying to be friends?"

"Yes, but that isn't enough. I'm not a good friend. I can't give you the companionship you deserve, not with all my responsibilities. As much as I'd love to shirk those and spend more time with you than with anyone else, I can't."

"I'm okay, I am used to entertaining myself."

"No. I don't like to think of you alone," he paused in thought. "You need Tamsin."

FOURTEEN

Mallan

The mists of Alcara crept to the shores beyond Cailloch, the air had taken on the first notes of cooler weather. Mallan noted the lapping of the water along the bank picked up. The ferry was drawing near.

Tamsin was the only one in his employ he waited for with patience. It was she that revealed his destiny, and for that he owed her. She could be late without repercussion, a rare reprieve in Mallan's eyes. There were very few who could defy him and suffer no consequence. If he didn't need the witch, he wouldn't tolerate her insolence. Mallan needed her more than ever, for Imara's sake. She was the only one he trusted to befriend his Starling, and steer her in the right direction discreetly.

The bow of the ferry broke through the fog and slowly emerged to the shore. Mallan rolled his eyes when he spotted the witch who beamed at him from the boat. It was a wonder Tamsin hadn't allied herself with the High Court, which aligned more with her outward appearance and bubbly personality.

With her vibrant blonde hair and deep magenta eyes, she sharply contrasted the dark looks that most of the fae of the Under Court had. Her manner of dress set her apart even further. Tamsin's uniqueness was the exact reason he thought Imara would warm to her with ease.

Tamsin stood as the boat docked. Her powder blue dress sparkled in the dim light, the front of the skirt barely reaching her mid-thigh looked more like a tutu until it sloped. To form the long trailing back of it. She made no move to exit the ferry, only stood there with her delicate hand outstretched in waiting. When Mallan didn't move to help her off the vessel, she cleared her throat.

"Really?" he scoffed. "You can levitate and you expect gallantry?" Tamsin only shrugged with the barest hint of amusement. Mallan shook his head and stepped forward to offer her his hand, grumbling as she slid hers onto his open palm and beamed again.

"See, it didn't kill you to be a gentleman," she giggled at his scowl. "Consider it a lesson in properly wooing a girl."

"I've no issues there, witch." Mallan found Tamsin's insolence more trying than usual. "I've a job for you."

"I'm at your service, as always, my Lord," she bowed, becoming more subdued when she realized his visit wasn't one of leisure, or to scorn her for her taste in partners. "What can I see for you?"

"I don't need your visions today, but your personage. I need you to befriend Imara."

"She's here then?" Mallan nodded in reply. A shadow crossed Tamsin's face, and unease settled in the air.

"What is it?"

"Nothing," Tamsin settled his worry. "Only, you can't pay people to be other people's friends. It just isn't done, and always ends badly."

"You're not being paid. I'm doing this for her. She needs more than ravens and servants to keep her company. You are the only one I trust with her."

Tamsin laughed, full bellied and long. "You surprise me, Lord Mallan. Of all your people, you trust her with me? You aren't afraid I'll corrupt her with my wanton ways?"

"Do you want this or not?"

"What's in it for me?" Mallan growled, the witch truly tested him. "I'm kidding, big guy. Of course I want to meet her. I could use someone other than my coven to cavort with. Though, it wouldn't hurt if you let me have five minutes with Braxar," she wiggled her eyebrows.

"Not a chance," Mallan ran his hand over his face, more than ready to get back to Shadowmire, but there was more he needed from her. "I need you to coax her to choosing me. She's stubborn, sentimental. I want her to be mine by the solstice, do you understand?"

"Of course, but you must grant me full access to her without hovering. Trust in my methods."

Mallan seethed inwardly. He didn't like giving up that control to anyone, but he was willing to do as the witch asked. It was for a greater purpose. "Be at the estate in the morning. Imara will be expecting you."

Tamsin danced like a child on the gritty shore of Cailloch as Mallan turned to smoke away home.

FIFTEEN

Imara

Mallan had summoned his witch, Tamsin, to the estate. Imara didn't know what to expect with her arrival, though she had her theories. Tamsin, or so Mallan said, would be a good friend because of all the beings in the Under Court, in Sylphea even, she knew as much as he did. He assumed she would hit it off with Imara the most and thought the witch's companionship would benefit her.

Imara hadn't ever had real friends, other than the people she considered family at Sconza's. According to Mallan, the servants and maids didn't count, or weren't enough. She needed at least one friend worthy of her. Her opinion of worthiness differed from his, and she had no issue befriending the lower fae that worked in Shadowmire. Although she drew the line at the goblins. She'd never get over their part in how she got there.

Agreeing to meet Tamsin was more humoring Mallan and keeping the spirit of their fresh start alive than it was a true desire to meet the witch.

Her mortal mind already predicted everything she thought she needed to know about Tamsin. She'd be cantankerous, old and bent, with wiry hair and long bony fingers curled from the ravages of time. Everything fairytales taught Imara witches were. She was certain they'd share no common ground. The impending introduction left her cold. Nervous and cold.

"What does one wear when meeting a witch?" she asked herself as she stared into the wardrobe, feeling overwhelmed. Everything provided for Imara seemed either too formal for a casual meeting, or too casual to meet someone Mallan held in high regard.

"You're meeting Tamsin?" Fern's delicate voice made Imara jump.

"Yes. Mallan insists I need friends. Friends who aren't maids. I disagree. You ladies are plenty company."

"That is kind of you, Mistress. Lord Mallan is right, though. You need a friend you can leave the estate with. We maids don't get to." That bit of information hurt Imara's heart. The maids and servants had no life outside their work, and no one should live like that. She'd have to take that up with Mallan and have it fixed. "I'd suggest dressing up more than you expected to. Tamsin might leave you feeling underdressed."

"She's a witch, how fancy can she be?"

"You'd be surprised," Fern sidestepped around Imara and looked in the wardrobe. After a minute, she pulled out a dress Imara never would have considered for the day. A gray dress, with a scoop neck and lantern sleeves, the fitted bodice embellished with shimmering crystals giving way to a full tulle skirt. It was definitely less formal than others she'd worn, but nicer than what Imara would have chosen.

～

IMARA CHOSE NOT to meet Tamsin in her suite. It felt too personal to have a stranger there, especially one she was so unsure of meeting. It was one of her sanctuaries in Shadowmire, a place where she didn't have to mask happiness to keep Mallan's coddling at bay. Her place of mourning, when maids weren't about to report to their master, to grieve Lorn, who she still missed so much it hurt.

That night, the night she lost the love of her life, felt ages away. Yet, the memories sat fresh in Imara's thoughts as if they'd just happened. Time hadn't lessened the pain. As long as her dreams chose him as their star, which they did more often than not, she didn't think it ever would. She hoped he'd visit her in her sleep forever; she wasn't ready to let him go.

Being in the Under Court, Imara's dreams had become more vivid than ever. Sweet visions of Lorn and their stolen life together. Dreams that felt real, breaking her heart when her eyes fluttered open in the morning and he wasn't there. Dreams which left her blushing and hot from phantom hands on her body in ways that never happened.

Then there were the dreams of Mallan, that left Imara tingling and wanting, made her curious if how he made her feel there would match up in real life. Above all, those dreams left her conflicted. They threatened to incinerate the vow she made against him. Her heart ached with the guilt she felt desiring her husband's murderer.

Imara couldn't go to Mallan for answers about why her dreams were so lifelike, either. His obsidian eyes always seemed to read her every thought and need. He read between lines far too well for her liking. She didn't dare ask the maids, either. They reported to Mallan, though they were often amused by the way Imara dared stand up to the fae when no one else did.

It was the conundrum that ultimately led to Imara actually agreeing to meet Tamsin; she didn't know her the way anyone else in Shadowmire did. She had no expectations of her, and could be an unbiased ear. At least that's what she told herself, knowing the introduction would have happened no matter what. Mallan got what he wanted, mostly.

Imara waited for Mallan's witch in the music room, sitting on the bench with no intention of touching the beautiful instrument. The longer she waited, though, the harder it was to deny the temptation the piano before her presented. She caved, plucking away at the keys of shining gold and ebony, and reminisced about her time on stage.

All those harried nights of performances, the rushing back and forth in a crowded backstage, and making hasty costume changes on the go; Imara missed them. She missed the thrill of stage lights shining on her and singing her heart out.

Her hands could go over standards and scales on any set of ivory keys with her eyes closed, and Imara did. She let herself imagine the warmth of the lights washing over her body as she hummed along with the notes. Imara felt she was far from ready to be the Starling again, yet the tune drifted through her and brought a sense of wholeness she hadn't felt since her wedding night. A musical bandage for her soul, which still felt tattered despite her efforts to find peace.

Imara got lost in the cathartic moment, her hands drifting from one song to the next without bothering to acknowledge the world around her. In her mind she was back at Sconza's, Lorn beaming at her from the audience while she entertained the dregs and well to do of Ocean Fare alike. She could practically smell the bitter ale and cheap whiskey served there. Even the sawdust floor.

Her fingers only slid from the piano after she ran out of songs she knew by heart, resting them in her lap and keeping her eyes closed against the real world. A slight smile curved her lips as she savored the feeling and let the warm memories brew.

"Don't stop on my account," a sultry voice jolted Imara back to reality. She opened her eyes to see a woman leaning over the end of the piano, her big magenta eyes framed by thick lashes and tipped in gold, shimmered with amusement.

Imara flushed under her gaze, embarrassed she'd been surprised. "Are you Tamsin?" she asked, skeptical that the beauty before her could be a witch. This woman was the complete opposite of the withering crone Imara painted in her mind's eye. Young, petite, and curvaceous, she put Tilly's beauty to shame with her gilded appearance. Tight golden curls bounced on her shoulders, and her bronze skin glowed under intricate and fascinating ruby colored runic tattoos. Sheathed in a sleeves golden dress that hugged her every plentiful curve, and arms and fingers adorned with shining gold jewels, she looked like an idol to be worshiped.

"Not what you were expecting?" Tamsin confirmed, twirling in a circle, the skirt of her dress flared out to reveal hidden sheer panels. She knew exactly how staggering she was. The kind of woman that belonged on the arm of someone powerful, like Mallan. Surely Tamsin would have been a better match for him than Imara, a lowly human. Yet, according to him, destiny had other ideas.

"Far from it," Imara laughed at her own expense and stood, offering her hand.

The witch glanced at her outstretched hand and rolled her eyes before coming around the piano herself and wrapping Imara in her arms, "I'm more of a hugger." Tamsin smelled like honey, wildflowers, and amber. Everything about her defied the dark world around them, a ray of sunshine cutting through the constant clouds that hung over the Under Court. Imara found she liked her more for it. "I can't tell you how excited I've been to meet Mallan's destined," she quipped as she pulled out of the embrace.

Imara's face twisted at the reminder, one she knew she would be constantly reminded of.

"Did I say something wrong?"

"I'm not on the best terms with the idea, is all. I had someone. Someone very special in my life and I'm in no rush to replace him."

"I'm sorry," the way the words fell from Tamsin's lips was as if she already knew the whole story. Like she knew every ounce of Imara's pain and truly regretted it. "When things are shown to me to foretell, there's no detail of the fallout. I couldn't have known all those decades ago what life you might have had outside of it. I'm only shown what I need to see."

"You?" Imara blinked. This woman, Tamsin, she was the one that told Mallan they were destined. It was unbelievable. She couldn't have been much older than Imara herself.

"Don't hate me."

"I don't," she swallowed. "Like you said, variables are unpredictable." The air became palpable with things unsaid, marring the pleasant meeting. Instead of letting it hang, Imara shifted to some light humor, "You look good for your age."

Tamsin gave a full bellied, enchanting laugh, "Thank you, I try." She hoisted herself to sit on the piano and looked down at Imara. "I rather like you. Knew I would."

"What? Did you foresee us being friends?" Imara wondered what all Tamsin had seen about her, a little unsettled that she had such an ability. The power to know the future could topple kingdoms and raise the lowest up high. Such a gift had the potential for mass destruction in the wrong hands.

"I don't look into my own fate. Witches who do it go mad when they learn what waits for them. I've trained hard not to see anything that could lead me down that path, for that reason, I don't offer services to friends," she looked pointedly at Imara. A warning she didn't have to give. Imara had no interest in knowing what lay ahead for her. Her life already had been too damaged by fortune telling.

"Isn't Mallan your friend?"

Tamsin laughed, falling back on the piano and righting herself again, "Mothers no. I work for Mallan, and despite a dalliance or two, that's where our relationship ends."

Imara had the unsettling thought of Tamsin being paid to be her friend, forced to be her friend in order to not upset her boss. She wondered if they could ever compose a true friendship that way. Further more, and perhaps even more unsettling, Tamsin's candor about her relationship with Mallan. A dalliance or two? Her spine stiffened and Imara's mind flashed with the invasive dreams that haunted her, the way Mallan's hand felt against her throat. She swallowed hard. It shouldn't have upset her, or shocked her, to learn their relationship wasn't always strictly professional.

"I'm sorry, does it bother you I've slept with him?"

Imara's eyes shot to her lap, ashamed that on some level, it did. It shouldn't have.

"It's fine," she whispered. She held no claim on Mallan, not really, despite Tamsin's vision of Imara and Mallan being destined. He was fae and had lived lifetimes before Imara even existed. He would continue to live lifetimes after her mortal life ended. Never mind her growing attraction to him, an attraction that proximity aided. It would be an uphill battle, she knew that, but Imara was determined to fight it.

"Don't worry, Imara. That was long ago. Besides, I much prefer goblins to fae."

"Really?" Imara's face scrunched at the thought. She loathed the goblins and couldn't, even in her wildest dreams, think of them that way.

"Oh, yes. They're mindless, eager, and take orders really, really well," Tamsin's eyes gleamed mischievously. "A perfect combination to feed my ego, which demands to be worshiped. Besides, they're gloriously endowed and don't tire easily." Imara couldn't help blushing, never having known what being with a man was like.

It was strange to imagine Tamsin, so perfect and endearing, paired with the monstrous creatures made of smoke and nightmares. She could have had anyone, mortal or fae, and she chose them.

"Enough about boring old men," Tamsin hopped off her perch, her hands reaching out to Imara with wiggling fingers in an invitation to join her. She didn't wait for her to accept them, instead grabbing Imara's hands and pulling her from the bench. "Let's go have some fun," she quipped, moving them towards the door.

Imara, swept up in Tamsin's eagerness, yelped a laugh. She got the distinct feeling that when it came to the witch, you simply went with her lead. She was a force to be reckoned with.

SIXTEEN

Imara

They stood at the threshold of Shadowmire, a sense of nervous excitement wrapped around Imara. She hadn't left the estate or its grounds since her arrival, and Tamsin wanted to take her exploring. The vast grounds stretched out beyond the door, glorious under a gray velvet sky that blanketed everything as far as the eye could see.

Steps behind her, Tamsin argued with Mallan. "You can't keep her locked up in Shadowmire forever, Mallan," she dared to address him casually when no-one else in his employ did. "How can she belong here, in the Under Court, if she doesn't experience more than the estate?"

"It's too dangerous," he rumbled.

"I'll be with her. Do you honestly think I can't handle myself out there? I may look like sugar and spice, but I've a wicked bite. You know I do."

"She can't."

"I say she can," Tamsin retorted. "You said it yourself, stud, she's got fire." The witch splayed her fingers and waved her hands about in emphasis.

Their bickering grated on Imara's neves. "I want to go," she whirled around and tried not to snicker at the sight of them. Tamsin, the tiny thing she was, floated before Mallan to meet him head on, a delicate, pink polished finger waggling in his face. Mallan looked like he wanted to swat her away like an insect.

He turned away from the witch and approached Imara, his face etched in deep concern, "Starling, there are creatures out there far worse than the wraith. Creatures that will not hesitate to slaughter on sight."

"Then send a goblin with us..."

"Imara!" Tamsin protested. "When I said I enjoyed the goblins' company, I didn't mean outside of some carnal fun. They're dull as bricks."

"Tamsin," Mallan bit, "I thought I told you to stay away from them. I don't need them distracted."

"You're no fun, big guy."

"A guard," Imara demanded. "Just one." She hoped the negotiated protection would sway Mallan.

"He keeps his distance and minds his own business, unless he's needed," Tamsin added.

"Deal," Mallan agreed, though was none too pleased about it.

"You won't regret it."

"I better not," he shrugged out of her grip and rolled his shoulders, his tense neck cracking with the motion. His dark eyes hardened, unhappy he didn't get his way. He'd conceded anyway. With a twist of his hand, he summoned a goblin in a puff of smoke. The blue scaled creature's goat like eyes looked about bewilderedly, a leg of lamb half lifted to his mouth, which was coated in grease.

"You are to escort Tamsin and Imara on their day out, keep a close eye but maintain distance, unless intervention is necessary," Mallan ordered. The goblin dropped the food and gave a salute, then stood at attention to wait for further instruction.

Mallan left with a curt nod of his head, unable to look at the witch in his employ. He didn't like being bested.

Tamsin couldn't contain her excitement. She bounced on the ball of her feet, clapping, "We're going to have so much fun!"

"Where are we going?"

"Brine Bay."

"What's there?" Imara wondered.

"Shops, food, and best of all, a beach." Tamsin took Imara's hands in hers and jumped with each word.

"Should we change?" Dressed as they were, they weren't exactly beach ready.

Tamsin scoffed, "No. No place is worth going to if you don't make an impression."

Brine Bay was a small coastal village just northeast of Shadowmire, its rocky shore shimmered with amethyst colored silt that caught the weak rays of the sun daring to peek out through the clouds. The village itself defied gloom in all its quaintness. Made up of white stucco buildings crusted with moss and salt, barnacles surrounding their foundations said that the tide rode high into the village. Gardens dotted the rooftops, the greenery peeking above the eaves.

Lower fae bustled about the buildings, paying no mind to Tamsin or Imara as they strolled through the sandy streets adorned with tide pools and various small sea creatures that the receded waters left behind.

The pair perused shops, and ate greasy, meat filled pastries from a vendor with gilled ears. Imara discovered a cafe that served strange green teas that tasted like kelp and rich coffee laced with sea salt and caramel. It was surprisingly normal, almost like any Morrean town or village that sat near water.

The more Imara saw of the Under Court, the more beauty she saw in the dismal atmosphere. Even the fae she'd once found strange or frightening held her fascination.

After spending some time taking in all that the village offered, they took to the beach before the tide could return to claim it. There was one thing they needed to take care of first. Their goblin guard.

"Hey, Goaty," Tamsin flirted, dumping the armload of gifts that all the shopkeepers insisted on bestowing them to gain favor with Mallan's honored guest at his feet.

"Shalver."

"Goaty. Watch our things for us while we pop down to the beach."

"Shalver stays with you." He wasn't the brightest goblin.

Tamsin wrapped her lithe arms around one of his bulking biceps and batted her pink eyes. "Please. I'll make it worth your while if you do this one tiny indiscretion for us. Mallan will never know." She placed a light kiss on his scaled cheek. Shalver's knobby Adam's apple bobbed and his goat-like eyes brightened. Before he could respond, Tamsin unwrapped herself from his side. "Thanks, Goaty!" She gripped Imara's hand and dragged her toward the beach.

THEY SAT feet away from the gray crashing waves, watching the sea fae. Selkies frolicked in the surf, leaping high into the air and sending glittering sprays of seawater hurtling toward the clouds. Their play single-handedly seemed to brighten the dreary day, despite the storm in the distance, their joy was proof that all was not as it seemed in Mallan's court.

The mystical creatures scampering in the waves had her wondering if there was even the slightest chance that Imara would find some semblance of their happiness in this dark place. A sliver of her soul hoped so, hoped for something to make the Under Court worth being bound to.

The longer she watched them, the more inspired Imara became. Inspiration turned into a melody she became lost in.

"We're lucky to see them."

"Huh?" Tamsin pulled Imara out of her thoughts.

"The selkies. They don't come down to the Under Court territories often. I don't even know why they're here now. It's not one of their migration seasons."

"So, they just show up randomly sometimes?"

"Rarely," Tamsin stretched her feet into the glittering sand, her crimson tattoo dancing over her skin as if to escape the grit. "Where were you just now?"

"Thinking about a song, I think." She cocked an eyebrow at Imara, who nodded toward the selkies in response. "They're so joyful, so beautiful. It's like I saw music in my head because of them."

"Willing to share?"

"I don't know, it's more an idea or a feeling. Not a real song or anything," Imara tucked her legs against her chest and swooped her windswept hair behind her ears. She couldn't share something that didn't exist, could she?

"Try, for me. Please," Tamsin batted her eyelashes and pouted her lips as she tugged on Imara's arm.

Twisting her ear to the sky, Imara honed in on the melody that swept through the air and over the crashing waves; on the wings of crying gulls. The song revealed itself to her quietly, slow and sad rather than the joyous notes she'd heard watching the selkies game.

. . .

COME HOME.

Fathoms below the night sky
Where the sea folk play
Beneath the waves
Come home

AN UNSEEN HAND guided Imara from her seat in the sand, her feet traipsing toward the shore until the surf washed over them with foam and discarded kelp. She danced there, the hem of her gauzy dress soaking wet, as the story unfolded. Imara was oblivious to the world around her, a vision on the purple sands in a crystalline dress that matched the stormy water before her. She barely saw the gathering sea birds scattered on the beach, each one cocking their heads in interest. Scarcely noticed the horse-like heads of kelpies bobbing in and out of the water, wanting to listen but hesitant to get too close. Imara didn't pay any attention as the selkies came ashore to shed their seal skins and join in her dance.

COME HOME

To the watery kingdom
Where shattered hearts with no crown dwell
Beneath the proud waves
Come home

"IMARA!" Tamsin's urgent call finally pulled her from the fantasy. Terror laced her pink eyes as she slowly lifted a hand and pointed behind her.

Imara turned to see a creature with brindled moss colored flesh and large black eyes rimmed by a thin stripe of mint. Its body was slight, though strong, with long taloned, webbed fingers and toes. A slight swell of breasts marked the creature as a female. Algae and kelp were woven into her waterlogged hair, the color indiscernible. Scalloped ears poked from between the locks and plants. Her entire body was covered in a thin dress that appeared to be made of water. She was beautiful and terrifying.

"Imara, back away from the nixie," Tamsin urged in a hushed tone.

The surf sloshed up Imara's legs, soaking her dress more, as she stumbled back a step before the nixie's cold hand clamped around her wrist. Imara gasped, fearful of what the creature would do. She let go, retreating a foot with her webbed hands in the air. "Don't go," her voice was a whisper, as if speaking out of the water strained her throat. "Please, keep singing."

As Imara watched the nixie retreat, she noticed more of them lining the shore. With a trembling breath, she picked up where she left off.

COME HOME
> *Our wayward queen*
> *Free your home from grief*
> *Restore the glory of Sylphea's seas*
> *Come home*

THE WORLD FELL silent when Imara finished her song. Only for a moment, though. Then the sea itself seemed to erupt in applause, and the sky thundered along. The creatures gathered along the shore slipped silently into the bay, but only after bowing as a sign of thanks. But the nixie that spoke remained, "Thank you for sharing," she gasped, removing a piece of kelp from her water tangled hair and tied it around Imara's wrist. She bowed, hand over chest, and dove back into the choppy waters.

"That was incredible!" Tamsin shrieked, grabbing Imara's wrist to inspect the kelp left by the water fae. "The nixies don't like anyone, and they gave you one of their most prized gifts."

"Oh," she eyed the new bracelet in wonder. Imara turned her wrist to inspect it, as she did the kelp transformed, becoming crystal-like, shining and smooth as jade. The veins of the plant morphed into golden threads and the water droplets that clung precariously to the surface had changed into glittering diamonds. "Why would they do that?"

"Who knows? Maybe they really liked the song."

Lightning flashed overhead, violent and angry, tearing the sky in half with its crack. The storm had arrived. In seconds, the sky unleashed a torrential deluge. Tamsin cackled gleefully, throwing her arms wide and spinning before clasping Imara's hands in hers and forcing the girl to dance.

They danced and sang in the storm until their bodies were heavy, their dresses were soaked through with rain and clung to their bodies. They tumbled together into the sand, wrapped in a friendly embrace, giggling like schoolgirls until the rain subsided. Only then did they leave that beach, still euphoric from what had happened.

Tamsin and Imara allowed Shalver to transport them back to Shadowmire, coated in rain and sand. The minute their feet landed the marble floor of the foyer, they dashed from the black cloud, eager to escape him. Their laughter echoed against the vaulted ceiling as the pair made for the stairs, their rain-soaked clothes dripping every step of the way.

Their delight came to a screeching halt in the sitting room. There, in one of the high-back chairs, sat Mallan. He was not alone. On one couch sat two females, both pale and dark featured; feminine versions of Mallan. They were nearly indiscernible from one another, if it weren't for the beauty mark that sat squarely between the breasts of one, on display thanks to her plunging neckline. On the other sat another female, autumn locked with eyes like cinnamon set against creamy umber skin.

The dark-haired fae with the beauty mark sneered at Imara, looking over her like a bug to be squashed. The female next to her stared indifferently, her eyes glazed with boredom. The third, didn't even look at her, ignored Imara's existence entirely.

Moving like fog, Mallan drifted from his seat and crossed the space to where Imara and Tamsin trembled from the chill that finally settled through their wet clothes. Imara, though, trembled from more than being wet. The strange women in the room had her quaking.

Mallan looked them over, his eyes gleamed as they passed over Imara, lighting over every curve of her water logged dress revealed. Until they landed on the bracelet left by the nixie and widened before flashing to meet Tamsin's. Her eyes flashed in wordless response, to which he nodded and calmed.

"Mother, Michaela, Auren," Mallan flanked Imara's right and addressed the women before them. "Let me introduce my guest, Imara Cawthorne." Her head snapped toward him, she hadn't expected to hear her married name from his lips. Imara faced the women once more while he continued, "Imara, this is my mother, Rhanda," he gestured to the woman with the birthmark, "my sister, Michaela, and her friend Auren." He gestured to the other dark-haired woman and the one sitting alone, respectively.

"It's a pleasure to meet you all," Imara greeted with a

cautious and slight curtsey. "Please forgive my appearance, I'm afraid we got caught in a storm during our outing."

Rhanda stood, arms crossed tightly under her chest and her onyx eyes fixated on Imara. Judging her. She marched toward her son, a sneer spreading on her painted lips, and sniffed the air as she stopped. "A mortal, Mallan?" she questioned with a haughty air. "You house a mortal in the suite across from yours? Don't you know what kind of message that sends to the court? I promised that suite to Auren."

"Imara is my chosen, Mother. My destined as foretold. The suite belongs to her until she chooses otherwise. The guest suites downstairs will be prepared for your stay. I believe they'll be satisfactory."

Rhanda scoffed, glancing over her shoulder at her companions before returning her critical stare to Imara. "Fine, have your fun, my boy. Mothers know your father had his share of it with mortals too, before he realized that was all they were good for. Though he never dared bring them home. Auren and I have centuries of time to wait out one measly human whore."

Michaela and Auren exchanged vehement looks as Rhanda dressed down Imara, their judgment seemingly in line with hers. The vinegar in their glares put her right back in Bott's, where everyone treated her like less than dirt because she was a bastard. To those women, being mortal was just as bad, and their hurtful judgement set a quiver in Imara's chin.

She wouldn't let them see how their cruelty affected her, and before tears could spill, Imara turned and dashed into her suite. Tamsin followed, keeping her arm protectively wrapped across her shoulders.

"So sensitive," Rhanda mocked. The others scoffed at the jab, their harsh tittering chased Imara all the way through the doors, which closed just as Mallan let loose a warning growl.

"Don't listen to those bitches," Tamsin crooned as she led

Imara to the wardrobe. "Jealous, conniving, power hungry sluts. Thats what they are. Auren's an idiot. Michaela hates Rhanda, jealous of how she dotes on Mallan. And Rhanda is furious she can't keep Mallan under her thumb and lay claim to some of his power."

She helped Imara out of her wet dress and sat her on the settee before flitting away to answer the knock at the door. Moments later Fern rounded the partition in the witch's stead, her path taking her right to the bath. Soon, the sounds of splashing water and the scent of eucalyptus and roses filled the air.

Muffled whisperings from the other end of the suite filtered through the loud, rushing water. Imara strained to listen as Mallan and Tamsin argued, but the roar of the filling tub drowned out any chance of comprehending what they said. That was, until the water stopped, leaving only the sound of their voices to fill the air.

"I need to know."

"I will look into it," Tamsin promised Mallan moments before appearing around the folded screen, a bright smile attempting to hide the tension emanating from her. "Come on then, let's get you soaking."

"What was that about?" Imara pried.

Tamsin's face faltered for a split second, "Nothing. Mallan's angry with his mother, of course. I just assured him I'd take care of you while he handled them." The answer she gave didn't match the end of the argument Imara overheard.

"I don't really care how they feel," Imara deflected any suspicion from her voice. Tamsin didn't need to know she didn't buy her excuse. "He chose me, I haven't chosen him. I'm only bothered that what I am is all they see. The story of my life, not being good enough for one reason or another. I thought those days were past me."

"They are. Trust me," Tamsin remarked. "Like I said, they're jealous bitches. Hopefully dinner will go smoothly after Mallan tears into them."

"Dinner?"

"Of course. Rhanda insists on eating as a family when she visits. Since you're Mallan's des…" the look Imara gave Tamsin had her changing her word quickly, "… honored guest, you have to be there." The witch grasped Imara's shoulders and herded her to the bath.

"I'd rather not," she dug in her heels, suddenly heated. Imara could easily imagine the frosty reception she'd get at the table. Rhanda's cool glare and the tittering in each other's ears as they glanced sidelong at their target. It didn't matter what Tamsin said about them. Imara couldn't do it. She turned away and headed into the main suite, no longer feeling the need to bathe.

"Don't be that way," Tamsin appeared before Imara and crossed her arms, her eyes flashing bright. The room hummed with the sudden breeze that swept through and coiled her golden curls around her head. "Don't let them win. You are a powerful woman, with powerful allies. Never forget it, never let others forget it." The strange wind died with her words and the room fell silent.

"Was that a prophecy? I thought you didn't do that for friends."

"No," Tamsin calmed. "No, sweet Imara. That was the truth," her slender hand cupped the girl's cheek. "Please join us for dinner. If not for any other reason than for me, so I'm not infinitely lonely. Who knows what stupidity I'll get up to if I have no one to commiserate with? I might have an orgy with the goblins on the table to cure my boredom. Right on the main course."

A snicker escaped Imara. The image of sweet, bubbly

Tamsin swarmed in a writhing mass of scales, claws, and horns among dripping candles and whatever succulent delights were on the menu was absurd to think about. Mallan's eyes flaming at the scene and his mother's prudish sensibilities being assaulted were priceless to imagine. Imara would pay to see that. "I think the fallout would be worth missing," she teased with a shrug.

Tamsin's mouth hung open, "Imara! Do you want me to be banned from Shadowmire?" The look on her face had Imara doubling over, steadying herself against the witch to keep from falling over. Her face blurred from the tears gathering in Imara's eyes, but not enough to hide her reaction when she realized the joke. "Not funny," she pouted.

"It's a little funny."

CHAPTER

SEVENTEEN

Imara

Imara headed to the banquet hall with the sense she was underdressed and covered in bugs. She'd made the mistake of letting Tamsin dress her for dinner, who decided that Imara must wear something spectacular to make Mallan's family and guest choke on their appetizers.

The dress was a sheer pale pink, long-sleeved piece with a full skirt and glittering flowers embroidered on the delicate fabric layered over what Imara could only think of as lingerie in the shame pink hue. The corseted bodice of the undergarment was boned, structured immaculately and drawn tight enough to make breathing difficult until her body adjusted to it. Tamsin only accessorized the look with a diamond and pink pearl diadem.

The witch dressed herself near the same, her dress form fitted and in gold hues, only forgoing the tiara. Together they made a head turning pair. A golden goddess and a blushing princess. Seductress and virgin.

On top of her already frazzled nerves over dinner with the

145

women who judged and hated her so, and her almost scandalous dress, Imara worried Mallan would be angry at how late they ran. Did punctuality equate to a promise kept in his eyes?

Every ounce of anxiety Imara tripled as they approached the banquet room, the doors already wide open. Then again, as they crossed the threshold, and she glimpsed the impatience Rhanda wore like a weapon.

"Finally," she sneered as Tamsin and Imara entered the hall. Her disdain transformed to disgust when she took in what they wore. Michaela and Auren eyed each other with smirking glances, only adding to Imara's embarrassment. Mallan growled a warning directed at Rhanda.

"Sorry, we're late..."

"But perfection needs a grand entrance," Tamsin cut Imara off. The witch leaned in to her ear, "Never apologize for being late," she whispered, leading Imara to the empty seat next to Mallan.

He stood from his seat at the head of the table, "And worth the short wait," he added, sliding in the chair after she sat.

The rest of dinner was cast in a tense air. Mallan's family behaved themselves, mostly, for the rest of the meal, keeping their sharp tongues sheathed other than to comment on a dish or make innocuous small talk. Still, their eyes glared, throwing the daggers their words couldn't, wouldn't dare to in Mallan's presence. Family or not, the Lord of Shadowmire wouldn't hesitate to unleash his wrath on them if they did.

Even then, the light conversation had nothing to do with Imara. She silently observed as Rhanda spent her voice on embellished stories about herself, or overselling the accomplishments of Auren, who paled at the praise. Her eyes continually shifted between Mallan and Michaela, unsaid words passing between her and the latter.

Mallan kept a close watch on the women. His dark eyes

rolled every time he detected any sense of exaggeration. He wasn't impressed with her lies, or anything she had to say about Auren.

Tamsin also watched the other females, though with a more defensive stare. She looked ready to rip scalps from heads if they said the wrong thing, and met their sharp glares with a warning in her own. All the while, she peppered the one sided conversation and incredulous smirks painted on her lips.

It wasn't until after when everyone was sated from the lavish meal and settling in the sitting room that the conversation steered to a place that acknowledged Imara existed, if only to point out her flaws. Rhanda revelled in comparing Imara to the far superior Auren.

"Imara," Rhanda gave the girl a long lockdown her nose, "you've been awfully quiet this evening. How are we supposed to get to know you if you don't deign to join our conversations?"

Imara opened her mouth to apologize, then thought better of it when Tamsin scrunched her face like she knew what was coming. "I didn't exactly see a good moment to interject myself into the dinner discussions. It would have been rude of me to prattle endlessly about my mundane existence." The witch snickered behind her hand.

Rhanda's face flashed red. She composed herself quickly, "Don't be silly," she flicked her hand indifferently. She swallowed thickly before her next words, "You are my son's chosen. That alone says you must be more extraordinary than any old mortal. It only makes sense to want to get to know you." Her eyes narrowed, colder than the deepest winter. "So tell us, what makes you a better match than a fae of good breeding?"

Emboldened by surviving the insult to Mallan's mother, Imara's spine stiffened. "Well, I was born to an unstable, single, teenage mother in a home for women with nowhere else to go. There, I was looked down on for being a bastard until they kicked me out when I turned sixteen. So, I wouldn't say I'm all that special," she met each of the fae female's eyes, determined to not feel ashamed about her upbringing. A flicker of something close to sympathy crossed Auren's face for a moment before her expression turned as blank as the others.

"You're too humble, Starling," Mallan interjected with smoldering eyes. "There's so much you left out."

"Oh?" Michaela studied her nails. Imara couldn't tell if she didn't care about or didn't believe Mallan's claim.

"Truly, she is," he affirmed. "Imara is a prized chanteuse. One of the best in Morrea."

His belief flustered Imara. "Morrea is so big, it's hard to say," she argued. She didn't want to delve into that part of her life with Rhanda. Her career, while closely tied to Mallan, felt too sacred to share with the vile woman, only because it led to unpleasant memories of late. Imara felt a strong urge to protect Lorn, and herself from fresh grief, by keeping it close to the vest.

"Come now, Starling. It's how you came into my life, after all. Mother surely would be interested in that story," he smirked.

Did Mallan mean to upset her? Intentional or not, a sharp pain sliced through Imara. She couldn't hold her tongue and unleashed it back on him, keeping her fire filled eyes locked on his. "It's true, I was once a chanteuse, prized in the slums of Ocean Fare. It was there I met the man of my dreams, poured my heart and love out on the stage until the day I married him. That same day, he was murdered, and goblins kidnapped me for their Lord and master." The group remained in awkward silence after she finished, no one knew what to say.

Tamsin tried to ease the tension. "Imara really has a lovely voice. She gave quite the performance for the sea fae in Brine Bay today, getting a token from the nixies in return," she motioned to the bracelet peeking beneath Imara's sleeve, drawing attention to it. "They aren't generous with their gifts, as you know, unless the recipient is special."

There must have been something else behind Tamsin's words that Imara couldn't decipher. The females paled as they beheld the sparkling gold and green bracelet. The gift from the nixies unsettled them, perhaps even scared them. Mallan angered. He didn't like it one bit.

Before Imara could ask what everyone tensed for, Michaela stood, "I think it's time to retire for the night. Would you walk with me, Auren?" The cinnamon eyed woman didn't hesitate, eager to get away.

"That is a good idea," Rhanda added, getting a sour look from her daughter. Without another word, the three of them left the sitting area.

When they disappeared from sight, Imara burst, "That was low, Mallan."

"I'm sorry?"

"Making me relive that. Making me tell your mother, who hates me for no reason other than I'm mortal, about my life. About how we met. If you really wanted a clean start with me, you wouldn't have done that. And you won't do it again."

Imara didn't give him the chance to respond. She stormed into her suite, leaving Tamsin and the Lord of Shadowmire glaring at one another.

THE LIGHT from the fireplace danced on the golden vines as Imara turned the bracelet around her wrist. Questions ran through her head ever since the brief conversation in the sitting room.

The nixies impressed her with the gift, her mortal mind enthralled by what must have been simple magic to Tamsin, to the fae Imara found herself in the company of. That made her question why the others had such varied reactions to it. What made Tamsin boast about it, the horror on the other females' faces? Why was Mallan so angry with his witch over the gift?

The shimmering green and gold taunted Imara with secrets she expected to leap off the faceted leaves. They were almost audible, those non-existent answers she longed for, another invisible song thrumming through the cold jewels and seeping into her bones. Or perhaps it was her wishful thinking that threw her ears back to Brine Bay. The song Imara plucked from the salty air played in her head with foreign words and disjointed chords lost in crashing waves.

The fantasy built, adding dozens of voices to the music, rich baritones and soaring sopranos bringing new highs and lows. The gentle glow from the fireplace became like sun glitter frolicking across the ceiling. Imara could practically see the fae skipping through the waves there, beckoning to be joined, her name of their lips through the song. Imara. *Come back, Imara.*

It took everything in Imara not to heed the imagined call and flee back to the little village on the water. She couldn't resist joining in the music, though. She pushed up from her seat next to the fire to relinquish everything to the phantom chorus. The room spun around Imara, spinning lights and ethereal laughter driving her mad dance. There wasn't a corner of the suite where her feet didn't wander, that the song didn't fill. She kept going and going until she fell exhausted onto the bed, her heart thrumming and her skin tingling.

Somehow, it wasn't enough to satisfy. Imara wanted more from it. She wanted the soul freeing therapy that happened on the beach, the joy that simmered under the surface waiting to be let loose like it had then. She couldn't quite put her finger on what she was feeling, only that something was missing. Or she was missing something.

Without warning, silent tears slid down her cheeks and she realized she knew exactly how she felt. It was a homesickness. A feeling of having lost so much more than she already had.

"Well, that was interesting, wouldn't you s... What's wrong?" Tamsin sat next to where Imara lay curled up. "Didn't I say not to let those females get to you?"

"It's not them."

"Sure," she quipped.

"No, really," Imara sat up with a sigh. "I don't know what came over me. One minute I was trying to figure out what the fuss over the bracelet was about, the next I was dancing in a frenzy, and then crying and feeling incredibly lost."

Tamsin's eyes fell on the gift wrapped around Imara's wrist. "The sea song," she murmured in awe.

"What's that?"

"What's what?"

"What you just said. The sea song," Imara waved her hands in frustration. Tamsin was acting strangely, and though she'd only known her for a day, it seemed unusual.

Tamsin shook her curls and blinked rapidly, "Oh. It sounds like you somehow tapped into the sea song, the song of the sea fae mourning their greatest loss. Losing their queen."

"Alette."

"You know about her?" Tamsin looked even more shocked at the queen's name coming from her new mortal friend.

"Just what I read in a book a maid brought me. I asked to learn more about this place."

She nodded, "It's said that the gifts of the nixies, of any sea fae, are spelled trinkets imbued with the song. Their way of celebrating their world, and their way of marking those they consider friends. Allies."

"At the beach, you said it was a thank you gift for the song."

Tamsin shrugged, "Could be. Maybe they liked it so much

they think of you as a friend? Only time will tell, if you ever go back to Brine Bay with me."

Back to the bay. Those words sent shivers through Imara's bones, reigniting the song that haunted her. Come home.

Home. A place stolen from Imara time and time again. Bott's was home as a child, then Sconza's when she had nowhere else to go. Neither of those places would ever be home again. Then there was Lorn. Lorn should have been Imara's home for decades to come. She wanted so badly to grow old with him under a thatched roof, some place green and secluded. The Under Court didn't feel right enough to call home. The sea wasn't Imara's place either, though part of her longed to spend hours on its shores, frolicking with Tamsin, every day. It was the most carefree she'd felt in a long time.

"Nothing could keep me away."

The perky witch threw herself at Imara, a torrent of giggles, as she landed a kiss on her cheek. "I say we keep the day going. Have the maids bring us some desserts and lots of wine, and we will have our own little party. Plot our civil revenge on Rhanda and the girls."

"Civil revenge?"

"Yes, my dear, dear friend. We are going to kill her with kindness, and drive her mad with perfection. Plus, it'll be great fun to lord your friendship with the nixies over her."

"She wants to be their friend, too?" Imara chortled. She couldn't image the stuffy woman having fun, ever.

"Not in the least. Rhanda fears them. Anyone who isn't their friend should."

BEFORE IMARA COULD ENJOY her night in with Tamsin, she needed to, finally, rid her body of the day. She needed a bath, a slice of relaxation to mellow her soul. Then, maybe, she'd be able to enjoy the rest of the night. Imara sent Tamsin to procure what she felt they needed for their private party while she did just that.

She called Fern and Thorn to prepare a hot bath, as hot as they could make it, and lace the water with calming oils. The ever intuitive maids lit the chamomile, lemon balm, and lavender scented bathroom with dozens of dripping candles. Either they'd heard how poorly Mallan's family had treated Imara, or they simply saw the stress etched in her every cell.

The bathroom steamed like a late spring day after a rain storm by the time Imara readied to slip into the water. The heat enveloped her, turning her flesh pink on contact, and seeped deep into her bones. Imara's whole body sighed as the stress eased. The bath was just what she'd needed to unwind. She closed her eyes and drifted.

Brine Bay formed in her mind, the sea stretching out until it kissed the dark clouds on the horizon. Those clouds swooped in, soon enough the whole sky was swirling, foreboding. Lightning flashed with an audible crack, striking so near that the sky turned a blinding white for a split second.

When the light dissipated, dozens of sea fae populated the beach. Their eyes all reflected the stormy sky, full of danger and anger. Every one of them had their vision fixed on Imara. They wanted her.

She tried to run, but her feet sunk in the sand, glued in by invisible hands. There was nothing Imara could do as the fae began creeping towards her, descended upon her. She tried to scream, but nothing came. All she could do was whimper as she braced herself for their attack. Only they didn't. Mere inches from Imara, the sea fae froze in a tight circle around her, close enough to touch even though they didn't move to.

Anticipation built, Imara's heart thundering indiscernibly

from the storm in the sky. Time slowed as she waited, and waited, for them to do anything.

The nixie closest to Imara opened her mouth in a scream swallowed by the booming clouds, exposing her needle-like teeth. Her clammy hand clamped down on the mortal girl's wrist and her sharp nails dug into her soft skin.

Imara's eyes jolted open, a searing pain stretching from her wrist to her elbow. She could still feel the nixie's claws in her flesh as the nightmare faded to reality. Yet the pain didn't subside. It felt all too real, continued to burn long after the dream was fully gone.

Then she looked at her arm.

Tearing from the bath, Imara screamed at the very real pain that came with the kelp bracelet morphing into golden threads, dotted with green and white gems, snaking up her arm. It fused with her flesh, burned and twisted as it settled into place.

It was only when the transformation completed that the pain stopped.

Cradling her arm, Imara fled the bathroom, trailing water everywhere, and crashed into Thorn. "Are you okay, Mistress?" the maid wrapped her arms around Imara, steadying her.

"I don't know. My arm. The bracelet," Imara panted.

"Let me see," Mallan's voice came from behind the maid as he charged into the suite. He stepped around his servant and took Imara's arm in his hands. She caught a brief glimpse of Tamsin heeling him, her face masked in concern. "What happened?" he asked, running his fingers over the golden thread embedded in her skin, his eyes darkening.

"I fell asleep in the bath, waking from a nightmare with my arm in blinding pain. That's when I saw the bracelet change into this."

"Tamsin!" he barked in response, and his witch came close at the command. "Why?"

Her eyes glimmered with curiosity as she too ran her fingers over the transformed bracelet, although with more reverence than Mallan had. Her study of it took longer than his, as though she was truly learning its secrets. "Don't quote me on it," she said after terse minutes passed, "but I think it reacted to the water."

"It got wet before, in the rain, but didn't change then," Imara reasoned.

"Got wet, yes, but not submerged," she corrected. "That has to be it, the bracelet was a gift from Below. It would make sense it would react to being submerged."

"Will it harm her?" Mallan demanded, impatient for solid answers.

"I don't think so, Mallan. If the nixies meant her harm, they would have done so on the beach. They don't play long games."

"I need to know for sure, Tamsin. Get me answers."

"I'll look into it. I'll visit them myself in the next few days," she stammered. "I promise."

"See that you do," Mallan threatened.

EIGHTEEN

Mallan

Mallan summoned his mother, Michaela, and Auren.

He paced the sitting area, a low rumble in his chest. Every time he looked at his mother, the fire in his eyes spiked. His anger didn't phase her, she still sat relaxed on the couch with Michaela with cool cruelty and pride oozing from her. She never had had the decency to admit or even recognize when she was wrong. When she stepped too far.

The Mothers knew he loved his own, though he didn't like her. Her quest for power was misguided and warped beyond rational thought. She didn't understand what it was to have a destined mate, only one sought to further her own agenda. A legacy she attempted to continue with her own children.

It took long minutes of back and forth before his anger slaked enough to not want to shake her until her bones separated from her skin. It would solve so many problems for not only him, but his sister as well. To have their meddling mother out of their hair would ease their woes. Yet, he wouldn't give in to that urge. He was a monster, he'd admit that, but he wasn't a monster that committed matricide. There were lines one didn't cross and remain sane.

"Would you stop your pacing, you're giving me a headache and you'll ruin the rug."

Mallan pinched the bridge of his nose and blew out a heavy breath, "The rug doesn't matter, Mother." He was almost there, almost ready to look at her without rage taking over.

"What's really bothering you, son?"

His head snapped up, eyes wide and mouth agape, and he turned his attention to his twin, Michaela. She got up sometime in the past few minutes and sat with Auren, and rubbed her back gently. The Glass Desert beauty's face was long, her cinnamon eyes drooping. His sister met his gaze and shrugged, "I'm not touching that one, brother."

"What's bothering me is you, Mother," Mallan caved and glared at her.

"Me?" She batted her lashes and clutched her chest. "Is that the thanks I get for all I've done for you? All I try to do for you?"

Mallan spun, gripping his horns, and made for one of the empty chairs, falling into it in defeat. There was never any winning with her. He hunched forward, placing his elbows on his knees, and he templed his fingers at his mouth, contemplating his next words.

"You arrived unannounced, Mother, as usual, and insulted my destined as though she were some loathsome creature."

"If the shoe..." Mallan glared harshly at Rhanda, warning her not to finish her words. She swallowed hard. "I only want what's best for you."

"Imara is what is best for me, and Sylphea. As I've made abundantly clear for the past year, Auren and I will never match. You need to stop, especially now. Back off of her, and try to be nice."

Rhanda clicked her tongue, "Mallan, dear, you're blinded by

her face and figure clearly. I think you've spent far too much time in the mortal world and have forgotten a human and a fae can never be destined to one another. It's impossible." She shrank back a little with the glare Mallan returned, a look that promised violence if she uttered another thing against Imara. "But," she recovered, "who am I to question the great Lord Mallan? Go ahead and follow your cock. See where it gets you."

Mallan's mother stood, smoothing her skirt, "Come along girls," she ordered Michaela and Auren. "I think it's time we go to the rooms so generously given by my son and prepare for bed."

"That's the best idea you've had since you've arrived," Mallan bit back the words he really wanted to say as he watched the women saunter toward the stairs.

"We'll see you tomorrow," Michaela said, turning her gaze back on her brother just before she descended. Her eyes said what she couldn't out loud, *I'm sorry*. They were both trapped in their mother's web of ambition. Poor Auren, so sensitive and kind, had been twisted into the schemes as a power grab and forced to dampen her true self and adopt the cruelty of Rhanda. She had no choice, she gave up everything to leave the Glass Desert for her destined. She was at Rhanda's mercy just to be near her, and if she betrayed her benefactor, she'd have nothing.

A headache pounded into Mallan's head. Whether his mother would heed his request was uncertain. He stared blankly at the stairs, debating if he should go after the women, to ensure Rhanda would listen. It wasn't worth it. She was single-minded and went after her goals full force.

Rhanda orchestrated Mallan's rise to power from child-hood, giving him the best training and education. Her persis-tence turned him into a formidable machine that was bound to grab their queen's attention. Somehow, her plans never failed, as seen in his rise in the ranks and gaining favor with Ondine; becoming her consort and most trusted warrior. Even conceiving her children was meticulously planned, targeting a high-ranking general in Queen Ondine's retinue for his power and reputation alone. Love was a foreign concept to her.

Rhanda's scheme to pair him with Auren would be the first failure of her life. Mallan would make sure of that.

CHAPTER

NINETEEN

Imara

Tamsin came squealing around the folding screen, waving a small bottle in the air. "I found just the thing!" She leapt on to the bed, crashing into Imara in a fit of laughter.

Together they'd already gone through two bottles of sparkling rosé, the bottles discarded on the floor beside the bed. A tray of sweets, bonbons filled with Bordeaux cherries, vanilla Petit fours with decadent chocolate and fruit fillings, and a plethora of other pastries sat forgotten on the bedside table, most of the treats already gone.

"I knew I liked your maids," she exclaimed, and held the bottle out to Imara.

"I don't understand," Imara took the bottle, uncorking it and scenting its contents. She couldn't place what the light floral aroma reminded her of.

"It's grave lily oil. Wonderful for the skin, but highly controversial. You see," she poured a small amount of oil in her hand, set the bottle down, then rubbed the concoction into her skin,

160

"grave lilies only grow on the graves of mortals here in Sylphea."

"Mortal graves?"

"Morrea and Sylphea weren't always separated, remember?" Imara read about mortals staying in Sylphea before the two worlds were forced apart. They came and went, traders and tourists. Some stayed for long stretches of time, having fallen in love with the beauty and mystery of all things fae, or with some fae themselves. She didn't even think on if any had made their final resting place there, if they had fae that mourned them.

Tamsin grabbed the bottle of wine on the side table and took a swig. "Anyway, many high fae think the flowers are invasive, and horrible because of where they grow," she took another drink. "I say, we mix some of it in Rhanda's own bath oils. She'll never know it's there!"

"How is that revenge, exactly?"

"Oh, she's allergic. Didn't I say that?"

"No," Imara laughed and took the wine from Tamsin, taking a drink herself. "I think you've had enough of this."

"Whoops." Tamsin broke into a fit of contagious laughter.

"I don't want to hurt anyone."

"So she gets a little rash? Is that so bad?" Imara looked at her new friend incredulously. If there was anything she could guess about Rhanda, it was that she was cunning and petty. She'd likely blame the rash on Imara, either having figured it out or just wanting to taint Mallan's view of her. Not that she cared if he saw something other than wonderment when he looked at Imara. She could do with a little distance from him. "Fine, I'm too gone for better ideas."

"Maybe brainstorming fueled by sugar and wine was a bad idea?" Imara fell back on the pillows, Tamsin following and curling into her side. In moments, soft snores came from the witch, who in sleep looked so innocent compared to the fiery sex-pot she was when awake.

Sleep didn't come as easily for Imara. Her mind raced in cloudy drunken circles until the sky lightened. It was then, as she finally felt the fingers of sleep slowing the wheel her thoughts spun on, she heard a rapping at the window. The cadence of her heart picked up. After the wraith security had been increased around Shadowmire, but what if something had slipped by once again?

"Tamsin," Imara shook her friend's shoulder. The witch responded with a grumble and turned over. "Tamsin, wake up. There's something at the window."

"Hmmm," she sat up, rubbing the sleep from her eyes.

"There's something at the window," Imara repeated. The rapping sounded again, shaking Tamsin more alert. Her magenta eyes flared, and she leapt from the bed, flying to the window in question, ready to unleash her magic if need be.

Imara watched anxiously while Tamsin approached the glass. She placed her hands on the glass and inched her face close, fogging the window with her breath. "What is it?" Imara wanted to know.

"I can't tell. I'm going to have to open the window."

"Be careful," the concern something awful would come through the window put a tremble in Imara's voice.

"Don't worry, I won't let anything harm you." Tamsin unlatched the window lock and cautiously pushed it open. Not a second after, the witch squealed as a blur of black and white rushed past her.

Imara sighed in relief. Corvus landed on her bed and dropped something from his beak next to her. She picked up the offering, studying it. A rock, small and perfectly round, with glittering veins of quartz dividing it. "Thank you, Corvus."

"I take it you know this bird?" Tamsin accused after closing the window and perching on the sill. She glared at Corvus, death in her stare. "What did he bring you that required me waking so early?"

"A lovely rock," Imara held it up for Tamsin to see.

"Cute," the witch rolled her eyes and turned her attention to looking out the window. Imara shook her head at Tamsin's mood. She definitely wasn't a morning person. "That's it!" she exclaimed after a minute of brooding, and skipped back to the bed. "Your bird friend is a genius, or I am." Tamsin was practically dancing.

"Oh?"

"Ravens are notorious kleptomaniacs, they'll steal anything shiny to give to their murder, or some non-bird they've taken a liking to, right?"

"I don't think I'm following."

"Rhanda and those other bitches, silly. We let Corvus here in now and then, or give him access to your suite whenever he likes, and encourage him to go treasure hunting in their rooms. They'll go mad wondering where their things are disappearing to and, as long as he stays unseen and takes his prizes to the rookery, they'll never know."

Imara wasn't completely sold on the idea, theft didn't sit well with her. Or maybe she wasn't as into revenge as her friend was.

Noticing Imara's hesitation, Tamsin added, "If it makes you feel better about it, we can train him to bring me the gifts and I'll magic them to be returned after Mallan's family leaves."

"Ok. Let's do it." Imara finally agreed. The female fae would likely blame Imara for the missing items, but when they appeared among their possessions, hopefully they'd have some sense of guilt. The plan was petty enough to be harmless, and would have Rhanda and the others eating crow. Imara liked it.

· · ·

MALLAN HAD BEEN RIGHT. Imara needed Tamsin in her life. The friendship formed quickly and edged its way into her heart, filling a fragment of the space left behind by Lorn's absence. She'd never had someone like Tamsin as a friend, never a close female friend that brought life and fun. She was a bright spot against the perpetual gloom that settled over Mallan's lands and helped Imara see flickers of light where there was otherwise none. Tamsin brought the peace that Imara longed for, allowing it to flourish where her stubborn nature might have killed it before it had a chance.

The more at peace she became with her new world, the more like herself Imara felt. Lorn was no longer a shadow that sent her into fits of depression, glued to the bed and at war with the decisions she was making. Because of all the things she'd done since his death. Instead, his memory became soft and light, a warmth that soothed her soul and left Imara smiling.

The time spent with Tamsin even had Imara spending more time in the music room, the peace and happiness she'd found made the space hers instead of a gift Mallan used to win her favor. Over time, the tendrils of joy evolved into wings. Musical wings. Tinkering on the piano keys became lyrics in her head, which became humming, then a quieted song, and then, at last, a song that soared to fill every inch of the music room.

The wings of the Starling lifted and stretched in aching relief at being truly freed. Endless weeks of being caged by misery at long last over. The sea song, the dancing on the beach with Tamsin, and the tinkering before hadn't unlocked the chanteuse in Imara. It was at that moment, delving into her repertoire for the first time since before her wedding, that she was herself once more. With those robust notes of old, Imara realized something. While Lorn had been her heart, her everything, it was song and music that had always been her home.

It didn't take long for Imara's full voice to creep beyond the music room and draw some to the space. Their applause as she finished drew her attention straight toward them. "I'm sorry, was I too loud?"

"Never. That was beautiful," Mallan purred, his eyes shining with admiration. "It's remarkable what song does for you. You positively glow when it takes over. Seeing you as my Starling again warms me like you can not believe."

Imara's stomach soured, twisting against the reminder. Again. She forced the feeling away, easier than it had been to do before her agreement with him. Most days went by without feeling it. Then there were the days where the reminders were too heavy, and she had to fight against the remnants of the scared and tempestuous girl inside her. Imara knew Mallan saw when she warred with herself, he saw everything and dealt with it with graceful patience. Imara noticed a shift in him every time she won that battle, an appreciation for the effort she made to keep things amicable between them.

His patience showed her another side to him, not only with her struggle, but with keeping his family in check. He stood up for her against his mother and the other fae females, though Rhanda truly needed to be reminded the most, with a firm hand and soft words. That level of diplomacy shocked Imara. Their first meeting dug a scar into her memory, no matter how much she tried not to think of it. He'd entered her life as a nightmare draped in finery. Beautiful, but a monster that didn't hesitate with brutality. The way he dealt with the wraith still haunted her. Those visceral moments, when she thought of them, threatened to break her resolve to keep the peace with Mallan.

"Is there something you need?"

"No. I simply couldn't resist listening to you." He gestured to the bench, "May I?"

Wordlessly, Imara slid to make room for him. He sat next to her, pushing his cloak out so not to sit on it, his hand grazing hers for a moment as he settled. The brief touch jolted dreams to the forefront of Imara's thoughts, and her skin prickled. As quick as the sensation came, it left the moment it was over. The moment Mallan moved his hands to the keys and played.

His fingers danced across them, picking out a jaunty tune he'd played often when he had been Sconza. "Do you remember that awful drunkard from the club?"

"There were many, you need to be more specific," Imara laughed. There were so many patrons at Sconza's that fit that bill, often more than one a night.

"You know which one. The big man that thought he could fly and broke my piano."

Imara remembered. The man in question was a regular at Sconza's, harmless, except in the ring. Germain, a mountain of a man whose boxing fame swept far from Ocean Fare. He was a legendary southpaw with the heart of an artist and an unquenchable thirst for ale. It took at least four or five pints to even make a dent in his sobriety, which also made him a valued customer. No matter how raucous his drunken antics got, Sconza never permanently banned him from the establishment.

"I remember Germain, though I don't think he tried to fly; he was thrown off the stage," she shouldered Mallan. The fae lord only thought the man was awful because of one incident.

Germain had just won a match against one even more fierce than he was in the ring. He was celebrating, and on his tenth pint of Sconza's finest ale. The boxer was three sheets to the wind when he decided he needed to try his hand at being a chanteuse. Germain staggered onto the stage, lifting Imara into his arms for a quick spin around the stage before setting her down gently, stealing her spot at the center. Then he warbled a drinking song. His voice wasn't bad, per se, rather warped by drink and the late hour. The crowd loved it, as did Imara.

Sconza did not. The lanky man marched up to Germain with

fire in his eyes, lifted the giant, and threw him into the piano. Luckily, only the piano suffered any injuries. The boxer had a few scrapes, but nothing bad. His temper didn't rise either, instead he laughed until tears took over his face.

Everyone gasped when Sconza, not a small man, but small compared to Germain, threw him. In retrospect, Imara understood how he'd done it. He wasn't what he appeared to be then.

"True," he chuckled. "How could I let him interrupt you? You are my star."

"I was your star. Now, I'm just a broken girl that can sing."

Mallan looked away with hardened eyes, guilt flashing across his face as he continued playing with tense muscles straightening his frame. Imara hit a nerve she hadn't meant to. It seemed no matter how hard she tried to let go of the past, it was always there. Always brought back with some word or gesture.

"Sorry. I didn't mean to blame you. There's just a part of me that still feels empty compared to before. I'm not sure I'll ever feel complete again," Imara gripped his shoulder to reassure him. Mallan didn't respond, just continued to stare ahead with a clenched jaw.

Imara did the only thing she could think of to ease the tension. She sang along. As the music flowed, she kept glancing at Mallan in her periphery, watching as his tense guilt slowly eased and threw himself into the song. His movements were fluid, smooth and elegant, like watching the music come to life through him. Glimmers of the man he pretended to be rose to the surface, the inexplicable connection Imara shared with Sconza came rushing back too. Once again, they were chanteuse and showman. The Starling and her maestro. An incomparable pair, just as they'd once been.

Nothing, no one, could ever deny the chemistry the pair of them presented during performances when he'd joined her. The audience fell rapt every time. They'd sit as far on the edges of their seat as possible, as if being pulled in by the snare of some siren, and would do anything to get as close to her as they could. Those performances left Imara and her boss shooting for the stratosphere, high for hours on end.

Imara had to admit she missed that version of them. The easy relationship she had with Sconza, fueled by a shared love of music and strengthened by her grateful heart. If it hadn't been for him, for Mallan, Imara could have had a very different fate. He, as Sconza, had been her best friend, her confidant, and the man she knew would be there for her through thick and thin.

All of that had shattered with the truth. But there, sitting at that golden piano, the music flowing between them, that old feeling knitted together. Imara could almost see it, the shard of their bond fitting like puzzle pieces, not perfectly but enough to see the picture.

Their connection would never be the same as it once was. There would always be cracks and imperfection that came from the truth. Those differences made them an entirely new creature. One she unexpectedly came to want.

"What is it, Starling?" Mallan's question interrupted her thoughts. She hadn't realized she'd stopped singing, that she was just staring at him with new eyes.

"Nothing," she tucked her hair behind her ears, "I was just remembering how good we were together. Back at Sconza's." Imara placed a hand over his, and he stopped playing.

His eyes fell on their joined hands, reverent shock reverberating across his face. Moments later, his sight met hers again, "We were good, weren't we?"

"The best." For the first time, Imara felt a shred of something real with Mallan. Something other than hate or anger, or irritation, or just tolerance. An ember of how things were, and a promise of how things could be.

"There is something," he admitted, breaking eye contact and fingering the keys again. "I was going to ask later, but it feels right now."

"Hmmm?"

"I'd like you to accompany me to the High Court for negotiations?"

"I don't know if that's a good idea." Imara wanted to say yes, to see more of Sylphea than she already had. The problem was she knew the history between Mallan and his counterpart in the High Court. Lord Khryton wouldn't like her presence there. "Why don't you take Auren or your family? Or all of them," Imara suggested. She could use a few days of not tiptoeing around them.

Ever since her sleepover with Tamsin, she'd done her best to avoid the three females. She'd been able to keep away from Auren and Michaela, who kept to themselves other than at dinners. Rhanda, however, was like a plague. She was everywhere, trailing her son most of the day and inserting herself into his business. She'd also spent a fair amount of time undermining Imara, trying to break her down.

"My mother's focus is currently on harassing my staff and goblins about some missing jewels. You're welcome, by the way."

"For what?" Imara held in her amusement. Corvus took to her and Tamsin's plan with little effort. He'd been swiping trinkets from the three of them, taking them to the witch or the rookery for safe keeping.

"Keeping her off your back. She insisted you were the one behind the missing pieces, until I interjected, assured her you'd never been to their suites, and reminded her she misplaces her jewels in strange places. So, of course, she has everyone searching the entire estate." Imara smirked, shaking her head. "Besides, with these negotiations, I want you there."

"Won't my presence be a problem, considering the treaty you have with them?" Imara couldn't imagine Lord Khryton taking her presence in his court lightly when it was he that started the treaty. "Proof you've broken your accord with him?"

"Imara, I have no doubt your presence will disarm him, and may even make him second guess starting a war he knows he can't win."

She still didn't understand why Mallan wanted to take her with. What difference would she make in negotiations between two powerful fae? There wasn't a reason she could think of that she would make Lord Khryton hesitate. "Why? What do I have to do with any of this?"

"You live in the Under Court, Starling. The negotiations affect you because of that. Besides," he added, noting Imara's hesitation, "is it so wrong for me to want to spend time with you? To want to include you in all aspects of my life?"

"I guess not," an unsure smile lifted the corner of her lips. Mallan's confident reassurances did little to ease the writhing doubt snaking through her veins.

CHAPTER

TWENTY

Imara looked forward to going with Mallan to the High Court, couldn't wait to see more of Sylphea during a potentially long journey. Her imagination went wild with ideas about all the new things she would get to see. She lost sleep over deciding what to wear. Imara hoped that if she looked the part of a lady, Lord Khryton wouldn't look on her with disdain. He'd be appeased enough that he wouldn't have a fit of rage at Mallan and incite a war.

She hated war, hated the dread it filled all it touched with. The years waiting for Lorn to return to her were torture enough without the threat of fighting breaking out between opposing nations. It had been her greatest fear when he enlisted, that she'd lose him too soon. A fear that came true, though not from the ravages of war.

Imara was ready early the morning they were to leave, her trunk packed with more than what probably needed to accommodate the unknown. All she had to do was wait for Mallan to say it was time to go, giving her plenty of time to mull over what she would wear. She didn't want to underdress, or overdress, and did not know what weather to expect in other parts of Sylphea. In the end, she chose a simple and elegant outfit that travel wouldn't muss; a cornflower blue, high collared, sleeveless dress. She was just fastening the silver clasps on the midnight blue fitted jacket when the knock came at the door.

"Are you ready?" Mallan greeted when she answered, holding out a hand for her to take.

"Yes, very much so," she pointed at the trunk waiting next to the door before sliding her hand into his.

"You won't be needing that."

"I won't?" Mallan smirked in response to Imara's confusion, only to pull her in close and wrap his arm around her. His conjured smoke swirled around them, dashing Imara's hope to see more of Sylphea. She felt silly even, for thinking he would travel any other way to the home of his enemy. Still, the disappointment stood.

But, as the clouds dissipated from around them, what she saw was not disappointing. They'd appeared just inside a courtyard beyond golden gates, before them a shining palace with gilded spires and faceted windows that winked in the foreign light. The bright sun was blinding after so long under the gloomy skies of the Under Court where the sun rarely peeked from behind the clouds and even when it dared shine, its brightness paled. Imara's eyes had grown too used to the dim of Shadowmire.

Blaring horns sounded moments after their arrival, and soon a troop of bronze armored guards flocked from the palace with their tall spears. Behind their ranks, a dumpy man dressed in refined regalia marched, red faced and huffing.

"You had to cause a scene, like always, Mallan," he wheezed, pushing through a row of guards.

"Nonsense, Vikard, I'm expected."

"To arrive in two days by coach, as civilized fae do," the portly man seethed and turned a shade redder.

"Your master knows my preferred method of travel, and the day I was to depart. Would you rather I transport directly inside Illumia?"

"That is not allowed," Vikard went from red to purple, and reached up to his left ear. Imara was surprised to see it rounded, like a mortal's, but it wasn't naturally so. The edges had been darkened with spiraling veins of black that stretched into the canal. His ear had been marred by magic.

"Who knew Khryton would be so upset over your ear?" Mallan replied wryly. "Would you just take us to him, Vikard, or would you like a matching set?"

Vikard stammered at the threat, "Us?" It was as though he'd been blind to Imara's presence until Mallan drew his attention to it, garnering another fit. "Mallan, what nonsense is this? Bringing a mortal to Sylphea? To Illumia? What are you trying to pull?"

"She is a guest in my court, Vikard. She will be treated with the same courtesy as me," he growled, bending his face down into the steward's. "So take us to see him, or I will take your other ear before finding my own way to Khryton."

"You step too far, Mallan," the shorter fae quaked at the repeated threat before turning on heel and motioning for them to follow.

Half of the guards fell into step with Vikard. A guard reached for Imara's elbow, eliciting a deep and feral snarl from Mallan. The guard shrank back, falling behind to join the men taking up the rear.

Imara tried her best to see everything while they walked through the courtyard. The yard surrounding the palace was stark, made of shimmering white stone, but they moved too quickly through for her to see the finer details of the stark golden decorations and identify the white flowers that grew around them.

Vikard led Mallan and Imara through the grand entrance and to a large room where an empty throne sat on a high raised dais. The room was extravagant, decorated in tones of gold and white, celestial and gaudy in a way that felt showy and cold. Maybe it was that Imara had grown used to the dark of Shadowmire, or maybe it was something else, but the room didn't feel right to her.

The portly steward left them with the whole of the guard that escorted them, which seemed like overkill to Imara. The hatred and distrust of the Lord of the Under Court ran deep in these fae, that much was obvious.

Minutes later, Vikard returned, this time appearing next to the golden throne. "Lord Khryton and his son, Lautrec," he announced simply.

Khryton, a formidable man with sharp blue eyes and golden shimmering skin and hair, strode across the dais to take the throne. He was tall, though not as tall as Mallan, and built like a warrior, oozing strength and power. His son, Lautrec, a younger, leaner version of the man, followed close behind him. There were differences that set them apart. His golden hair flowed to his shoulders, and he had well trimmed facial hair. His eyes, while also blue, were deeper and softer.

Lord Khryton sat on the throne, his shining blue eyes passed over Mallan in a guarded manner, glaring indignantly. But as his eyes passed over Imara, he faltered. A moment of disbelief crossed his angular features. Her presence, as Mallan predicted, influenced him, but not as she anticipated. He didn't look horrified or angry; he looked genuinely shocked to see Imara before him. Almost as though he'd seen a ghost.

Mallan snickered at his foe's reaction, although he recovered himself quickly. He'd unnerved Khryton and knew it. He enjoyed it. Whatever animosity lay between them, Imara thought, was fathomless.

"Mallan," Khryton greeted curtly. "Thank you for agreeing to these negotiations, though it would have been nice if you had kept to the agreed time."

"A misunderstanding, I'm sure," the dark fae dismissed the accusation. "It's good to see you, young Lautrec. Has your father already grown so old that it's time for you to learn how things are ran?"

Khryton sneered, though kept diplomatic composure rather than rise to the insult. "I suppose this young woman is the guest you mentioned? I'm surprised to see she isn't quite fae."

Mallan nodded once, glee lighting his face. "Khryton, Lautrec, allow me to introduce Miss Imara Cawthorne, of Ocean Fare." Khryton paled, swallowing audibly.

Imara curtsied before the fae of the High Court, "Lord Khryton. Lautrec. It's an honor to be here to witness these negotiations between your courts. Making my home at Shadowmire will certainly benefit from learning more about yours."

"I'm sorry? You, a mortal, are making your home at Shadowmire?" Lautrec looked to his father, bewildered.

"Yes. I've found myself here with no safe home to return to in Ocean Fare. Mallan has been gracious enough to offer his home as mine. I know it goes against the treaty you have with him, but I assure you Mallan means no ill by doing it."

"You assure me?" Khryton laughed. "Young lady, all you can assure me is that Mallan is not to be trusted to keep his word. Bear that in mind regarding whatever he has promised you by bringing you here, illegally, I might add."

"I know about the treaty," Imara reiterated.

"Then you know the severity of him breaking it," Khryton scowled.

"The treaty was shredded long before I brought Imara to

Sylphea, Khryton, and you know it," Imara's host accused the golden fae, pointing a long finger at him. Khryton ruffled under the scrutiny, and even his son seemed shaken by Mallan's words.

"Your words mean war, Mallan."

"Please," Imara cut in, "can't your courts forget the treaty and make a new one? Keep the peace?"

Khryton stood and glowered at Imara and Mallan, "The treaty is there for protecting mortals. For your protection, Tilly!" his voice boomed, filling the throne room. Imara shuddered from the power she felt come from him. That was nothing, though, compared to the shock she felt at hearing her mother's name come from Khryton's lips.

Before Imara could respond, could gain some clarity on his slip of the tongue, Mallan pushed ahead of her and took hold of her wrist. "I guess it's war then," he laughed as he swept them away in a cloud of smoke.

"What the Hell was that about?" Imara shoved away from Mallan the moment his transporting smoke cleared.

"Khryton is misguided. The Under Court poses no greater threat to mortals than his own court does."

"Not what I meant. He called me Tilly! Why would he call me my mother's name?"

Mallan smirked, his dark eyes shining mischievously, "It's not my job to keep track of what or who Khryton does."

Imara's eyes threatened to spill her emotions to the floor. "You are an asshole," she shot with as much vinegar as she could muster to keep the tears at bay. She didn't want to deal with Mallan, or his half answers. His insinuations. The response he gave was vague, vague enough to not be a lie. But that didn't mean he wasn't omitting information to have the upper hand. That hurt Imara.

Before she lost control of herself, she turned to flee to her suite.

Mallan stopped her before she reached the stairs, appearing before her in his smoke and blocking her path. he countered every move she made to go around him perfectly, as if they had choreographed it.

"You used me!" Imara shoved against his chest. She became fed up, tired. "You used me as a pawn in your spat with Khryton. I don't like it."

"True. I knew your presence would throw him off guard and present myself with the opportunity to reveal his deceit."

"Why? I want to hear you say it?" She had her suspicions, but she didn't dare to say them out loud.

"Can we discuss this somewhere more private?" Mallan gestured to the stairs. "I think it would be for the best."

Up they went, the air between them heavy. Imara felt his eyes boring into her from behind until they reached the glass tower. There, he made his way to the window and stood looking out over his land, his hands clasped behind his back.

"I never intended to keep my end of the bargain with Khryton, as I knew he never meant to refrain from the mortal world himself. I may be considered evil, but he is no angel himself, no matter how much he says he is."

Imara worked her lip, listening to what Mallan offered. She expected learning from him what she was thinking. "I knew," Mallan continued after a pause, "Khryton would be your sire. Or rather, the sire of my destined. I had to monitor him when I learned it. He may say he made the treaty to protect mortals, but he doesn't think highly of them. I worried his reasons for even deigning to mate with one were for some darker purpose.

"When my spies told me your mother was with child, I had

to take steps to protect you from whatever machinations Khryton had for you. I cloaked Tilly, and you, from him, leaving breadcrumbs of a tragic end for you both. I'm not sorry about what I did. I would do it again and again, given the chance to." Mallan turned, looking Imara in her crystal eyes, seeking reassurance and only finding her frustrated with his story. His face fell when he saw the scowl painted on hers. He cleared his throat, "I thought I was saving you, and I was wrong there. Had I known your life, your childhood, would have been so tortured, that is where my actions would have taken another path. I never would have left your mother alone if I knew the abuse you'd suffer. I would have cared for her with respect, ensure you were raised without want for anything. Especially not the love and protection you deserve."

"So you knew how awful Bott's was, and you just left me there?"

"What else could I have done? Khryton spied on me as much as I did him. If I interfered once I set it in motion, he would have found you. It only took me so long to approach you after they kicked you out because I had to make sure his men weren't snooping. I did, however, protect you from the worst dregs on those streets, made sure the ones that wouldn't be deterred by your fire, stayed away."

Mallan's full confession set Imara off balance, and doused the ire from his deception into an ember. She understood why he did what he did, though she still didn't like it. She didn't appreciate being used. It made her feel like the roach the ladies at Bott's treated her like.

There was nothing to be done about Mallan's past choices, the consequences Imara and her mother suffered had already played out. Forgiveness wasn't an issue, at least not from Imara, she'd forgive the fae for what he did. He couldn't have known what horror lay in her future when he began his plot. But then there was Tilly, who suffered torment and belittlement for love, and became destined to live her life being told she was a liar. Delusional. She didn't deserve that.

Imara's mother had an affair with a fae, not an angel as she had thought. She could see why Tilly would make that assumption, Khryton's shimmering appearance made him look like an angel. It was fitting she knew she wasn't the liar everyone said she was. Tilly deserved some closure, to be justified that she'd been in the right all along.

When Imara didn't respond to his tale immediately, Mallan worried, "I guess this means you're back to hating me?"

Imara's head rolled as she released a deep breath and reached out for him, taking his hand in hers, "No. As much as I should be, I'm not."

"Can I make it up to you?"

"No," she said firmly, though another idea populated in her mind at the offer. "But there is someone you can make it up to, and maybe win a little more favor from me in doing so." He quirked an eyebrow, a silent plea to tell him what to do. "You saved me, protected me. Now, it's time to do the same for my mother."

TWENTY-ONE

Imara

The woman in the mirror stared back at Imara. Dressed in fine clothes suitable for any upperclass citizen of Ocean Fare, modest in cut and color, she looked serious. If she didn't bear Imara's face, she shouldn't have recognized herself.

The wardrobe was filled with spectacular pieces Imara never dreamed of owning. Still finding the one that portrayed her in a way the matron of Bott's would approve of proved harder than she thought it would be. It was imperative for her to make a good impression. The women at Bott's never took kindly to visitors they deemed as wretched. Poor, shabbily dressed, unclean, or immoral, all the things that described the very women they cared for most of the time. Given how they kicked her out, Imara didn't think they'd even let her in the door if they didn't think they'd benefit from it.

The dress she settled on was a cream colored, high collared with full sleeves that pinched tighter past the elbows to fit her forearms, which Imara paired with a black overskirt.

Demure gray pearl buttons decorated the cuffs. Then to ensure she wouldn't get turned away, Imara donned a luxurious fur-lined cloak that only the wealthiest in Ocean Fare could afford, and a jewel studded crucifix brooch to hold it closed.

Imara was still gaping at her reflection when Mallan appeared behind her in the mirror. "I must say, I don't think this look suits you, Starling."

"Sort of the point, it suits Bott's. My history with the home won't make getting in the door easy. This," she gestured to her clothes, "will help."

"I will glamour an appearance similar then."

Imara turned from the mirror, she never agreed to him joining her. She only needed Mallan to send her there. "I'm doing this alone. You're my transportation, and that is the end of your role unless I need you otherwise," she chided. "Use your abilities to get me close enough to Bott's to not arouse suspicion and come back when I call. That's all."

"I don't like it."

"You don't have to," she rolled her eyes. "You just have to accept it and realize I won't be in harm's way at all. I can handle people."

Mallan warred with the idea of leaving her unguarded. "Fine," he reluctantly agreed, "but you must do one thing for me in return."

"Really?" Imara scoffed. "As I recall, you doing this for me is not a favor that I need to repay. This is an amends that has to be done."

"The conditions of visiting your mother are, true, but not the condition of me leaving you unprotected. I'm going to need another agreement in order to do that." Mallan looked Imara in her eyes with a burning question. One she thought she knew all too well.

"I can't give you what you want, Mallan," she retorted. She wasn't prepared to swear herself to him.

"Refusing me before you even know what I ask?" he smirked. "Very presumptuous of you, Starling. I was merely going to ask for your help with the solstice celebrations coming up. I hold a ball for the Under Court every year, and I was hoping to add a concert to the festivities."

Imara's heart skipped, and her skin warmed. She was certain he'd ask for something else, but she didn't expect that. He knew her weakness, her love of music and song, would make it something she couldn't refuse. The promise of a stage had her beaming.

"Good," Mallan accepted her wordless answer, and called upon his smoke.

"I'm nervous," Imara admitted, looking to Mallan for reassurance. They appeared in a nearly empty alley with coal stained walls a block away from Bott's. No soul witnessed their arrival, save a lone, scraggly, gray cat that lapped at a dingy puddle. The dirty water was enough to make him stand his ground when they appeared, though he hissed and continued to keep a close eye on the pair.

"Don't be. Your mother will be happy to see you. Plus, I will be there in a heartbeat if you call."

"But what if they turn me away?"

"Come back here, call me, and we'll bypass the door and go straight to your mother's room." Mallan had pitched the idea before they left as well. Imara didn't think it was a good one then, it still wasn't.

"I don't want to scare her. I'll think of something," she took a step toward the alley's entrance. "Here goes nothing,"

"Remember, just call if you need me for anything." Imara gave Mallan a slight nod and turned the corner onto the street.

Imara's heart pounded in her ears as she walked the short block to her childhood home. The familiar sights of the neighborhood had changed little, if at all. Small, dirty children played in the gutters, women hung laundry out of their windows, and vagrants scattered along the street to beg. Imara felt their eyes following her, their desperation marking her fine clothes and cloak, assessing her as a tempting prospect. She'd never felt so out of place there.

It wasn't long before she reached the stone steps, guarded by iron posts, that led to the door of Bott's. The old iron knocker on the chipped font door felt heavier in Imara's grasp. She never thought she'd step foot in the place after they threw her out. She never even considered returning to visit Tilly, though that had more to do with the matron than her mother. Imara didn't want to see the inside of Bott's again, and was certain she'd have been denied entrance had she tried before.

The door opened, revealing the matron, Agnes. She'd aged a good deal since Imara had last seen her, when the woman had escorted her out of Bott's Home for Troubled Women to fend for herself on the streets. Her flaxen hair had more gray in it and wrinkles had formed at the corners of her eyes and mouth. Agnes's face still looked perpetually sour.

"May I help you, Miss," Agnes's eyes ran over Imara's fine clothes with greed, noting the brooch longer than any other part. There was no recognition in her steel eyes, only the gold she hoped Imara would be offering.

Imara smiled saccharinely, "Agnes, it's good to see you again."

The woman covered not recognizing Imara with a generic answer. "What can I help you with?"

"I'm here to see my mother, Tilly."

The hope in Agnes's eyes filtered away as familiarity took over, her mouth agape. "Imara, my dear, how lovely to see you! You certainly look well."

"I believe the last time we saw each other was when you dropped me off downtown with nothing but the clothes on my back," Imara jabbed and the matron paled.

"The years have been kind, I see," she deflected. "Fortune not found in these walls found you as I knew it would." The lie slid from the pious woman with ease. Imara could only scoff at her hypocrisy.

"Hardly. My mother," Imara touched the brooch on her cape, reminding Agnes of what she risked losing if she didn't let her see Tilly. What she hoped Imara would offer for the care given to her mother all those years.

"Yes, of course," her simple brown skirt swished as she shoed Imara into the foyer. "Can I get you anything, tea or coffee? Perhaps some pastries?" Agnes plied with fake hospitality, a kindness she never showed her charges and reserved for important visitors. She saw Imara's upper class appearance as dollar signs. She'd offer Imara anything to dip into her purse.

For Tilly's sake, Imara took advantage of the offer. "That would be delightful. Would you bring us some coffee and cakes? Tilly would love them."

Agnes swallowed hard, a hesitant false smile wavering on her lips. "Do you remember where Tilly's room is?"

Imara tilted her head in a half nod. She knew where to find her mother. The room had been hers for many years too, though it was barely big enough for one person. Their room sat at the top of the stairs, where Imara headed promptly after Agnes went in search of refreshments.

Tilly's door looked just as Imara remembered, perhaps faded from time, but the same. Tilly had painted an homage to her celestial lover, with a pair of golden wings and hearts, to mark the room as hers. Looking at the tribute, Imara realized that her mother had lost her mind, just a little, because of her father. She froze, perpetually locked in a love-sick stage of adolescence, as though his affection had stunted her mental growth.

Imara knocked on the center of those wings twice, paused, and then knocked three times. It was a pattern she and Tilly developed just for them. A code of sorts that only they understood. A piece of comfort, knowing the person beyond the door was the other.

No answer came.

She knocked again. This time a faint welcome drifted through the wood, "Come in." It was strange that Tilly didn't bound to the door and welcome her daughter with a bright smile and a tight hug as she used to. A troubled knot formed in her stomach. Tilly had always loved company, especially Imara's. The call through the door felt like a snub, like Tilly was punishing her for years of not visiting.

Smoothing her skirt, Imara followed the command and stepped back in time as she entered the room. Like the exterior of the door, the room had barely changed since the last time she saw it. The wood floor grayed more from age and squeaked just beyond the threshold. That stupid spot had snitched on Imara more than once when she tried to sneak out during the night when she should have been asleep. Bott's was an old home that held countless adventures for a little girl surrounded by those that didn't want to be her friend. Her imagination led her to explore every dark corner. Hunger had her climbing in every kitchen cupboard in search of Agnes's best treats, stealing them whenever Imara could. The switching when caught was always worth it.

Ratty patchwork curtains hung above the slim bed, rustling in the slight breeze coming through the window. Tilly sat expectantly against a threadbare pillow, her eyes oceans of tears that glittered with happiness. Yet Imara's heart twisted at the sight of her mother. Tilly's waifish body told the tale of illness and hardship. Her once vibrant, raven hair hung limp and dull around her frail shoulders, wrapped in a moth-eaten knit shawl she'd had since Imara was small. Maybe longer. It had once been beautiful, woven with golden thread that had long since faded, and clasped with a sun brooch that had since disappeared.

"My little Angel," there was no strength behind her smile. "You've come back." Tilly's shocking appearance threw Imara so much she lost all words. She could only offer a forced smile. She didn't want her mother to see the worry that wanted to take over.

Sitting on the edge of the bed, Imara took her mother's hand. It seemed to weigh less than a bird, a pang of guilt coursing through her heart at the realization. A jolt of fire came on its heels. Agnes didn't bother to mention Tilly's fragile condition. It was likely she hadn't even noticed, or didn't care. Imara wanted to rip the woman from the home and toss her to the streets herself, not that it would do any good. Ousting her wouldn't bring in a better matron. Ocean Fare didn't care enough about lost women to do anything about the mistreatment. If they had, changes would have come a long time ago.

"What brings you back?" Tilly asked with the eagerness of a small child.

Imara didn't know where to start. Did she tell her mother about the life she led on the streets of the city, her singing career, her wedding? Or did she stick to what had happened to her since arriving in the Under Court? The only thing she was certain of was that Tilly had to know what brought Imara back, questions about her father. There was always the chance her mother would feel attacked if she brought up the man that sired her.

Before Imara could answer, Agnes burst in without knocking. She was never one to ask permission to enter one of her charges rooms, she felt entitled to revoke their privacy whenever she felt like it. Which was all the time. The older woman bustled in and placed a tray laden with iced biscuits, crumb cakes, and aromatic coffee on a little table near the bed, knocking over a framed picture of Tilly and her daughter. She didn't bother uprighting it.

"Is there anything else I can do for you?" Agnes played the helpful, pious act up. She was working hard for the money that wouldn't come.

"No, Agnes. You've done quite enough," Imara seethed, shooting sharp eyes at the woman.

Agnes's pleasant facade faltered at her tone. She knew she messed up somehow, lost any chance of a hefty donation. That was all she needed to understand. The woman sneered at Imara and Tilly, and with an icy voice she announced, "Visiting hours will be over in ten minutes."

"Visiting hours will be over when I say they are, Agnes," Imara fired back. She'd lost the last of her patience for the matron. "Unless you want to find yourself on the wrong end of my ire, or my friend's. Trust me, I have many new friends more powerful than your imagination could comprehend, and they will defend me and whomever I ask them to." The threat was half empty. Imara didn't actually know if Mallan would do what she told Agnes. But that didn't mean she wouldn't evoke his power.

The matron, seeing a new side of Imara, a side that would fight her, hurried away, slamming the door behind her.

Imara's anger boiled, breaking any doubt about where to begin in pieces. "I met Khryton," she said matter-of-factly, bypassing uncomfortable questions and getting straight to her point. She hoped using his name would springboard Tilly into opening up.

"You, you," her words stumbled, and Tilly fluttered an emaciated hand to cover her shocked expression. "You met Khryton?"

"You know the name?"

Tilly nodded her head fervently, "I always hoped you'd meet him. Every girl deserves to know her daddy." The confirmation sent an odd wave of relief through Imara.

"I met him, briefly," shelf out the details how. Details that would probably upset Tilly. "An acquaintance took me to meet him. He seemed surprised to see me, called me by your name. I don't think he knew I existed." It was a lie, he knew Tilly had conceived, but thanks to Mallan, he thought they'd both died until Imara showed up in his court with his enemy. Tilly didn't need to know that either.

"No, maybe not. I can't say if he did for sure. He stopped coming to me before I knew I was pregnant. Though I never stopped hoping he'd come back. That we could be a family." Imara knew that already. Tilly pined for Khryton her whole life. "I'd love to see him again."

Her mother's wish gave Imara an idea, or completed an already forming one. She knew the minute she saw Tilly, saw her illness ravaged body, that she couldn't leave her behind in that horrible place. She'd been imprisoned there far too long, under false accusations. The only insanity Tilly was guilty of was immaturity brought on by heartbreak and trauma brought on by abusive accusations. Imara's mother had been wronged, and she was just as guilty of adding to Tilly's pain as anyone else was.

She wouldn't stand by when she could at least make some sort of amends.

"I think I might be able to make that happen," Imara looked into her mother's eyes, once mirror images of her own. "If not, the least I can do is get you out of this awful place. I have a friend that can help." Imara called for Mallan. He'd come and collect her, as promised, and she would convince him to take Tilly, too. It would take some bargaining, but Imara wasn't leaving Bott's without Tilly.

After summoning Mallan, Imara prepared her mother for his arrival. "Now, this friend, he might look scary, but I assure you he's going to help you. He will not hurt you," just as she finished those words, Mallan appeared in his cloak of smoke and all of his nightmarish beauty. He filled the room, bumping into the table and spilling the untouched treats.

"Tilly, this is Mallan, my friend," Imara introduced the fae.

"A pleasure, Tilly," he bowed and took her hand, placing a kiss on it.

"Mallan, we're taking her with us. I won't take no for an answer."

"I didn't think you would."

Imara was pleasantly surprised it had been so easy; that he didn't offer any resistance to do what she wanted. She helped her mother to her feet, noting once more how light she had become, and another stab of anger toward the matron took hold of her. Tilly huddled close to Imara, passing an uncertain look at Mallan. "It's okay, Mom. He's like Khryton," Imara hoped the comparison would soothe Tilly's fears.

As Imara sided up to Mallan, Agnes walked in unannounced, railing about the clatter she'd just heard. Her words died on her thin lips when she saw Mallan. Her eyes went wide, taking in the terrifying and beautiful fae. Agnes's shock turned to fury, "You're in league with the devil!" she accused.

Mallan certainly looked the part of a demon. Imara herself had briefly thought that's what he was, and she was content to let the matron think it, too. "Like I told you, Agnes, I have powerful friends." The fae lord whisked them away before anything else could be said. Imara held no qualms about Agnes seeing him, his powers at work. She wouldn't dare tell others what she saw. They'd mark her as crazy as she had marked Tilly.

TWENTY-TWO

Imara

Tilly rested comfortably in Imara's suite, she looked like a doll against the massive bed. After taking an immediate liking to the maids, becoming enamored with their pastel skin and wide eyes, and enjoying some tea, she fell into an easy sleep.

It pained Imara to see how frail her mother was. Even breathing seemed like a struggle for her. She couldn't sit in her room and watch Tilly without wanting to cry, wanting to go back to Bott's and pulverize Agnes for what she'd done to her.

Instead, she followed Mallan to his suite, cozying up on his couch and watching the flames he summoned just for her comfort. "The healer says Tilly is extremely ill, that she probably doesn't have much time," Mallan stated woefully as he sat next to Imara.

"I was afraid of that, even though it's easy to see. I want to make her happy in what little time she has left."

"Of course, Starling. Anything. Just tell me what she needs."

"Khryton. She needs Khryton. Send for him," Imara knew it

was a big ask. The negotiations didn't even happen before war was being declared. But it was the only thing she knew would give her mother the happiness she deserved.

"I can't do that, Imara. Not now, not with war looming."

"You can and you will. Those negotiations failed because of you. You goaded him. You knew who I was to him and used it to get under his skin."

"You're mad? I thought we'd resolved this?"

"We did, mostly. But, things have developed since. I don't like that you used me, that I have already processed. This is about Tilly, Mallan. Let there be peace, if only just for a day, to give her closure. A shred of a happy ending."

"Imara," he chided, "it's a bad idea. You don't know him like I do."

"And that is your fault, too," Imara placed a hand on his knee, and made a final plea, "My mother deserves closure before she dies. It's the least you can do for me after everything else. You owe me."

Mallan stood, breaking contact with her. "I owe you nothing," his gaze narrowed when he looked down on her. Imara's insistence for Khryton to visit truly bothered him. However, she would not give in, the visit had to happen.

Imara realized she needed to give him something big in return for this, if she was going to convince him to do it. It was time to change tactics and offer what she was so reluctant to .

"Please? Mallan, I'd do anything for her," Imara got up and wrapped her arms around the fae, resting her forehead on his chest and digging her hands into the back of his dark robes. Looking up through her lashes, she quietly asked again, "Please? Do this for me. For Tilly. There has to be something, anything, I can offer for this favor." It was cheap and low, using what he desperately wanted from her. She knew it was, but after years of being tormented and emotionally abused, of being told her great love was a fairy story, Tilly deserved her last moments to be with her lost lover.

"Would you be mine?" Mallana ran a sharpened nail gently over Imara's cheek, light enough to feel but not so hard as to leave a mark on her.

Imara shivered beneath his heated stare. To deny she felt something for Mallan would have been a lie. There were feelings there, different from the pure love she had with Lorn. Lorn was easy to love. With Mallan, those feelings were complicated, conflicted. She couldn't allow herself to give in to them, not the way he wanted her to. Imara swore she'd never be his, and didn't intend to go back on it.

"I...," shame averted her eyes, both from the feelings she dared not admit to herself, and for denying Mallan what he asked. Her torn heart felt like a failure, having gotten Tilly so close to her happiness and it not happening, all for denying Mallan. She couldn't stop the disappointed tears from falling.

"Starling, don't cry," he wiped a tear from Imara's chin. "I will call for Khryton. Tilly will get her happy ending, if you offer me one simple thing. A chance. A chance to win your heart. You don't need to swear yourself to me unless you want to. Just give me the chance to win you."

A chance. Nothing more, no strings attached. For her mother, Imara could give Mallan that, even knowing she would never choose him. She could at least let him feel like she might. "A chance then," Imara nodded. "We have a deal."

"Starting with a seal?" the question in his coal eyes asked more than that as his hand slid through Imara's hair to the nape. She responded with a lift of her chin, she was giving him a chance to court her.

His lips pressed to hers, caressing reverently for only a moment before parting. A promise, and a seal that surprised Imara. With his desire to make her his, she expected more. Not the gentle affection, so welcoming and sweet. It left Imara wanting more.

It felt strange to Imara to be sitting at Mallan's desk waiting for Khryton to arrive. Malian had done what she asked and summoned his foe, who was more than hesitant to accept the invitation. Mallan refused to tell the golden fae why he was being called to Shadowmire, which didn't help. He couldn't resist messing with Khryton.

"It'll be beneficial to us both," he hinted, dangling a carrot of another chance at negotiations. Reluctantly, Khryton agreed to meet, though he did not know he wouldn't be dealing with Mallan at all.

Imara's mind wandered over the upcoming meeting with her father. Her father, another strange sensation gripped her with the thought. It was a phrase she never thought she'd use. She'd long ago written off ever meeting the man that sired her.

She ran her hands over the smooth glass that covered the intricately carved desktop depicting whorls of clouds and flowers. The beautiful and impressive piece of furniture mesmerized Imara, and she grew lost in tracing the lines of the carving with her eyes when a knock sounded at the office door. Moments later, a goblin with a spiked cockscomb and golden eyes entered. Imara glimpsed several bronze clad guards from the High Court.

"Lord Khryton," the goblin garbled.

Looking into the goblin's eyes, Imara gave a nod. The creatures still made her uncomfortable, but that was nothing compared to the flight of wings that settled in her chest with the announcement of her father's arrival. The goblin turned and pushed his way through the retinue of guards Khryton brought with him.

Imara heard Khryton before she saw him, "I don't know what sort of games you're playing at Mal..." his curses died in his throat when his eyes landed on his daughter instead of the fae he expected. His shock switched to relief at the unexpected sight. "Imara, I was expecting to meet with Mallan."

"I know. I'm sorry for the confusion, but I'm happy that you came."

"You can thank my son for that. Lautrec convinced me to come, to give negotiations another chance. It's smart of Mallan to use you as proxy, smart but dirty."

"You're not here for negotiations, Lord Khryton," Imara stood and came around the desk to stand before her father. "I asked Mallan to send for you, for my own reasons."

"To what do I owe the pleasure?"

"It's more what you can do for me," she countered. Khryton arched a golden brow. "Follow me, please." The Lord of the High Court fell into step behind Imara as she exited the office, his entourage of guards joining behind him when he passed them.

"Where are we going?" Confusion laced his tone as Imara led him past all the formal rooms on the main floor and up the stairs.

"My suite," Imara looked over her shoulder with a sly smile, baiting him into admitting if he knew what she was to him.

"Imara,' he stammered, "I don't know what your intentions are, but I think there is something you should know."

"I'm your daughter," she replied bluntly, stopping at her door. She turned and looked Khryton in the eyes, "I know."

"I'm confused, you know? Then why are we..."

"I have a request of you, one I hope you'll consider." Imara interrupted, studying him and trying to find anything familiar about him. There was nothing. She was a pure copy of Tilly. "That being said, I ask that your guards stay out here in the sitting area. I don't want them overwhelming her."

"Her?"

Imara only beamed at Khryton, then flung the doors to her suite open and waltzed inside. "Mom," she called, "there's someone here to see you." She turned her attention back to her guest, Imara couldn't wait for her mother and father to lock eyes on one another. She hadn't told Tilly to expect company, though she knew Imara was trying to get in contact with Khryton. Imara wanted to surprise her.

"Mom?" Khryton's blue eyes went wide and rimmed with tears. Imara only nodded, holding back her own tears at his reaction. That was all he needed to hear. Khryton surged past Imara, who turned to watch the events unfold, and searched the room. When he spotted Tilly sleeping on the bed, he flew to her side immediately, falling to his knees there and caressing her cheek. "Tilly, my Kite, my Love," he whispered gently to rouse her.

Imara kept her distance, hugging her arms around her body and observing the reunion. She couldn't believe the coincidence that her father's pet name for Tilly was that of a bird. Kite. It was another thread that connected her to her mother, both birds in the eyes of the fae that cared for them.

She was barely close enough to catch the moment her mother's eyes fluttered open, only to widen as a weak smile broke across her face. She became filled with so much joyful light, more than Imara had seen in her before. "Khryton? Is it really you?" her wispy voice, hardly loud enough to hear, was filled with hope and disbelief as she reached for him.

"Yes, I'm here. I have you." He gathered Tilly's delicate hands in his own, kissing them over and over, letting tears of joy fall unabashedly.

It was then that Imara stepped forward, grasping her father's shoulder with care. He looked back at her, only long enough to acknowledge her, before turning his attention back to his lost love. "I'll leave you two to catch up. Please come find me before you leave. I want to discuss some things with you." Imara didn't need him to answer, she knew he'd find her after the gift she just gave him. She only hoped that he'd agree to what she wanted from him.

Imara left her suite with her soul singing. For what it was worth, Khryton truly seemed to love Tilly, even after all the years that had passed. As long as the next part of her plan went well, everything would be perfect.

Then she saw Mallan, looking as though he were waiting for bad news, waiting in the sitting area. He sat hunched over with his hands clasped in front of him, his eyes staring a hole in the oriental rug beneath his feet. His usually stony face was long as drawn. He heard her approach and his dark eyes shot up briefly, full of a fire that could burn down cities.

Notably, strangely, Khryton's retinue was mysteriously missing from the sitting area. "Where are the bronze boys?" Imara tried cracking his focus.

"They're smart enough to get lost when I tell them to," he replied without shifting his gaze.

"Do you really think Khryton is making nefarious plans while reconnecting with Tilly?" Imara curled up on the couch next to Mallan, tucking her feet under her. His ire sucked away her cat that got the canary smugness. She didn't understand why he couldn't just let go and let her have the win.

"I wouldn't put it past him. No situation, no person is beneath being used as a stepping stone for him."

"Trust me, Mallan. Khryton has nothing but my mother on his mind." He shifted his feet, looked up, and rolled his eyes at Imara. It was clear he would not move, let alone listen to her while her father was in her suite. In his home. Mallan wouldn't relax until Khryton was gone from Shadowmire, and the Under Court.

Imara knew his state of mind, she'd been there herself before agreeing to wipe the slate clean with Mallan. She didn't miss that perpetual state of anger and grief that had ripped her to shreds for far too long. She also knew she had to get him to relax or he wouldn't be receptive to what she planned on proposing to Khryton and him. To do that, she had to distract him from focusing on Khryton, improve his mood, and ensure he was with her when her father came looking for her.

"Come on," she stood, reaching for Mallan's hand. "Come with me to the music room."

"Not while he's in there," he motioned to the door with his head. "He needs to be watched."

"Then get someone to watch my door. I want to practice, and I want you there with me," Imara tempted, but he made no move to budge from his watch. She dropped his hand, "I can't believe you," she scoffed.

"What have I done this time," he bit.

"This! This stubborn insistence to watch Khryton. So what if he's in your house, in my suite? He's not going anywhere for a while. You didn't see how he lit up when he saw her, Mallan."

He scoffed, rolling his eyes again. "You don't know him. You don't know how he thinks, what he wants. He's a master manipulator."

"So are you. Or have you forgotten because I gave you a fresh start, a chance at my heart, all the things you did to get me here?"

"Starling,"

"No. You claim to want a chance at my heart, but you can't trust me? Indulge me, just a little?" Mallan's eyes lifted to hers, sharp with a new fire in them as he growled a warning. She struck a nerve questioning his word. "Then prove it. Prove you trust my word, get a damn goblin up here to watch my door, and come listen to me practice."

"I trust you. I don't trust him."

Imara let out a heavy breath, "Fine. I'll head up by myself, but I don't know how I'll concentrate without someone there to support me. Keep me focused and not worrying about Tilly." She walked away, slowly. Mallan grabbed her wrist, and she had to rein in the grin stretching across her face before turning back to him.

"You're trying to manipulate me?"

"What can I say? It's a family trait," she shrugged with a smirk. "Is it working?"

With a snap of his fingers, a bewildered yellow and blue fleshed goblin appeared in a cloud of smoke. "Keep an eye on Imara's suite," Mallan ordered.

"We'll be in the conservatory if need be," Imara added off hand just before Mallan transported them away. She hoped the goblin would remember and tell Khryton if he asked after her.

They appeared right outside the music room. Imara reached for the handle, proud of herself for getting Mallan to budge from the couch. Everything was going according to plan. But Mallan reached around her, grabbing the handle first, and blocked her from entering the room. He pinned Imara between him and the door, his campfire smell sucking the air between them away and filling the cracks until he was all there was to sense. Looking up through her lashes, she saw Mallan's face was set in stone.

"Do not manipulate me, Starling. You might not like the consequences," he breathed her in, savoring the closeness. The intimacy.

Imara's head spun, she couldn't hear anything but the thudding of her own heart and couldn't feel anything but the buzzing of her body's reaction to his nearness. Despite his harsh expression, she wasn't scared. She should have been. That's what Mallan did, he terrified. Yet, the effect on her was as though she'd had too much wine and wanted even more. A bad, drunken idea from getting too close to his power.

She sucked in her bottom lip and tried to find iron in her will, to shake the forbidden desire. Imara had to remind herself that he'd just done the same thing to her, manipulated her. "It's not fun being used, is it?" she shot back. "You manipulated me into helping you rile your enemy. I was just playing your game. So, if you can't handle it, don't start it."

He leaned in closer, lowering his head level with hers and unleashed a low heat inducing growl, the corner of his mouth lifting to reveal his fangs. Imara met the challenge, fought the wobble of her knees to stand her ground against him. She couldn't, however, stop her heart from racing, or her breathing from quickening. The desire pooling low in her belly.

Mallan wouldn't break her. His stare failed to make Imara cower, and she'd be damned if she let it take what little control she had over her feelings away. The way his dark eyes smoldered and flicked from her eyes to her lips and back, told her he struggled against his own.

"I'd have you away from my daughter, Mallan, unless you want to lose a limb," Khryton threatened. They'd been so rapt in their standoff they didn't notice him arrive. Mallan whirled at the sound of his foe's voice, loosing a wall shaking roar.

"Mallan!" Imara barked. His outstretched arm from inches from striking her father and dropped as he stepped back. He heeled at her command.

Khryton chuckled, amused at seeing the formidable dark fae halted with a single word, "Seems I'm too late to take your balls away."

Imara crossed her arms, glaring icily at the fae before her. "In the music room, now, both of you."

"I won't go anywhere with him," Khryton seethed. "Whatever you wanted to talk about will not be done in his presence."

"I never thought I'd ever agree with anything he had to say," Mallan quipped.

"We all need to talk. If either of you has any shred of real care for me, you'll humor me." Mallan moved to open the music room door, giving her a nod of his head and holding Imara's gaze with a look of awe and pride. He was smart enough to know he wouldn't win that battle. Khryton, however, hadn't flinched. Imara fixed her sapphire eyes on him, taking his blatant refusal as a slap in the face, one she intended to volley. "I get it if you don't feel you owe me and sort of fatherly feelings, but if you truly love my mother, if you ever loved her, you will go in that room and hear me out."

Khryton wavered on his feet, as though debating whether he'd listen. She thought her father was about to prove Mallan right, who'd gloat about it in his own way for days to come. But, after a long minute, and a deep sigh, he took the first step towards the door.

Khryton and Mallan stood at the opposite ends of the music room, matching expressions and body language. Contemptuous and unrelenting. Neither were happy about being in the same room, or about not being the one holding all the power. They were powerful males, leaders, rulers used to giving commands and being feared. They weren't used to acquiescing that power to anyone, let alone a half mortal girl less than half their size.

Imara took a seat on the piano bench, letting her fingers glide over the cool keys and pluck out a few notes out of habit before setting her hands in her lap. "Call off this war."

"Over my dead body."

"I can arrange that," Mallan growled, taking a step forward. Fear fell over Khryton's face as he pressed himself against the wall he stood by.

"Enough!" Imara dropped her gaze to her lap, focusing with all her might on the tightly woven silk of the dress she wore to keep herself from crying from frustration. At her order, Mallan's heavy steps stopped, once again halted with one word from her. "Why? Why must this war happen?"

"Mallan broke the treaty knowing full well the consequences, war or relinquishing his lands back to me. I'm certain you know him well enough to know he'd never pick the latter."

"Damn straight."

Imara glared at Mallan, a silent warning. "As did you," she countered her father, her gaze shifting back to him. "My existence is proof that you didn't keep away from the mortal world."

"But..."

"No, Khryton. No excuses. You both broke the treaty. If the consequences are war or giving up your lands, neither of you are gaining a thing. War is senseless, both of you would likely feel the toll deeply. Over what? Nothing that really matters anymore. That's what."

The silence was a blade, ready to slice them all open. The males in the room with her were gorgonized, didn't even seem to breathe when Imara finished her tirade. Neither made a peep in response, their silence filled the space and threatened to crush Imara. It wouldn't though, Imara's spine was iron, as was her determination to get a peace accord struck, however temporary it may be.

Imara's hopes of their cooperation waned thinly at their silence, and she felt certain she faced a losing battle.

"My mother is gravely ill," Imara began anew, "and doesn't have much time left, according to Mallan's healer. She needs rest and care, not to be stuck in the middle of a pissing contest between two over-egotistical fae. She deserves peace in her final days."

Imara stood and crossed the room to her father, looking up at him with steel in her bones. "And she deserves a taste of the life you once promised her. Take her home with you to the High Court. Let her live out whatever time she has left with you. I know nothing will make her happier, or will help her cling to this life and give her more time than she actually has."

She then turned her attention to her friend, tears in her eyes, "Please, give my mother some happiness before she dies. Stop this fight."

"You know I can't deny you anything, Starling. Not anything you ask. I will keep the peace for as long as possible."

Khryton chuffed in his corner, eyes skeptical, but he wasn't about to be outdone by Mallan. "Of course, my darling girl. I will welcome Tilly to my home and there will be peace. On one condition."

Imara couldn't believe her ears, "Are you kidding? Are you really so selfish that you need more from this deal than you're already getting? Keeping your lands, avoiding war, Tilly," she listed off everything he benefitted from just saying yes. What more could he want?

"I am indeed selfish and want more. I want to get to know you, Imara. I want you to come home with us, Tilly and me."

Imara wanted to know her father better, but she didn't want to leave Shadowmire. "I can't. I've already given my word to Mallan to stay here. A promise I can't go back on, but I can promise you the opportunity to get to know me more. I can visit the High Court, and there will be opportunities for you to come here to see me."

"I can understand you keeping your word with reputable

folk, but the Under Court doesn't work that way. Mallan doesn't work that way," Khryton scoffed.

A low growl came from Mallan, "The same could be said of the High Court."

"But," Khryton stammered, obviously afraid of Mallan, and covered, "I admire your willingness to do so. All I ask is that you stay safe and know I'm only a summons away if I'm needed. Your brother too." Imara read between the lines, *if she needed him to save her from Mallan and the Under Court.*

So far, Mallan had proven to be a man of his word. Imara had little reason to think she'd need her father's help, but she appreciated the offer. A huge weight lifted from her shoulders. She didn't need to worry about war for a while, and Tilly was going to be happy and cared for by the man she thought she had lost. That was all Imara wanted.

"Good. Now," Imara tugged the document and pen tucked into her pocket out, "all that needs to be done is for you to sign this agreement I drew up and we will be all set." She walked back to the piano and unfolded the paper, laying it flat on the instrument.

"You've been busy, Starling," Mallan whispered as he leaned in to sign the paper.

"You aren't the only one with plans," she jabbed back playfully.

"Full of surprises," he commented, cupping her elbow and leading her a step away to make room for Khryton.

Imara's father eyed the movement warily, obvious distaste in his gaze as he signed the accord. When he finished, he handed her the paper. Looking over it, Imara chuckled. Khryton made sure his signature was more prominent than Mallan's. Even in peace, he had to be better, go bigger.

Imara pulled away from Mallan, "Thank you, both of you. This means so much." She folded the paper and tucked it away in her pocket and patted it. She'd gotten two powerful fae to bow to her whims, and it felt good. "Now, if you'll excuse me, I'd like to spend some time with Tilly before she leaves for the High Court."

Khryton hurried to her side and offered Imara his elbow, "Let me escort you. It will be nice to be with my girls."

"I'd like that too," she smiled and turned her attention to Mallan. He'd plopped himself at the piano and plucked at the keys, his face sour and defeated, eyes blazing holes into Khryton. "I'll see you at dinner then?" Mallan's reply came as a short nod. Imara understood he wasn't ready to talk and left him to stew.

"That was impressive, Imara," her father commented when the door closed behind them.

"Who knows, perhaps the pair of you will find you like peace and it will extend longer than either of you ever imagined it would."

Before Khryton could answer, a cacophony of notes blared from the music room, as though many keys had been struck at once.

TWENTY-THREE

Mallan

Mallan glared at the splayed piano keys displaced by his outburst. Imara tried his patience with the stunt she pulled. She'd gone behind his back and made a deal with his enemy. He had no choice but to honor it, or else he'd push her away again. Risk undoing everything that he had accomplished already.

He could deal with that, with the curveballs she threw. The budding relationship with her father, however, he couldn't. He couldn't have her seduced into believing in his charm and outward goodness. He had to believe she'd see the tar that made his soul, that she was clever enough to see through his veiled bullshit. Though her inherently good nature, her want to see the good in those around her, her sensitive heart encased in iron, might prove to be a problem there. The leeway and undeserved forgiveness she'd given Mallan spoke volumes about the reception she might just offer Khryton.

His fists slammed into the keys again, damaging them

further and sending a few scattering across the room. He roared into the silence, his hands fisting into his hair.

"Problems, brother?" Michaela slipped from the shadows and plucked a key from the floor. "You certainly will have one when Imara sees what you've done to her piano."

"How long have you been here?"

"Not long, I heard the discordant noise and investigated. I had to make sure Mother wasn't messing with this room."

"She wouldn't." Mallan eyed the mess he made of Imara's instrument, a knot forming in his heart. He waved his hand over the keys and watched them fix themselves, then plucked out a few notes to ensure they were in tune.

"She's certainly voiced the idea. You may not see it, but she'd still trying to undermine Imara. Mother insists she only seeks retribution for her missing jewels, but I know better," Michaela commented bitterly.

Mallan didn't want to speak of his mother, it only added to the throb in his head. "How's Auren faring?"

"She's bored, and cold," Michaela laughed. "Trying to stay out of Mother's path. The usual for her visits here. Imara fascinates her, I have to admit there is something about her."

"There is definitely something about her," Mallan agreed with a wistful air.

Michaela's dark eyes studied her brother, a smirk quirking her lips. "You really feel for her. Here I thought it was just the prophecy that had you wanting her. But it's more than that."

"What do you know of the prophecy?" Mallan wasn't aware his family knew what Tamsin had foretold decades ago. He hadn't shared it with many outside of his regents.

"Only what Auren sees around her, that she holds the destiny of Sylphea and Morrea in her hands. I figured it was the only reason a human would captivate you," she slid onto the bench next to him, taking the sheet music into her hands to study it. Michaela hummed a few bars, then laughed at herself. "I'll leave singing to her."

Mallan laughed with her. He enjoyed the moments where they could bond beyond the sight of Rhanda. They could be themselves, with no pressure to bow to her whims or be what she wanted them to be. Though his aspirations didn't stray far from his mother's, they strayed far enough for hers to rub him the wrong way.

"She's not all human, you know." It was safe for Mallan to confide in his twin, and pointless not to. She'd figure it out soon enough on her own, or Auren would and share with Michaela as she did everything. "No doubt you saw Lord Khryton on your way up here."

"You mean she's one of Khryton's many halflings?"

Mallan seethed at the reminder of how cozy she'd seemed with her father, how quickly she took to him. His fists clenched in his lap to keep from damaging the piano again and he chuckled sarcastically, "Don't tell Mother."

"As if she needs another reason to hate the girl. You keep my secrets, I'll keep yours. Like always." Even as children, only they knew each others deepest secrets and biggest dreams. "I won't even tell Auren, though she'll see right through me."

"You can tell her. I trust Auren. She's good for you."

Michaela blushed under her brother's compliment, but still her heart twisted as if he'd ran her through. She and Auren were destined for each other, but as long as their mother tried to push her cinnamon eyed love onto Mallan, they'd never get to be together. Rhanda controlled too much, almost never left Auren's side as she schooled her in how to be a proper wife to the Lord of the Under Court. Her pain wasn't missed.

"Soon, my sister," Mallan wrapped an arm around her shoulders. "Mother will have no choice but to give up soon enough. I promise."

"We'll see," Michaela slid from under his arm, stood, and wrapped her arms around herself. "I should get back, Mother will wonder where I've gone off to." She headed for the door, only to turn back and take in the music room one more time. Her eyes shone as she drank up the details. "Word of advice, brother. Ward this room from Mother. She's desperate, getting more so by the day as she feels you slipping from her grasp. I fear if she took that frustration out on this room, not even your magic could restore it."

He responded with a nod; it was a good idea. He could always count on his sister to point out what he'd failed to see. "Thank you," he offered, only to be met with an indifferent shrug before Michaela left him alone once more.

Mallan would ward the room, protect what was most precious to Imara. But first, he needed to see Tamsin and urge her to work faster on the girl. The sooner Imara chose him and became transformed, the better. Not just for his plans, but for his sanity as well. His sanity, and Michaela's.

TWENTY-FOUR

Imara

Tamsin was late.

Imara hadn't seen her friend since before going to the High Court. The witch had been busy in Alcara, the independent island where the witches of Sylphea lived. They belonged to neither court, though the witches individually had their allegiances to them, and still they lived in harmony with one another. Imara couldn't wait to visit Tamsin there someday.

They arranged to meet on the rooftop garden, though Tamsin had pushed to venture to Brine Bay again. Imara wanted to venture out of Shadowmire again, but she couldn't shake the feeling that Tamsin had ulterior motives for returning to the seaside town. Like she had planned to take Imara there for something other than fun.

The approaching concert Imara agreed to was also preventing Imara from doing much other than haunting the halls of the estate, alternating days of rest and practice for the event. She couldn't afford to traipse across the Under Court and risk coming down with something. The solstice celebrations were important to Mallan, and with the High Court being invited, they were more important than ever.

Usually, it didn't bother Imara when others ran late. But she needed someone to interact with, that wasn't Mallan or the maids. Even though Auren was cordial enough, Imara still didn't trust her. The one moment between them in the sitting area had been just that, not significant enough to say she'd changed her mind about the cinnamon eyed beauty. The stress from feeling pressure about the concert and worrying endlessly about Tilly made Imara desperate to let off some steam and impatient to see her friend.

Tamsin hardly ever arrived on time for anything. Her excessive pickiness and need for perfection were practically a signature. "It does no-good to be an incorrigible flirt and look like you don't care about your appearance," she'd once said. "You have to be the complete package."

Incorrigible was definitely the way to describe the witch. There wasn't anything anyone could do to sway her once Tamsin made up her mind.

Wending through the rooftop garden while she waited, Imara eyed the dark bands of rain cresting the horizon and willed Tamsin to hurry. The approaching storm looked nasty, with bright bolts of lightning cutting to the earth every few minutes, and Imara didn't want to get caught in it. If she didn't have a concert to perform soon, she wouldn't have minded.

Watching the hypnotic dance of lightning in the distance, Imara didn't hear the soft crunch of gravel behind her.

"Beautiful, isn't it?" Turning, it surprised her to see Auren alone again. She wore loose fitting white slacks and tunic style top under a heavy oxblood cloak. "The storm? It's lovely. In my homeland, we worship storms, sacred for the life giving water gifted from them to the Glass Desert."

Auren looked at Imara with no trace of malice in her eyes or in her tone. "Auren. What brings you to the garden?"

"I'm waiting on Michaela. She's looking for something in the library, and I thought I'd wait out here, surrounded with beauty and color rather than old books." She looked back towards the glass doors leading into the library, searching for her friend. Imara never saw them apart from each other, and rarely without Rhanda. But, being alone with her on the rooftop, Auren didn't seem as prickly as when she was with them. There was a vulnerability about her that Imara didn't see before.

"I'm waiting for Tamsin," Imara explained without prompting and turned her attention back to the horizon.

"Have you heard anything about how your mother is faring from Lord Khryton?"

Auren shocked Imara by asking how Tilly was doing. That she was continuing to talk to her, even. "No, I haven't."

"I'm sorry," her sincere tone drew Imara's attention back to Auren. Her cinnamon eyes seemed to plead with Imara, to say more than her condolences about Tilly. All she could do was look back at Auren, curious about her. A wind swept through the garden, fierce and cold, a warning of the storm to come. Both women shivered, despite the warm cloaks around their shoulders. "No matter how much time I spend here, I never get used to the constant cold." Auren laughed, breaking the strange tension between them.

"Isn't your home part of the Under Court?" Not having experienced much outside of Shadowmire, Imara imagined the whole of the court to be like Mallan's home environment, cold. Brine Bay had been cold. Warmth wasn't something she associated with the place.

Auren laughed again, "Yes. The Glass Desert hides in the rain shadow of the Cailloch mountains, far from these costal areas. We're a different sort of fae there, meant for heat and fire. For sweeping desert winds and sun showers warmed by centuries of hot weather. Sand and succulents, with bright springtime buds, and reptiles on scorched rocks. Pink sunsets and golden mornings."

"It sounds lovely, especially the warm part."

"It is. You should visit it sometime. I'd love to show you around. We could ride fire tulpars across the desert sky at midnight, our way lit by their wings. It's one of the best things to do there."

"What are fire tulpars?" Imara was still in disbelief she was having a civil conversation with Auren. She'd been certain the fae hated her as much as Mallan's family, but if that was true, would she bother talking with Imara to just pass the time?

"Great horses with wings made of fire. There are other breeds of tulpar across Sylphea, but it is ours in the Glass Desert that flies the fastest." Auren studied Imara in silence, a warm smile on her face, "Though, I don't suppose you're fireproof? That could be an issue," she laughed.

"No, sadly I'm not," Imara joined in the laughter. In other circumstances, she might have liked Auren.

A caw cut through the air, followed by a flapping of wings. Soon enough, Corvus's ghostly body peeked over the edge of the garden, something glinting in his beak. Imara held her hand out for him to land on, though she was cursing him silently. There wouldn't be any way to conceal whatever trinket he had on him. He usually took his treasures to Tamsin, though with her arrival imminent, she supposed he was looking for her.

"Hello, Corvus," she greeted.

"Corvus?" Auren repeated, taking in the bird's unusual, piebald coloring. "You named a raven, Corvus?"

"I know, the name is redundant. I already got an earful about that from Mallan. But it fits, doesn't it?" Imara posed the query to the bird rather than Auren as she opened her free hand for him to drop the gift he brought, a fire opal brooch. His feathers ruffled and his feet danced up her arm, proud that he'd brought her something. Imara just hoped Auren didn't recognize the piece of jewelry.

Auren's eyes widened when she saw what he deposited in Imara's hand, "Is that my brooch?"

"I don't know," Imara hesitated, and handed it to Auren. "Is it?"

"Looks like we've discovered who's been nicking jewelry," Imara swallowed hard as Auren's eyes narrowed on Corvus. She didn't know how to explain it. "I'll have to let Mallan know to search the rookery for their hoard. I should have known it was a raven, I saw one flying out of Michaela's window the other day. They can't resist shiny things."

"Their hoard?"

"Yeah, if one is getting in and taking shiny things, more are, too."

"Do you leave your windows open?"

"Not me, Michaela and Rhanda do, though, sometimes the maids when they clean," she admitted with annoyance. "I think it's cold enough as it is in my room with the fireplace going."

"I'll talk to the maids, and Corvus," Imara added, poking at the bird's beak. He snapped gently at her fingers and flew across the garden, lighting on a tall planter and cawing angrily. He didn't like not receiving praise for the gift, as Tamsin usually did. She often rewarded the bird with bits of carrion or seeds.

"You know," Auren began, "you're not what Rhanda says you are. You're okay. It's safe to say I rather like you even. I want you to know I'm sorry for being so awful when we first met. Rhanda's judgement clouded my own. With everything she's done, I owe her. It's easy to get wrapped up in her ideas."

"I get it." Mob mentality was something Imara was all too

familiar with, on a small level. Agnes had warped so many other's minds to think like she did.

"Auren," Michaela's rich voice called from the library window. She climbed through, out onto the graveled garden path, a book in her hand. Stone faced, she made her way across the roof to where Imara and Auren stood. "Everything okay?" she asked as she approached, a strange look written on her face.

"I'm fine, Michaela. I got distracted talking to Imara."

Michaela's eyes widened, her lips pulling in as she nodded. "Here's the book you wanted. I knew it was in there, you just didn't look hard enough." Her eyes looked over Imara, giving away absolutely nothing to what she was thinking. Michaela gave the book to Auren, their fingers grazing, lingering for a moment. "Or was that the idea?"

Auren shrugged, donning a sheepish half grin and batting her eyelashes to complete her confession. The blush on her cheeks deepened, "You know me so well, M."

"You're lucky Mother hates the library," she smirked before turning and heading back inside. The quiet red-head watched the statuesque, ebony haired beauty as she went, eyes glinting with mischief and wanting. The chemistry between them was palpable.

"She's something," Imara commented to test her theory.

"Yeah, she is," Auren sighed.

Imara could read between the lines well enough to see the truth about Auren and Michaela. They loved each other, but Rhanda used them as pawns in her schemes to control her son. Auren was likely being used to forge some high-powered alliance, and Michaela was being forced to watch her mother try to give the woman she loved to her brother on a silver platter.

She reached out and touched Auren's shoulder, "You're lucky."

Their eyes locked and Auren's face softened more, a smile gracing her lips. "I should go," she said after a minute. "It was nice talking to you. I mean it."

"You too. My room is open anytime you want to do it again. The fireplace in my suite is the best it seems."

"I might take you up on that," she beamed at the promise of warmth and good conversation. Auren turned to head into the estate, pausing just before going inside and looking back at Imara. "Good luck, by the way. With the concert. I'm looking forward to it."

"You mean break a leg?" Tamsin popped up in a cloud of pink smoke, perched daintily on a bench close to where Corvus pouted. Her eyes bore into Auren. "Good luck is bad luck in the theater, right Imara?"

"At least in Morrea it is." Imara confirmed.

"Oh, I'm sorry," Auren's face fell a little at the mistake. "Break a leg," she said with a small wave as she disappeared into the library.

"What was that about?" Tamsin shoved off the bench and floated toward Imara, lighting on her feet with a twirl. "How awful was she? Be honest."

"Not at all," Imara received an incredulous look from the perky witch. "Really. I don't think Auren is like Rhanda at all, and I don't think she'd be friends with Michaela if she was."

"I'll be the judge of that," Tamsin huffed, crossing her arms. "You are too sweet to see..."

"I'm serious. We need to stop."

"But..."

"Tamsin!" Imara barked her name as a command, one she would see obeyed whether the witch liked it or not. The wind kicked up, as though to punctuate Imara's serious tone, fluttering the leaves and whipping her hair. "Auren and Michaela aren't threats, and Rhanda is taking her frustrations out on the staff. We are done."

Tamsin trembled from the sudden cold wind and accompanying rumble of thunder. Imara had never seen her cower at anything since meeting the witch, not even Mallan. She stood toe to toe with the formidable fae on numerous occasions and played with fire by skirting his rules. Especially with the goblins. Imara never expected her resistance to fall so easily, "Fine, spoilsport." She turned back and plopped back on the bench next to Corvus, joining him in his pouting with her eyes flickering.

"Auren saw Corvus bring me her brooch, so even if she was awful the whole thing would still be done. She'll pass on the recommendation to keep windows closed, but I don't think she'll tell anyone which bird was doing most of the thieving."

"You can't know that."

"No, I can't. But I'm trusting my instinct on this. Having a little faith. My gut tells me we can trust Auren and Michaela. If it'll make you feel better, talk to them yourself. Then tell me if I'm wrong," Imara challenged, shooing Corvus away and sitting next to Tamsin. The raven flew off toward the rookery.

"We could at least continue with Rhanda," Tamsin wasn't ready to let go of vengeance so easily. "Come up with a new tactic?"

"I don't know. I don't know if I want to do anything, or if it's worth the effort. No matter what, Rhanda will continue to push Auren at Mallan and be at my throat because she perceives me as in the way. She won't care that my position with him is my decision, and I won't change my mind. I'm not his to claim."

"Yeah, but it could change. I know you like him," Tamsin assessed intuitively. Against her best wishes, Imara had grown fond of Mallan. Their relationship wouldn't shift to anything more than friendship, of that Imara was insistent on. The only reason she even forgave him was because of Lorn, otherwise Imara never would have opened up to the fae. Yet, part of her would always hate him for stealing her life from her, no matter how close they grew.

Imara sighed deeply, "You're right," she admitted. "Some days, I feel like I have my old mentor back, and being Mallan's friend becomes as easy as breathing. But nothing will ever take away what he did to me, and there's always a reminder of it lurking around."

"You win. No more schemes. They were fun though, right?"

"A little. They didn't get us anywhere though, did they?"

"It was a good way to kill time," Tamsin suggested. "Being stuck here can't be all that fun? What are you going to do for fun now?"

Fat raindrops splattered against the delicate leaves surrounding them, telling Imara it was time for them to head inside themselves. She stood, offering a hand to Tamsin, "For now, I have a concert to prepare for."

She slipped her silken hand into Imara's, interlacing their fingers as she screwed her mouth to the side, "Well, that sounds like a lot of work and no fun."

"It is a lot of work," Imara laughed. "But for me, it's a lot of fun too."

TWENTY-FIVE

Imara

The week leading up to the concert had Shadowmire in a flurry of activity that Imara never expected to see. Mallan ordered the ballroom to be renovated into a grand concert hall. The kind of stage she and Sconza had dreamt of turning his club into on late nights after closing and deep into a bottle of whatever he had on hand. More often than not, she ended the night in tears, worrying about Lorn's safety, and whether he'd still love her when he came back. If he came back.

Knowing, in the aftermath, who Sconza truly was, the memory of those nights turned Imara's stomach. How tortuous those nights must have been for the man who sheltered her, who believed she was his destiny, to sit there and comfort Imara and her longing heart. As Mallan, he'd never have held his tongue or held her with friendly arms to ease her plight. Mallan's strength to keep his facade whole showed a will stronger than iron.

Imara's excitement built as she watched the renovation,

until the morning Mallan posted his goblins outside the closed doors to the hall, with orders not to let her pass. "Why have you locked me out?" she complained, several times before that day was even through.

"You'll see it before the concert, I promise. Until then, be patient. Let me surprise you with the final details," he teased and pressed his lips on the back of her hand.

"As long as there are no more roses, or orchids," Imara played back. She truly had enough of them after the extravagant apology that nearly fractured her, even though they were beautiful flowers.

"No, Starling. Those are for apologies. I have something better in mind for this hall after you've cast your spell over all of Sylphea's most influential fae."

A searing hot stone lodged in Imara's throat. The most influential fae of Sylphea? Mallan had made it seem like the only attendees would be his closest allies, with the recent invitation extended to Khryton, Tilly, and Lautrec. Invites he'd made for Imara so she could keep her promise to get to know her family, and spend time with Tilly. Then there was the ball to be hosted afterward, which had even more guests. It was all starting to feel like too much.

"What is it?"

"I am curious where you plan to have this ball, though, when you've turned your ballroom into my concert hall?" Imara shifted her focus to the floor, tracing the intricate bolts of gold shooting through the marble. She couldn't look him in the eye, afraid he'd see her true worries.

Mallan arched a brow, a smirk playing at the corner of his mouth, "Your concert hall?" He liked Imara claiming the hall as her own, her growing comfort in being in his home. "But I think there's more to it than that."

"There's nothing, Mallan."

"Liar," he rumbled quietly, and the knot in her throat grew. Mallan didn't like liars, and Imar knew her only saving grace was what she represented to him.

"I'm sorry," she quieted.

"Don't be," Mallan lifted her chin, forcing her to look into his coal eyes. "I'm not angry, Starling. How could I be angry with you? I'm amused." He closed the gap between them, the heat from his body wrapping around Imara. "First, the ball will be somewhere, and I promise you'll like it. Don't worry about that. Second, worrying about a location wouldn't have you so wound up. Third, I am Mallan, a fae of nightmares and scoundrels," he lowered his head until his lips brushed Imara's ear. "I can taste your delicious fear. "

Imara's knees threatened to crumble, feeling his breath in her ear, the vibration of his words seemed to run in her veins. She sensed his words meant more than their face value. He didn't just see through her lie, didn't just taste the edge of her fear. He tasted her beyond her dread, intimately.

"No," her response came breathless, revealing the effect he had on her. His fangs flashed in a duplicitous smirk. In all her time in Sylphea, she never heard him referred as that: *fae of nightmares and scoundrels*. An appropriate title. He was Ondine's favorite, her right-hand man. She'd loved him, leaving him alive after he'd failed to secure her victory. The rest of her Generals didn't receive such a pardon.

After a nervous release of breath, Imara continued, "I didn't know how big these solstice celebrations would be. I thought it would be more intimate, not an even for all of Sylphea."

"It's all in your honor."

"It's intimidating." Imara buried her face in his broad chest, almost too afraid to confess her fear. Surely it would seem trivial to him. "I've never sung for what's essentially nobility, Mallan. My audience has always been the dregs and outcasts at

Sconza's; maybe a few rogue members of the upper class. I never had to mingle with those in power. What if I'm not good enough?"

Mallan rested his chin on Imara's head, his hushed voice rumbling through her skull, "You are more than good enough, Starling. You'll see. They're going to love you, just like I do."

His words rang with an honesty she hadn't felt since meeting him. He meant them with every fiber of his being. He loved Imara, not just because he was told they were meant to be together. That made his words weighty. They were heavy, like a chain wrapped around her neck, dragging her to the depths of a stormy sea. Imara didn't know if she could survive them.

An old, familiar friend greeted Imara the morning of the concert. Anticipation. A buzz somewhere between excitement and nervousness filled every inch of her like lightning. She'd suffered through weeks of preparation, and couldn't believe the day had finally arrived.

The feeling doubled when she glimpsed the dress she was to wear for the concert as Imara passed through the suite to start her day. The violent plum gown, so dark it seemed black, that Mallan selected for the night. Off the shoulder, with a band of lace flowers above the sweetheart neckline of the bodice over a skirt of miles of tulle. The dramatic dress had a touch of regality when paired with the radiate tiara of silver and black pointing to the heavens and leaden with diamonds.

If that wasn't spectacular enough, Tamsin promised an addition to the ensemble during the performance that would blow everyone's minds. Snow-white wings, tipped in silver, would be glamoured on Imara's body at the height of the concert.

Imara worried, when Tamsin revealed her plan to her, that the wings would be a giveaway to her relation to Khryton. Mallan wanted all attention on her, not on Khryton, whom he still held a lot of animosity toward. So, they decided to keep that part of her identity hidden, even though it might give the Under Court and the High Court reason to unify.

Tamsin assured her no one would even entertain the idea. The sight of wings appearing on Imara would be merely a spectacle. Many high fae had them, even Mallan could manifest a pair himself. He certainly had no relation to Imara.

Though tempted, Imara resisted the urge to run to the gown and run her hands over it in giddy anticipation of wearing it on stage. Other priorities took precedence. She still needed to see the concert hall.

Imara didn't even bother to change out of her nightgown before racing down the three flights of stairs, only stopping once she reached the closed concert hall doors. Eager to see the space where she would perform that night, she wasn't about to wait for Mallan to tell her when she could. She restrained herself as long as she could. If she had to wait any longer, she'd burst.

"Damn it," Imara cursed, finding the door still locked. She wasn't about to let that stop her. She squatted eye level with the keyhole, hoping to catch just a peek inside. That was fruitless. She screwed her mouth to the side and worried her lip, cursing every story she'd heard where the hero could spy through a lock.

Still, she wouldn't give up. With no clue how to do it, Imara pulled pins from her braid, determined to pick the lock. She jammed them into her target, wiggling them about and praying for a stroke of luck, only getting increasingly frustrated the longer it took.

"Trying to get a peek early, Starling?" Mallan laughed after clearing his throat. Imara jumped at the sound of his voice, bolted to her feet, and attempted to hide the pins behind her back.

"Mallan," she greeted. "It's the day of the concert, I think I deserve to see my venue before my audience does."

"That you do," he reached down the collar of his shirt, pulling out a long silver chain with a small key dangling from the end. Even though the key was simple, nothing spectacular to it, it was the most beautiful key Imara had ever seen.

Imara reached for the key as Mallan pulled the chain from his neck. She was anxious to get her hands on it, only to have it yanked out of her reach. "Hey!"

"Not so fast, I want to see your face when you see it." He stepped between Imara and the doors with one simple instruction: "Close your eyes."

"It's too early for you to be this frustrating," Imara grumbled, but obeyed his command and closed her eyes. Her stomach flipped when she heard the key turn in the lock and the door creak open. She hadn't been so excited about something in a long time.

Moments later, Imara felt Mallan move behind her and place his warm hands over her eyes. "I'm not peeking, you don't need to do that."

"I need to be sure. With you, I never know what to expect," he teased with a whisper on the outer shell of her ear, releasing a whole new excitement in her. Before she could respond, Mallan began ushering her forward. A few steps into the hall and his hands slid off her eyes, "Keep them closed until I say so," he ordered with another whisper.

His footsteps echoed off the walls. The refurbished space's acoustics were perfect. Imara listened, rapt, until his feet stopped. She heard a grunt, and then, a few moments later, he gave the order she longed to hear. "Open your eyes, Starling."

Imara gasped at what she saw.

In the minutes before the concert, all that separated the audience and stage was a heavy, gold velvet curtain, trimmed in black ropes. Opulent and elegant, a far cry from the barrier-less, worn, beer and sawdust scented planks of the stage at Sconza's. Standing there, waiting for the goblin turned stagehand to draw the curtains open, Imara's heart became a frightened doe snared in a hunter's trap. Not even steady breathing could calm her anticipation, her fear, or the intangible magic that coursed through her.

From the moment she opened her eyes at Mallan's command, she felt transported to a dream. He had transformed the once darkly beautiful ballroom into a concert hall worthy of the finest palace. The time frame of the makeover didn't leave time to replace the shining black and gold marbled floor, or the smoky chandeliers, but the room looked completely new, regardless. Plastered gold walls and enormous crystal sconces wrapped the room in a warm glow. Mallan had a handful of rows of plush seating installed near the stage. Otherwise the concert would be standing room only with as many guest Mallan invited.

As promised, there were no roses or orchids to be seen. Instead, the stage dripped with calla lilies in the purest white, rich purple, and deep black. Timid violets peeked out between the trumpeting flora, along with sprays of baby's breath and fern fronds. Orbs of floating light of varying sizes completed the stage.

It was more than Imara had ever dreamed of. Even as she prepared for the curtain to draw back, her head swam from the beauty that would surround her as she sang.

Heavy footsteps sounded from beyond the curtain, and the air shifted as the humming chatter of the audience hushed. They were more than ready to be reprieved from the anticipation their host had created. His wide spread invitation practically became a scandal whispered across the land, a wild fire unlike any seen before in Sylphea. The High Court and the Under Court coming together peacefully under one roof hadn't happened in their histories. The last time Sylphea had been united was in the age of the Three Queens. It was the promise of a new era that had everyone buzzing.

"Welcome, all, to Shadowmire," Mallan's voice, muffled through the curtain, slipped easily to a showman's cadence. "To what I hope is the first of many performances like this." The crowd cheered, sending another surge of emotion through Imara. "Without further ado, allow me to introduce Imara, my Starling."

As her name rolled off his tongue, Imara took a deep breath, rolled her neck and shoulders, and shook off her nerves. In the seconds it took for those golden walls to part, she transformed herself into the Starling. Mallan's songbird was prepared to introduce herself to the rest of Sylphea. Then, as the floating stage lights bobbed into place, Imara took that initial step into her spotlight and unleashed the first of many notes to come.

Summon the devil
> *With a grazing hand*
> *A despaired queen*
> *His to command*
> *But he's undone by her eyes*

. . .

Just like that, Imara got lost in her own songs. It seemed like she'd barely began when the notes introducing the final number cut through the otherwise silent hall. Every bar, bridge, and chorus had completely enthralled the crowd.

Merely a dream
A breath on a cheek
A silent demand
A shivering touch
Ghostly embraces
To screaming your name
Give in...

At the second verse, Tamsin's glamour fell over Imara, unleashing her very own pair of dove-like wings that glowed and shimmered under the spotlight. The resulting shock that swept through the audience carried her to new heights.

Breath stolen and ragged
Beaded sweat so sweet
Sleep of satisfaction
Led to dreaming deep
A place in memory
Eternal bliss to keep
I'm giving in...

Imara's heart drifted back to the ground at the song's end. The silence gaped, then gave way to thunderous applause.

"You are perfection, Starling," Mallan hushed, bringing her

back to reality as he placed a bouquet of the decorative flowers in her arms. Warmth spread across her cheeks from the euphoria caused by the adulation. Her first concert in the fae world had been a success, and she couldn't wait to mingle at the ball.

But first, she needed a costume change.

TWENTY-SIX

Imara

The concert left Imara on a high, one like she hadn't felt since...

She shoved the thought aside, refusing to let it fully form. The intrusive memories were certain to deflate the cloud she found herself on, and she didn't want that to happen. She wanted to celebrate her triumph on stage, fully enjoy the afterparty the ball promised to be. If the concert was the main course of the night, the ball Mallan promised was to be the dessert.

After the curtains closed once more, Mallan transported Imara to her suite where she wasted no time sloughing off the Starling and donning her gown for the ball.

Tamsin helped Imara select the dress she'd wear for the event, insisting it had to contrast that of the concert. When she brought the form fitting, strapless, mermaid style garment that began white at the neckline and bled down in an ever darkening shade of red until it grazed the floor in a pool of oxblood, Imara couldn't wait to wear it.

She turned before the large mirror in the wardrobe, looking nearly as ethereal as Tamsin. "I'm not done with you yet." Tamsin held out her slender hand and soon a choker made of white satin ribbon adorned with sparkling rubies appeared. "This is for you." She spun her fingers in the air, signaling Imara to turn toward the mirror.

The moment Tamsin set the choker against her throat, Imara couldn't help but place her fingers on it as her friend tied the ribbon, letting the ends cascade down. "It's stunning, Tamsin. Thank you."

"Just a little something to complete the look," she shrugged. "Let's not keep your new admirers waiting."

It was time to head to the party. Tamsin opened the suite door and began ushering Imara down the stairs to the main floor in silence. Something was off with her. Tamsin wasn't one to not advocate being fashionably late. The further they got from Imara's suite, the stranger the witch acted. She fidgeted with her gauzy skirt, which mimicked the pinks and purples of dusk, and with her golden and pink locks, which never failed to gleam in any light.

"Are you okay, Tamsin?"

"I'm fine," she beamed, though the gesture didn't reach her always expressive eyes, and paused at the top of the last flight of stairs.

"Are you sure, because you seem anxious?" Imara had never seen Tamsin anything other than confident. Something was eating at her. There was only one thing she could think of that was different about the ball, the same thing she had been nervous about herself. "Is this about the ball? The High Court being there?" Tamsin didn't say anything, just stared blankly at Imara. "It's okay if you are."

"Ladies," the call came from below, pulling their attention. Mallan waited at the bottom of the stairs, decked out in a fitted tailed tuxedo with oxblood accessories. "Do you mean to delay my celebrations? My guests have waited too long to meet the star of the evening."

Tamsin used Mallan's interruption to avoid answering and flew down the stairs to meet him. "Doesn't she look spectacular?" She bounced on the balls of her feet, bragging. Mallan chuckled, a half smile painted on his face and an appreciative fire in his eyes as they roamed over Imara. The look had her flushing, the heat in her cheeks grew hotter with every step she descended.

Before Imara could reach the bottom, Tamsin gave her a wink, "I'll leave you two to your grand entrance." She gave Mallan's arm a squeeze and flitted away to join the festivities herself.

She lighted on the bottom step and Mallan came forward, bowing his head. "Imara," he offered her an arm, "you look even more indelible than you already were."

Her stomach fluttered, metamorphosing into tingles that ran through her entire body. "Thank you."

"Are you ready?"

"Just point me in the right direction," she slipped her arm through his. She still didn't know where the ball was being held, and had no time to snoop before the concert. She couldn't wait to see what the rest of the night had in store.

"I can do better than that," he mused, enveloping them in a cloud of smoke and carried them away. When the smoke cleared, they stood at the edge of the upper courtyard behind Shadowmire. The space was lit by tall candelabras that dripped with wax and the same flowers from the concert hall. Soft music drifted in the air, though there was no band or orchestra to be seen anywhere. Between the lights, the courtyard bustled with denizens of Sylphea, dancing in tenuous peace bolstered by flowing champagne and rich hors d'oeuvres that highlighted the decadence of Mallan's hosting court.

Mallan escorted Imara down the steps to the lower level. Without the safety of the stage, the crowd suddenly felt overwhelming. Every eye on her hatched a new butterfly. She scanned the courtyard for friendly faces, finding few and far between. Lautrec watched them carefully while continuing to chat with a group he stood with. Near the bottom of the stairs was Tamsin, who kept her steely glare on Khryton, every ounce of her coiled tightly.

Khryton's eyes lit when Imara looked at him, and he downed the flute of champagne in his hand. He muttered something to Tamsin, who responded with a furious look and grabbed his arm. He shoved his way out of her grip and stepped toward the stairs. "Attention, everyone, and welcome our host for the evening, Lord Mallan," his voice boomed. "And the star of the night, my daughter, Imara."

Imara's stomach sank and every jaw in sight wagged, all for two others. Tamsin, who glowered at Khryton before storming off into the crowd, and Mallan, who growled under his breath next to Imara as he tugged at her elbow.

"We agreed that tonight would be about her," he bit at Khryton on approach.

"Things change," Khryton straightened the lapels of his jacket. "You can't expect me to not want to shout it from the rooftops that she is mine after her incredible performance."

"She is not yours," Malian growled again, his jaw clenched.

"I'm proud, is all I'm saying," he gulped in response. Khryton's boisterous facade waned under the threat. "I'd be even prouder to introduce her properly to the right people." Mallan tensed at his presumption.

"Why don't we leave that task to Mallan, it is his court hosting after all," Imara interjected before Mallan murdered her father and the treaty she struck fell apart. She may not have been an expert in court dealings, but even she knew he had no right to be taking any credit away from Mallan. The tension hanging over their heads thickened by the second, neither of them willing to concede anything. "I promise to save you a dance, though, Khryton," she added, hoping to appease him.

He sucked his teeth and rolled his eyes before bowing out, "I look forward to it," he said flatly.

As they disappeared into the crowd, Mallan's muscles slacked beneath Imara's hand. They wended through the courtyard, making a beeline to the opposite end, as far from Khryton as Mallan could get them. The whole time, Imara drank in the crowd, amazed at the fantastical appearances of the different fae from all over Sylphea. Lithe creatures, all with sharp ears and teeth, and unbelievable features that defined from where they hailed from, pawed at them and praised Imara as they passed. All the while, her escort refused lengthy introductions he felt were unimportant, most of those being from the High Court.

In the end, all their faces swirled together, each one becoming as unremarkable as the next, despite their fantastic features. Save for one introduction, the one Mallan spent the most time on. He was by far the most frightening, at first, his appearance menacing and dark behind a geometrically cut, obsidian, skull half mask with little of the beauty of a fae peeking through. The only parts of his face that Imara could see beyond the mask were his cinnamon eyes and a set of full lips lined in gray.

"Imara, let me introduce you to Samir, the Living Ghost of the Glass Desert. Samir, this is Imara Cawthorne of Ocean Fare, Morrea."

Samir, the Living Ghost. Even his title sent chills through Imara. Other than the wraith, of all the fae, high, demi, and everything in-between, he was the most otherworldly she'd encountered, as though he truly had one foot in the afterlife.

"A pleasure," Samir pressed his palms together before his heart and bowed. The silk smooth voice that came from him contradicted his startling appearance.

"Sir," she curtsied back, unsure of how to address him properly.

"Please, call me Samir, Miss Imara." He reached into the well-cut, tailed jacket he wore and pulled out a small, red, drawstring satchel. He gave a quick tug on the strings to open it, then he tipped it over his other hand. Out poured a fine, black, glittering sand. Rather than gather and spill from his palm, the sand took form. Imara watched in curious awe, anticipating the final shape it would take. In seconds he held a dagger of volcanic glass, its handle faceted as his mask, and its blade sharp and gleaming. "A gift," he smiled, "in thanks for sharing your beautiful voice."

Imara's hand trembled, reaching out for his gift, which he passed gingerly from his palm to hers. "Thank you, Samir. It's stunning."

"And dangerous," Mallan quipped in gentle warning. "The Glass Desert obsidian weapons burn as they cut, as hot as the lava they're born from, without cauterizing."

"Oh! Perhaps it would be best if I don't carry it about a crowded courtyard then," Imara observed, and her companions chuckled in agreement.

"Allow me," Malian waved his hand, and the blade disappeared in a small cloud of smoke. "There, safely deposited in your suite, Starling."

"Thank you again," Imara reached for Samir, intending to shake his hand, but he pulled himself out of reach.

"His position doesn't allow for contact with others," Mallan informed her when he saw the confusion on her face. "The

Living Ghost is a sacred role in the Glass Desert, a conduit between the living and the dead so revered there."

"I'm sorry," she began, only to be cut off.

"Nothing to be sorry about, Miss Imara. My lands and customs are foreign to you, as Sylphea had likely been until recently, being that you are from Morrea, that is. I take it your mother is mortal?"

"Yes, she is. She's staying in the High Court at the moment," Imara didn't want to disclose her mother's condition. She didn't think she could take the piteous looks that came with it.

"I would like to meet her," Samir swept his gaze over the crowd. "Is she here with Lord Khryton, then? Or has she run off with Rhanda, who also appears to be missing the soiree?"

"No, unfortunately," Imara replied somberly. When she hadn't seen her amongst the audience at the concert, Imara's soul ached. She'd hoped Tilly would have been there to see her perform. It was likely her last chance to do so.

"Rhanda, run off with a mortal?" Auren sauntered into the conversation, looking stunning in her midnight gown. "I think she'd rather take her chances with the nixie," she chuckled, greeting Imara with a kiss on the cheek and repeating the greeting with Mallan. Her gaze settled on Samir. Immediately she bowed and placed her palms together, "My Soul, it's humbling to see you, as always."

"My Flesh," he greeted in return, making the same gesture.

"Rhanda, to answer where she is, retired halfway through the first song at the concert. Some nonsense about having better things to do than listen to a sow pretend to be something it's not. Not that anyone agrees with her," Auren added quickly in Imara's ear.

Rhanda's rejection at the concert didn't surprise Imara, only highlighted her pettiness. She'd only attended in the first place to appease her son, to have a chance at finding another perceived fault to diminish Imara. Her need to push Auren on Mallan knew no bounds.

"No offense taken," Imara patted Auren's arm. Their relationship had shifted since their talk on the rooftop garden, becoming bonded in a sisterhood of understanding. They both were slaves to forces beyond themselves, deciding their futures.

"How are you enjoying the evening, Auren?"

"It's splendid, Lord Mallan. Truly. Who knew you had all of this refinement in you?" The tease showed she truly loved him as a brother. If only Rhanda would get out of her way so she could call him that and openly love Michaela. Rhanda's need for power blinded her to her children's hearts completely and had Auren chasing a pairing she didn't desire. "I was hoping for a turn on the floor with you, though."

"Later," he gripped her shoulder. "I have yet to give Imara her first dance of the night. She is my guest of honor, so I must be the first to dance with her."

"Of course," she nodded.

"I spy my sister over there," he ticked his head toward the stairs. Michaela stood there in a stormy dress, which matched her outward indifference. "How about you keep her company while you wait? I promise you are next," he winked. Imara couldn't help but wonder if he knew of their secret love.

"Let me join you," Samir said to Auren. "I don't believe I've had the pleasure of meeting Lord Mallan's sister. I should very much like to."

"I'd be delighted to introduce you," she replied, barely concealing her excitement. The Living Ghost and Auren took their leave, slipping into the crowd toward Michaela, both moving like spirits.

"Seems like Auren is changing her tune about you," Mallan quipped. The brief interaction Imara had with her had quickly left them more at ease with each other. The budding bond between them even surprised Imara with how it had bloomed so easily.

"We've talked, and found common footing. I'm excited to get to know her and Michaela better now that I know they don't see me as Rhanda does."

"You know," Mallan leaned in, "if my mother hadn't poached Auren from the Glass Desert, she'd be next in line for Living Ghost. It's why she chose her, she has the gift of ghosts; a powerful gift. She ensures the Glass Desert remains a part of the Under Court that way."

"They're at risk of shifting alliances?" Imara understood then why Rhanda pushed so hard for the match of Mallan and Auren. She was powerful, and Rhanda coveted power more than anything.

"Not in the least. Mother is paranoid. She thinks their proximity to the High Court places them in danger of being wooed away. But she doesn't know Khryton is paranoid as well. He fears death."

"Couldn't Samir have stopped her from taking Auren?"

"He could have, and would have, if he wanted to."

"Why didn't he?"

"Love," Mallan's dark eyes bored into Imara's with the one-word answer, shining and full of heat. The silence that followed enveloped them, shutting out the rest of the party as though they were the only two there. Imara had to look away to keep her composure. "Auren had more love to give," Mallan continued after she broke eye contact, "and Samir didn't want to trap her in a role that didn't allow for it. She'd have been miserable."

"That's easy to see, she is a truly genuine soul. I really do like her. She deserves the love she wants."

"So you know about her and Michaela, then?"

Imara gave a nod, "Why do you let your mother continue

trying to force you together? It's cruel." She turned to glance across the courtyard at the two lovers. They conversed, faces lit with happiness beyond compare, though their body language was secretive and tense.

"Have you met Rhanda?" Mallan's joke pulled her attention back to him. "She doesn't listen to anyone, especially not me. I don't want her punishing Michaela for interfering with her plans, or Auren for not complying. My mother is cruel, much more than I can be. I protect them by letting her keep on trying. Those days are numbered though, of being complacent about her plan. Soon enough, she will stop because she'll have no choice but to." He brushed a knuckle along Imara's jaw.

She swallowed hard. His explanation reminded Imara of the journey that brought them to that moment. His hungry eyes unwrapped the feelings she'd tried so hard to keep at bay. Her fickle heart threatened to ruin the night Mallan had planned so meticulously. She needed a distraction. "You promised me a dance, Lord Mallan."

"That I did, Starling," he took Imara's hand and led her out into the courtyard and among the throng of revelers already churning to the music. The other dancers shifted their paths to accommodate the lord of the Under Court and his partner, giving them the center of the floor and a wide berth. Many even stopped to watch.

Mallan released his inner showman under the watch of the two gathered courts, walking Imara in a great circle before pulling her in against his body. The warmth of him pressed on Imara, surprised her every time they were close enough to feel it. He was far from the cold that took up near every inch of the estate.

The closeness, Mallan's firm hand on the small of her back, and the light in his otherwise cool eyes made Imara gulp. The dance may not have been the best idea to distract from her torn heart. Those feelings, the guilt and the desire, swirled around as the dancers surrounding them did. To stop the chaos, to keep from destroying the celebration, her mind locked on the fae that watched. A performance, that was all their dance needed to be to keep her heart intact until the final strains of the song played out.

TWENTY-SEVEN

Imara

"May I have this dance, sister?" Imara heard from over her shoulder as the music ended. She twisted, finding Lautrec there, golden and smiling. He truly was a copy of their father, she noted, making it easy to see how Khryton had once swept Tilly off her feet.

"Of course, Lautrec," she accepted, then focused on Mallan again. "Thank you for the dance." Imara bowed her head, trying to keep her manners as she imagined they should be, though she truly wanted to move away from him as swiftly as possible. Her brother's invitation was more than welcomed. She needed a reprieve from the dark fae, it was becoming more difficult to control her feelings for him. It was only a matter of time before she could no longer deny what she felt. She might want to give Mallan what he wanted.

The lord of the Under Court wasn't happy to relinquish Imara over to the heir of the High Court, but he still slipped her hand into Lautrec's with a smile. The night was about Imara, the result of her brokering peace between the courts, not about old tensions. "I promised Auren a dance, anyway."

"I'll take good care of Imara," Lautrec tipped his head just before ushering her into another turn about the floor. Begrudgingly, Mallan stepped back to the edges of the crowd, keeping his eyes on the pair for a minute before seeking Michaela and Auren.

It was only after Mallan's watchful eyes were no longer on her that Imara could relax enough to give her attention to her brother. His bright eyes studied her closely, uncomfortably. Her peace lasted only a mere moment. The scrutiny in Lautrec's gaze forced Imara to look off over his shoulder to watch the other dancers.

We're like two sides of a celestial coin. A golden sun and the beautiful, mysterious moon.

That comparison drew Imara's attention back, relieved he'd merely been admiring their opposite natures and not judging her. "You definitely have more of our father in you than I do," she laughed. It wasn't the first time she'd heard herself described as moonlight.

Lautrec's eyes widened, then glinted, "You heard me?"

"Of course I did, you spoke. Didn't you?"

"No, I didn't," a sly smile played over his mouth. *I thought it though.*

Imara gaped at her brother, "How?"

"I think you may have some latent fae ability. The same one as I have, in fact. It's called the Blood Connection, a controversial ability to read the mind of blood relatives through touch."

"That's not possible. I'm not..."

"You are half fae, Imara," Lautrec pointed out the obvious.

"But, I've never..."

"Been able to hear thoughts before?" he chuckled. "I wouldn't imagine so, though I can't be sure. I've never met a half-blood from Morrea, only those born here. I can only guess that being here, at Shadowmire, in Sylphea, has awakened yours."

Imara mulled over his reasoning. It would make sense, the only hitch in his theory was that she hadn't heard Tilly's mind when she touched her. Unless her mother had been too weak for Imara to hear her, or the fact she was mortal made her immune. She didn't think Lautrec would know those answers either. But another question formed in her mind, "Do we share the gift with our father?"

"No," the answer was curt and led to long moments dancing in silence. Imara struck some nerve there.

Imara tried to use the Blood Connection to glean what he wasn't saying, but no matter how hard she tried, she heard nothing. "Are you sure you didn't put your thoughts in my head?" she prodded. "I get nothing but silence when I try."

His responding laugh was melodic, "You're new to this. You will not master it moments after learning it. Besides, I was blocking you. It's an essential skill for any creature in Sylphea to learn, though many do not."

"Could you teach me?"

"For a price," he teased. In Imara's mind, a shimmering image of Auren appeared, her red hair pulled away from her face, gentle curling tendrils coming free, and wearing a shimmering midnight dress that left nothing to the imagination, his thoughts taking liberties with what she wore to the ball.

"Sorry to say, but I can't help you there. Auren is spoken for." Imara looked over to where Auren danced with Mallan. They were deep in conversation, laughing with one another. They made a beautiful pair, though Imara knew the truth of their relationship.

"Competition?" Lautrec watched them as well.

"No." Imara said nothing more and looked back at her brother. It wasn't her place to reveal Auren's heart to anyone.

"I guess I'll just have to do it out of the goodness of my heart then," he winked. "Don't worry, I won't tell our father."

"Why wouldn't you tell him I have an ability?"

"Not this one," he said coldly, glancing over to where Khryton stood watching them. "Dad doesn't acknowledge the Blood Connection."

"He has a problem with it?"

Lautrec's eyes became distant, pained, "Why else do you think he hasn't so much as shaken my hand since my ability appeared?"

"So, we have other siblings?" Imara tried changing the subject.

"Many, in fact. Our father being somewhat of a whore," he laughed wryly, though his expression remained sour. "All of them half-siblings. None but myself are full high fae. There are a quite a few of them here tonight, if you're interested in meeting them. None are as interesting as you, though. I really am glad you came into our lives, and am looking forward to getting to know you."

"Me too," Imara smiled despite the chill his revelation sent through her. "Can you show me?"

Lautrec spun Imara, moving them across the floor to near the stairs where a group of fae, each of them dressed in gold, where he stopped. Lautrec wasn't kidding. Khryton was a bit of a whore and not one of them looked completely related. Including Lautrec, Imara now had seven siblings she knew of. And there were more, according to her golden brother. "Dear siblings," he crowed, "I'd like you to meet our little sister, Imara."

Imara gave a small wave. Lautrec introduced them one by

one, starting with a tiny half dryad female named Vine, who had pale green skin and hair, and large blue eyes. Next came Ubbe, a half witch with dark brown hair and deep purple eyes, he shared Khryton's sharp facial structure. Sorrel and Sabine were twin half banshee, both with long ink black hair and obsidian eyes, their skin had a slight golden sheen that marked them as half fae. Tello, he was a half elf with golden hair, green eyes, and longer pointed ears. Finally there was Zephony, a half nymph with golden curls that cascaded around her shoulders and deep brown eyes.

Each greeted Imara, though most of them seem indifferent to her.

Imara and Lautrec didn't linger with their siblings, but headed back to the dance floor, only to run into Khryton. Imara's stomach soured, Lautrec's revelation had painted her father in a new light. "It's my turn," he declared, not bothering to ask. His entitlement was another notch against him.

Lautrec conceded to their father, offering a bow to Imara, his eyes meeting her with unsaid apologies. She couldn't help but feel sorry for him as she watched his departure, not only from the dance floor. He left the ball entirely.

"Shall we?" Khryton pulled Imara's attention from her brother's exit as he headed up the stairs into Shadowmire. Her father waited with his hand offered out, his face an unreadable mask. With a nod from Imara, he locked his hand around hers, his grip firm and warm. The second his skin met hers, it felt like a great wave crashed over Imara, blinding her with a searing light. Her head swam with echoes of Khryton's voice.

"My daughter is amazing. Yet, such a disappointment." His critical thoughts of her floored Imara. As far as she knew, she'd done nothing in his presence that seemed to offend at the time.

A replay of Mallan swaggering into Khryton's court with Imara at his side flashed before her. Twisted visions of Mallan and her laughing and cavorting indecently, things that had never happened, taunted her father. That was the disappointment he meant. Imara had sided with his enemy.

Another flash and a circle of males appeared in a dreamy haze as Khryton spoke again. *"It appears any coupling between mortals and fae result in powerless creatures. Even when sired by myself. There's no reason we should fear their taking the side of their mortal families and rising against us."*

"What of their offspring, or the generation after that? Surely powers will appear down the line." A different voice echoed.

Khryton's voice replied, *"I don't think there will be cause for panic as that happens. As the mortal lineage becomes more and more diluted, the fae lineage will purify once more. By then, they should identify more with us. In time, there won't be any more mortals, the world will be purged of them and fae will rule everywhere."*

The scene faded, bringing Imara back to reality. A wave of nausea swept through her as Khryton came into focus. His prideful smile faltered, "Are you okay, my dear?" he asked.

There was no response in Imara. Khryton assumed Imara had no fae abilities, let alone the Blood Connection. He hadn't bothered to block his mind at all, and what she'd seen and heard left her feeling ill.

Khryton wasn't good. His world may of been the representation of what most mortals thought Heaven was, full of beauty, but what Imara saw in him as he spun her around the floor was something more akin to Hell. He was a liar, his motivations for the treaty hadn't been to protect mortals at all. He just needed Mallan out of the way to enact his genocide by breeding. That was more terrifying than anything she'd encountered in the Under Court.

Even at his worst, Mallan never frightened Imara the way her vision of her father's ambition for the world did. It left her wondering if she'd done the right thing in reuniting him and Tilly. Had he once been a man that deserved the adulation her mother gave him? Or had he seduced her with empty promises and false grace for the sake of an experiment? Imara hated the idea that Tilly was only as an incubator to him and clung to the thread of hope that Khryton truly loved her mother.

The ball became suffocating once she glimpsed into her father's mind. He'd ruined the party. The merriment rang false and the delicious foods turned sour.

"Are you okay, Imara?" Khryton repeated. Imara's eyes snapped to his, taking in the concern that etched the corners of his own. She wasn't sure she could even believe that micro expression was truly concern for her.

Imara needed to get away from him, as far away from him as possible. "Excuse me, Khryton, but I'm suddenly not feeling well. I think I should retire from the party." It was an easy white lie, a half lie. She wanted to stay and enjoy the solstice celebrations, more than she'd realized, but she couldn't bear being anywhere near Khryton any longer.

"Would you like me to escort you to your room?"

"Thank you, but no. It's unnecessary." Khryton merely shrugged, didn't insist on making sure his newly found daughter was fine. He didn't do the chivalrous thing and push that she accept or at least find another to escort her. He simply shrugged and turned away from Imara in search of someone more willing to entertain him.

Imara's emotions swelled and crested as she left the ball, threatening to sweep her away for everyone to see. The last thing she needed was to make a scene. It was a struggle to maintain an unhurried exit, or to accept kind words from those she passed. Every step, every second, the dam of her will weakened. She barely made it to the stairs before the angry tears appeared in her eyes, barely made it into the estate before they fell freely.

The instant the doors closed behind her, Imara ran. She ran

to the tower above her music room, only stopping there because she couldn't go any further. She threw herself against the thick glass of the encompassing window and pounded her fists against it.

Through hot tears, she looked out over the courtyard and watched the fae below dance, completely ignorant of the fact one among them was a monster. Her eyes found him easily. Every move he made, every fae he interacted with, made her wonder if they knew. She wanted to know who among the revelers were cohorts in Khryton's plans.

"Are you well, Imara?" Mallan's tenor vibrated against the glass. Imara had been so wrapped up in tracking her father she hadn't noticed his reflection appear.

She tore her gaze from the party, wiped her eyes, and smoothed her skirt in an attempt to compose herself. "I'm fine. I was just feeling a little overwhelmed is all," Imara lied, plastering an empty smile on for Mallan to see in her reflection.

"The party or Khryton?"

"Was it that obvious?" she asked. Embarrassment flushed her cheeks at the thought she'd caused a scene despite trying not to hurry out. Imara hated the whole party might have seen her emotional state.

"No. Not at all. You left after dancing with Khryton, and knowing him the way I do... it was easy to deduce."

"I didn't make a fool of myself?"

"You could never look the fool, Starling," Mallan's reflection in the window cleared as he stepped even closer. His hand grazed her shoulder, a whisper against her flesh that sent shivers down her spine. Imara sucked in a breath, biting her lip to keep herself from moaning under his touch. She hoped to keep him unaware of how he affected her.

He noticed. His light grip tightened, and he loosed a heavy breath. Stepping even closer, Mallan's body pressed to Imara's back, the hard lines of his muscles tensed at contact. Imara's body woke, electrically aware of the body beneath the thin layers of clothes between her and Mallan. Her mind flipped, grasped onto memories of intrusive dreams, and drove away her anger. She was desperate to feel something other than seething fury at her father. To forget. So, she gave in to the thoughts she'd shoved away, to the need to feel what his roughened hands felt like when they skimmed over her own velvety skin. She wanted to experience his fingers pressing into her flesh with passion.

Their eyes met through the reflection in the glass, the wanting in his met the desire taking over Imara. She held her gaze and lifted her chin to stretch her neck. Mallan accepted the invitation of her exposed throat with a wicked, heavy gleam that flashed over his face and brought his lips to the curve of her neck. His fangs grazed the flesh, unleashing a heat that galloped through Imara. A fire that raged and consumed her every thought. She closed her eyes against the burning ecstasy and let it take over her every cell.

Mallan's mouth blazed a trail across Imara's bare shoulders before stopping, prompting her to turn and face him. His reflection hadn't adequately depicted the beautiful hunger written on his face, a force of nature that quaked Imara to her very core. His hands wrapped in her hair and pulled Imara so close there was no space left between them.

They crashed into each other, mouths meeting in desperate passion with teasing tongues and gentle nips. Mallan lifted Imara, her legs wrapping around his body, and pressed her against the large window. The cool glass did nothing to temper the heat rising in her skin. His mouth explored, trailing kisses on Imara's neck, collar, and peaks of her breasts. His hand found purchase there his thumb grazing across her tightened nipple through her dress. She never wanted Mallan to stop, wanted to lose herself in the mindless bliss and never have to feel anything else again. Her desire grew, prodding her mind to wonder how closely her intrusive dreams would match with reality.

"Please, Mallan," Imara begged, writhing against him, willing to go further just to numb everything the ball had wrought on her. To wash away Khryton's evil plans from her mind. Imara needed the distraction and wanted desperately to forget it all.

"Are you mine?" He growled between kisses. It was a question Imara didn't want to answer, because that answer scared her. What it meant would tear her apart. She pulled his lips to hers to deflect the question. "Say it, my Starling," he broke away, panting. "Say you are mine and I'll give you everything you ask for. I will be your thrall, your lover, anything you want me to be. Just be mine."

His demand chilled the heat that pooled in Imara's center, and the moment passed. Her torn, confused heart felt like it was about to explode at the rush of coherent thought that planted itself firmly with his words. She almost gave in to the desire Mallan stirred in her, and it would have been a complete betrayal of Lorn's memory. The vow she made.

Imara wanted Mallan. She wanted to run from him. She needed his touch to wipe away the shame of being little more than a genocidal experiment. She had to stay true to herself, her word. There was only one thing to say. Imara looked up at Mallan through heavy lashed and whispered, "I can't."

TWENTY-EIGHT

Mallan

Mallan brushed Imara's cheek, catching the fat tear that rolled from her crystalline eye. Her pain, her conflicting feelings, wrenched his heart. That tender gesture rushed Imara from the cage of his arms, and she ran without looking back. He barely caught the new torture written on her features as she went. She didn't expect his reaction. Neither had he.

Slamming against the glass wall, his breath fogged on the surface and took him back to the day he finally entered Imara's life, though as someone else. He watched her on that street corner from the moment she claimed it. If he was honest with himself, that was the moment real feelings for the girl began to develop.

He should have swooped in a taken her from that snowy street the second she landed on it. But he couldn't resist watching the fire in her grow from an ember into a flame as she fended off the few he allowed to approach her. When he finally came to her rescue, and she looked up at the man he pretended to be with snowflakes caught in her lashes, her bright blue eyes full of courage though her body trembled, his plan changed.

Instead of immediately whisking her to Shadowmire, something in him cried to make her dreams come true before making her the Lady of the Under Court. To give her more time as a human, just a few years. Until she was of age.

The fun they had, Gio Sconza and his Starling. Mallan hadn't wanted it to end. That was the only reason he kept the illusion going for so long. Then she met Lorn and was happier than ever. The soft spot she made in his blackened heart couldn't bear to tear anything from her that made her so blissful. In the end, he had to. He had to stop pretending to be Sconza, had to break her heart, because the prophecy needed to come to fruition.

Mallan regretted every step that brought him to the night he stole her future from Imara. He should have taken her from the street corner to his home in Sylphea, never giving her the chance to meet Lorn. He let it go too far and knew winning her to his true self would be a battle the moment he decided how he'd rid her of the fool. It was the only way he saw Imara letting Lorn go had been to orchestrate his death. He'd been wrong there, too.

Perhaps if he had revealed his true form and home to her from the beginning, his heart wouldn't twist when hers did. He wouldn't care so much, and she'd already be his. Mallan would have given her what she plead for so desperately when he found her in the tower. All of him.

Thoughts of her rubied lips whispering his name, begging him to take her, haunted his mind. Imara's soft flesh against his hands, his mouth. The taste that drifted from her skin to tempt his fangs to pierce it. Mallan shuddered, his forehead pressed against the glass, as that fantasy played out in his head and made him ache.

Mothers he wanted her, was so close to having her. Then he had to open his mouth to appease his own ego. He had to hear the words from her.

"Damn, Lorn." Mallan grumbled to no-one and pounded a fist against the glass. He was the real problem. He was ultimately the one to blame in this tedious waiting game. If it wasn't for that mortal, Mallan's destiny would be his already. If Lorn hadn't been dead already, Mallan would kill him. Make him disappear from existence, so Imara would let go.

Mallan was tired of waiting. He knew what had to be done to get everything he ever wanted. Imara had to forget Lorn ever existed. The problem was, in order to forget, she had to succumb voluntarily to the spell. Lucky for him, he knew just the witch to lace Imara's thoughts with the idea.

CHAPTER

TWENTY-NINE

Imara

It was warm. Much too warm.

The doors to her suite pressed against Imara's trembling back, her chest heaved and her head spun. The encounter with Mallan in the tower looped in her memory. She still felt his roughened fingers sliding incrementally closer to where she needed them and his fangs on her neck. They were enough to flare the heat that refused to leave her skin. The heat that came with two-sided guilt.

No matter how easy living with Mallan had become, how a friendship had sprouted once Imara finally gave him a clean slate, the feeling of betrayal loomed. A place in her heart still burned for Lorn, and always would. Because of that, she could never give Mallan what he wanted. Imara could never be his, even if she wanted him in ways she shouldn't.

She wanted him. Imara wanted Mallan, though it was painful to admit. She wanted his skin against hers, to taste his lips and the salt of his flesh. Just thinking about it sent her

253

temperature rising, making the glowing fireplace uncomfortably unnecessary. The flames taunted her.

Too warm. Too hot.

With no way to snuff out the flames in the fireplace, she did the only other thing she could think of. Desperate to cool off, Imara stormed across the suite to open one of the oversized windows, stripping as she went and leaving a trail of clothes behind her. By the time she reached it, she only wore a barely there slip.

She flung the window open, letting in a cold breeze that swept over her and pebbled her skin. She relished in the frosty air, drank it in greedily. Still, the heat wouldn't fully subside. She waited, eyes closed against the world and her face lifted to the night sky and willed relief to come.

The door opened and closed. There was only one inhabitant of Shadowmire that dared enter her suite without permission. Mallan. The corner of Imara's mouth lifted as the devil on her shoulder recounted the way his muscled frame molded against her soft curves. Heat, glorious and tortuous heat that had started to subside, roared back to life. She square her shoulders and turned, "Mal..."

It wasn't Mallan that Imara saw.

Rhanda hovered near the suite doors, arms crossed over her chest and her eyes full of cruelty. Her unexpected appearance swept the fire from Imara's veins, from her heart, and replaced it with hoarfrost. The pleasant chill of the night became too cold, but Imara didn't bother closing the window before confronting the intruder.

"Most people knock before entering another's room," Imara crossed the suite to her dressing area and grabbed a robe, pulling it around her body as she made her way to where Rhanda stood.

"Most people aren't the mother of the Lord of the manor,"

she retorted, as though giving birth to Mallan had given her the right to be such a bitch.

"Still, manners," Imara wouldn't give her the pleasure of being right. "What are you doing here?"

"I could ask you the same thing."

Imara scoffed at Rhanda's audacity. She just wouldn't let go of the insult she felt at Mallan giving Imara the suite, at his choice of her over Auren. "It's my suite."

A dry and malicious chuckle escaped Rhanda as she stepped toward Imara. "My son is currently being a good host, seeing to the guests at his solstice ball that somehow turned into a celebration in your honor," she spit the word. "And here you are, in the suite that should be Auren's, undressed and waiting for someone. I may have spied on you a little at the ball, got there just in time to see you cozying up to the High Court's golden son. Then there's the matter of who I saw you leading to your room not too long ago. Did my eyes deceive me, or did I imagine you leading the ruler of the High Court to your suite some time ago?"

"What are you implying, Rhanda?" Imara clenched her jaw.

"You know very well what I'm implying. Which of my son's enemies are you sleeping with, or is it both? Father and son?"

"Neither of them," the accusation boiled in Imara's stomach, and she had to restrain herself from attacking Rhanda.

"Struck a nerve, did I? I don't think you'd be so upset if it wasn't true. And they say I have a nose for power." Rhanda smirked, checking her nails.

"I don't deny dancing with Lautrec, or that Khryton came to my suite in the past. But you are way off the mark if you think I'm romantically involved with either of them. I asked Khryton here to see my mother. Her dying wish was to see the man she loved her whole life, and I wanted to oblige her with that. She deserved to be reunited with my father. If you bothered to actually arrive on time to the ball, you'd have heard it from his own lips. Khryton is my father, making Lautrec my brother."

Rhanda's eyes went wide. It didn't take long for the shock of Imara's revelation to be replaced with something else, something vile. "So," she stepped closer to Imara, leaving barely any space between them as she sneered down at her, "you're in league with the High Court. I should have known. When my son learns of this..."

"Your son," Imara interrupted, "knew before I did. He introduced me to Khryton and Lautrec and knew he came to see me and my mother. He arranged it. Though, I'm regretting the introduction ever happened. Khryton is vile, the only fae I've met that's more toxic than you. The only thing good that came from learning who my father is, was reuniting my mother with her love, and the peace that was brokered because of it."

"That doesn't mean anything. You don't mean anything. As soon as he's done with you, the treaty will fail and you'll be slaughtered along with the rest of the High Court. Just you wait. My son will be with Auren sooner or later. You'll see," she smirked, "well, you won't because you'll be dead."

Imara wanted to tear into the poisonous female, claw her eyes out and lash her with the harsh truth of why she'd never get what she wanted. Mallan would never love Auren the way his mother wanted him to. He wouldn't do that to his sister, who was the one the Glass Desert heir was in love with. She couldn't, though. Imara understood the importance of protecting them from Rhanda, and she wouldn't betray their relationship. Or risk the budding friendship she had with them. "I'm in Mallan's life whether you like it or not, Rhanda. Get over yourself and stop meddling with your children's lives. One day, you'll be sorry you did."

"Careful, halfling, she growled. Mallan won't always be around to protect you, neither will Tamsin. I could destroy you in such a way it would look like an accident, so very easily. I promise you that."

The promise Rhanda made her reminded Imara of Mallan, of his strong conviction about promises. He likely got that from her. An idea formed in Imara's mind to drive home how futile the female's quest was. She locked eyes with Rhanda, keeping her tone low and steady, "You've no doubt seen the wraith head outside the gates, yes?"

"Of course," she scoffed.

"Did you know that head is a promise?" Rhanda shook her head, the strength in her waning under Imara's reinforced spine. "That wraith is a promise from Mallan to all of Sylphea, that anyone who even thinks of threatening me will suffer for it. I assume you know how seriously he takes promises."

The dark-haired beauty swallowed thickly. She knew without having to witness just how far Mallan would go when promises were made and broken. The threat of his wrath had Rhanda stepping backwards, retreating from the suite with no further conflict.

Only time would tell if it was enough to keep her in line, or if she'd find some new courage over something small, that would have her aiming for Imara's throat once again.

Just to make sure her night wouldn't be further interrupted, Imara quickly locked the door, sighing against it. "Dammit."

The confrontation with Rhanda was the topper to an emotionally tumultuous day, and the last thing Imara wanted. She'd hoped the retreat to her suite would have been the end. Even that proved to have surprising repercussions.

THIRTY

Imara

For three days after the concert and ball, Imara kept to herself, reverting back to staying in her suite and only accepting the company of a select few; namely the maids and Corvus, who still pouted when she wouldn't let him beyond the boundaries of the room and into the estate to search for treasures.

The solitude had been good for alleviating stress, but not so great for banishing torrid memories. Imara wished desperately she could disappear and reappear in a cloud of smoke, like Mallan and Tamsin. Her mind could be occupied with familiar songs in her music room, or she could escape to Brine Bay to distract herself. The freedom alone would have been worth any punishment, were she caught.

Instead, her thoughts were free to explore, unhindered by outside forces to torment her. The only relief came with pen and paper, emptying her heart and soul in poetic lyrics she'd put to music when she was ready to.

Sitting at the table, a pot of violet tea gone cold before her,

Imara scrawled every bit of love and pain inside herself out. A plate of blackberry scones and currants lay as forgotten as the tea. Once she started translating her tumultuous feelings into words, she became driven. Obsessed. Nothing broke Imara's focus on the lyrics before her, not even the rapping on the door.

It was only when pink clouds obscured her vision that Imara was forced to stop. Tamsin's magical smoke took Imara from her seat at the table and deposited her on the bed. Moments later, the witch herself appeared.

"So," Tamsin quipped, plopping down on the end of the bed, "why are you hiding from Mallan?"

"Hi. Nice to see you too, Tamsin. If you don't mind, I was in the middle of something." Imara knew seeing her friend was what she needed, a real distraction from the chaos that plagued her for days, but she wanted to get back to her words.

"Hi. Why are you hiding from Mallan?" she repeated.

"I'm not hiding from Mallan," Imara deflected. "He knows where to find me."

"Hiding from, avoiding; same song, different key."

Imara rolled her eyes at the blonde witch, she was in no mood to argue. All she wanted was to hide from the world, and try to forget everything that had happened after the concert that night. The way to do that was by making new lyrics.

"You've been avoiding him since the party, you can't deny it. He's already told me you've holed yourself in here since. And I'm pretty sure I know why," she leaned in, putting her nose close and inhaling. "Someone's been having fun."

"I don't know what you're talking about, Tamsin," Imara maffled, the events from the tower played in her mind. Mallan's fangs brushing against her flesh with every kiss he planted on it. Her body pressed against the cool glass as the fire building between them grew. Imara felt that heat rising to her cheeks again.

"That blush, and," Tamsin sniffed again, "those increased pheromones say different my friend. You can't hide things from a witch." The flush burned hotter, fueled by memories and embarrassment. Topped with shame that crumbled Imara's shoulders. The change in her demeanor had Tamsin scooting closer to her friend's side. "Oh, honey. What's wrong?"

"I'm so confused, Tamsin. His men killed my husband and kidnapped me. How can I feel anything but hate towards him?"

"Your destinies twine together, Imara. Sparks are to be expected. Besides, doesn't that sprinkling of anger just enhance what you're feeling? Make it all that much hotter?" Phantom hands gripped Imara's throat and the memory of fangs on flesh sent shivers through her once more. In her head, Lorn seemed to fade.

Imara ignored Tamsin's last comment. "Intertwined destinies or not doesn't change what he stole from me. To be honest, it only confuses me more."

"How so?"

"I don't know if what's happening is natural because of our destiny, or a subconscious decision I've made because it's inevitable. Thinking about that only makes me feel worse, like I'm truly betraying Lorn. On top of that, I'm leading Mallan on." Imara sighed, looking back at the table where she abandoned her therapeutic works. They called to her. It was the only thing that had eased the heavy guilt that coated her mind. "That's why I'm hiding from Mallan, why I've thrown myself into creating new songs. So I can let go."

"If you could make yourself forget your past, would you?" Tamsin asked. "Even just one part of it to ease your pain?"

"No. We need our past to learn from it. The memories can be painful, or glorious, but necessary either way."

"Not even to protect yourself, or someone else?"

The question felt loaded. How would someone even begin

to pick and choose what they remembered and what they didn't? Even so, Imara couldn't help but wonder how far she would go to end this self-inflicted torture. The words on paper would only work for so long.

"I don't know," the admission left a knot in Imara's heart.

Tamsin stood, something grim crossing her usually bright eyes, and walked to the door. As she placed her hand on the handle, she turned back and said, "Let me know when you do." Without another word, she left Imara alone to think about her chilling words.

What had she been trying to say? Was Tamsin saying she could make her forget? She hardly believed something like that was even possible. Force herself to forget something or someone from her past. What Imara said to her was the truth, she didn't want to forget anything, despite the pain it caused. Although, doing it to spare someone else was an entirely different thing.

Exactly who was Tamsin implying she needed to protect by forgetting the past?

Imara thought about her implication for hours without coming to an obvious solution. Beings far less delicate than herself surrounded her in Shadowmire. Not a single one needed her.

As soon as she thought it, Imara knew she was wrong. Mallan's face flashed before her, the disappointment and pain Imara caused every time she refused to pledge herself to him. She realized she was hurting him beyond mere irritation.

There was one thing that Imara couldn't deny Mallan was certainly aware of. She wanted him. She craved him, and not just on a physical level. They were bonding and becoming closer than they had been when he paraded about Ocean Fare as Sconza. Yet, she turned him away, often under heated and tantalizing circumstances, every time he asked. It was the one thing she couldn't do. Wouldn't do, because of the guilt it brought her.

The hard truth forced her to evaluate the carrot Tamsin dangled, and she came to a heartbreaking conclusion. If Imara wanted to truly move on with her life, and actually give Mallan the chance she said he could have, there couldn't be any traces of Lorn left. She had to forget him, as selfish as it sounded, to have peace. She knew it was the ultimate betrayal of the perfect love they shared so briefly.

The walls of the suite closed in on Imara, as if to punish her for even considering letting her husband fade away completely, and pressed her into a ball in the middle of the bed until she couldn't breathe. When her body couldn't give anymore, she shattered. Immobilized and empty, everything stopped existing, all for the heavy weight of the spider-silk thin threads that connected the pieces of her together across infinite galaxies. Strong enough to keep her from drifting irreparably away, yet so delicate that one push could sever the lines and snatch recovery from Imara.

It was only when Imara tugged at those gossamer threads, urging her pieces home to her, that tears came. They flowed along those invisible lines, like tiny stars winking in her emptiness. Beacons for the shards of Imara lost on that dark sea. A final mourning for Lorn, her great love, because if Tamsin could do what she implied, if she could erase anything from Imara's past from her mind, she would ask her friend to take her husband.

THIRTY-ONE

Imara

The sun set and rose again, then stretched to its highest point, sleep never coming, before Imara felt the last sliver of herself lock into place. Before she was ready to see if she would, in fact, be saying goodbye to Lorn for good. With swollen eyes, crumpled clothes, tear-streaked cheeks, and a head filled with cotton, she pulled herself from the bed to find Tamsin, hoping she had come to Shadowmire.

If Imara had been allowed, she'd go to Alcara, Tamsin's home island in Cailloch and have the witch weave the hinted spell over her. Mallan was strict about where she went. He insisted an escorting guard accompany her wherever she went. But Alcara was one place Mallan had forbidden her to go, even with an escort. His reasoning was thin, and made little sense to Imara, especially with the peace treaty still in place. The witches that lived on Alcara were neutral between the courts, the only territory in Sylphea that was.

The witches of the island held no allegiance to either Khryton or Mallan. Collectively, their interactions with the courts were made on individual levels. They picked whom they swore allegiance to and that choice could change on a whim. The only ones they were loyal to were themselves. Witches banned together. She couldn't wrap her head around why Mallan would have an issue with her going to Alcara if the witches were indeed that neutral.

No one was more disappointed by the decree than Tamsin. She longed to take Imara to her island home and introduce her to the coven. Show Imara the wonders there, and many other places in Sylphea, including other places Mallan prohibited her from visiting. Devs Willow Wood, the home of the goblins, was on that list, as well as any place north of them. Imara suspected it was Tamsin that was truly the reason the woods were forbidden, given her fondness for his soldiers and Mallan's order for her to leave them alone. It was an order that her friend defied as much as she could, according to the stories she'd tell Imara, which led Imara to question if Tamsin was as loyal to him as she claimed to be.

Her search for Tamsin hit a block the moment Imara opened the door to her suite. Thorn stood just on the other side, hand raised to knock, with startled eyes. At first she thought it was her own unexpected appearance that shocked the maid, but Thorn's expression didn't change as she greeted her. "Miss Imara," she stumbled over her words, "you have a visitor." Her wide blue eyes darted to the side and back, showing there was someone beyond the frame of the door.

Imara peered around the door and saw there was indeed someone waiting. Samir sat in the high-back chair furthest from the suite. No wonder the timid maid looked so alert. The Living Ghost's otherworldliness could unease anyone not used to him.

His cinnamon eyes met Imara's, and he stood. He wore a dark cloak over his lightweight desert garb, made for weathering the grueling heat of his home, yet still he visibly shivered as he wended through the furniture to greet her at the door. Thorn quickly scurried away when he approached, leaving them alone to talk.

Samir flashed a bright, sharp smile as he bowed his greeting, keeping his eyes locked on Imara, taking in every detail of her disheveled state. The way he analyzed her set her on edge, and she crossed her arms in front of her as though it would hide her wrinkled clothes and sleep deprived eyes.

"I don't mean to discomfort you," he noted the shift in her confidence. "I am merely concerned. Have I come at a bad time?"

"No, not at all Samir. I had a rough night is all," Imara stepped aside to allow him entrance. "Please, come in and sit by my fire. Shadowmire, while beautiful, is dreadfully cold."

"Thank you," Smir's face lit at the invitation. "In all my years coming here, no one had offered me a warm hearth to sit next to."

"By all means then," Imara offered with a smile.

She followed Samir to the fireplace, settling on the edge. "What brings you here, to me?" Imara could understand why Samir would come seeking Mallan, as he was his Lord, but didn't have any idea why he'd seek her out.

"I have a message for you," he said, sitting cross-legged on the floor before her.

"A message?"

"More someone wishes to speak with you," not wasting any more breath, Samir dug into the folds of his cloak and brought out his satchel. With deft fingers, he opened the bag and poured the fine black sand onto the floor in front of him. Bits of sand sparkled in the firelight as if recalling their former lives as shards of obsidian formed by fire. When the bag emptied, he placed it back into his cloak and meditated. He was summoning a spirit.

A lump formed in Imara's throat as she watched reverently. She couldn't think of anyone in Sylphea she knew of that had died. Her immediate thoughts flew to Tilly, but she was certain she hadn't passed yet. Imara was sure her father or brother would have sent word if she had.

The grains of sand shifted, rising into the air slowly and settling back into the pile. Over and over they repeated the pattern, every time rising higher. Soon, with each new rise, the sands whirled into a nondescript form until that form became clearer and clearer.

Imara gasped when the sand stopped its dance and settled into its final shape. Though there was no color, the for the sand took was undeniably that of her mother.

Devastation rolled into Imara's heart, springing tears to her eyes immediately. Tilly had passed from her illness and no one bothered to tell her.

"Hello, my Little Angel," the sanded form of her mother said, her voice strong and vibrant as it had been in her youth. "Don't cry. We knew this was coming, and I am free now."

"I know. I know. It's just, no one said anything to me. I didn't know," Imara sniffled, wiping away her tears.

Sorrow etched Tilly's barely there features, "I know. But I am here now. Here, saying my goodbyes," regret laced her words.

"I'm glad you asked Samir for this, I'm glad I could give you happiness and peace in your final days." The look of regret crossed Tilly's face again. Even as ghostly sand, Imara's mother was easy to read. Whatever she wasn't saying, she was reluctant to share. "What happened?"

"The High Court was a dream, they attended to everything I needed and wanted. Khryton was everything I remembered."

"But?" Imara pushed.

"He was only everything I remembered for a few short days. Then he came around less and less until he never came at all. I figured he was busy, there had to have been so much on his plate as Lord of the High Court. I didn't mind so much, I had plenty of lovely company. Your brother, Lautrec, he came and saw me all the time. He read to me, showed me fantastic things I'd never dreamed existed," a light smile appeared on the corner of her mouth and she chuckled a little. "He even left me an orb connected to his own vision the night of your concert. Seeing you onstage like that was a blessing. You were so beautiful and vibrant, it filled me with so much joy to see you living your dream. I only wish I could have been there in person."

"From what I can tell, Lautrec is a good man."

"He genuinely is," her face soured. "Not like his father at all."

Imara's heart sunk. After what Lautrec revealed at the ball, she didn't think her opinion of Khryton could sink lower. "What happened?"

"A few days before the concert, a maid helped me to a window so I could look out over the gardens. Khryton has beautiful gardens. Anyway, I saw Khryton out under a large magnolia tree, his hand up the skirt of some girl as he buried his face in her neck. To make it worse, as if he sensed me watching from above, he looked right at me and smirked before turning his attentions to her breasts. He had no remorse at being caught."

Imara's blood boiled. She'd sent her mother to be loved and cared for by the man she had been in love with her whole life, only to have it thrown in her face. It's not that Imara expected he never moved on after thinking Tilly died, she had many siblings after all and Lautrec outed him as a whore. But he could have had the decency to make her mother his world for just a short time.

"After the concert," she continued adding on to the cruel tale that Imara couldn't imagine being able to get worse, "Khryton came to see me one last time." Tilly went quiet, her ghostly hand fisted at her mouth. Imara's instinct was to reach out for her, hold her mother, and tell her it would be okay. But, it wouldn't. The fact that Tilly stood there in a whirl of sand, screamed she wasn't.

"Mom?"

Tilly shook her head, "I just need a minute." Her mother turned back and forth, as if pacing, her spectral arms wrapped around her body. After minutes of tense silence, she faced Imara again. "There's no easy way to say this, so I'll just say it. That night, he came into my room, sat on the bed, and whispered a secret to me. *'I never loved you, you were just a means to an end. An incubator in my experiment to wipe out man. An experiment that went very well.'* I started crying, screaming at him. I was inconsolable. It turned into a match of who could out scream the other when he began yelling at me to be quiet. Then he hit me," she paused, Imara knew if she could cry she would have been. "He kept hitting me, over and over, climbing on top of me. He reached for a pillow, and..." she broke off, stifling a dry sob.

Imara didn't need to hear the rest to know what happened. Khryton smothered her. He murdered Tilly in cold blood, revealing what a monster he truly was.

The hate she held in her heart for him after learning the truth about her conception multiplied a thousand times. Imara had come to terms that he was vile and cruel. Even with the truth that she was an experiment in his plans to wipe out mortals. What she couldn't handle was that revelation that spilled from her mother's lips. From the lips of the ghost of her mother.

"I'll kill him."

"My little angel, no. Don't become like him. You're too good a soul to do that."

"I'm not as good as you think," Imara spat.

"You are. You are destined for great things, my beautiful girl. I love you."

"I love you too."

The sands that gave Tilly form wavered, "I have to go now, darling. Please remember me well and let go of the hate. It will only eat at you." The air cleared and the sand settled into a neat pile before Imara could respond.

Without being focused on her mother, Imara remembered Samir. She looked at him sitting there before her with his eyes still closed and wondered if heard any of what transpired. His eyes opened, and his serene expression told her he didn't.

The Living Ghost stood, dug the red bag from his cloak once more and opened it. "I am truly sorry for your loss," he said with heavy eyes. The spry look Samir had when he first arrived was gone, the message he delivered had sapped all the energy from him.

"Do you hear your messages?" Imara asked, she had to know for sure.

"No, no need to worry there. Messages are private, personal. Only their recipients should hear them."

Imara nodded at his response. "Thank you for bringing her to me," the words came out bitter, scorched by the means of Tilly's death.

"Of course. If there is anything you need, Lord Mallan needs, we are at your service." As he bowed his farewell, the sand swirled once more, forming a cloud that enveloped Samir until he became one with it. The cloud drifted across the suite and under the door. He was gone.

Imara's world felt raw, jagged. All she wanted was revenge

on her father, but Tilly made her promise not to go after him. She thought Imara was the angel she nicknamed her. Though her promise was unspoken, Imara wouldn't kill Khryton. But she never said he wouldn't die because of her.

The peace treaty, as far as Imara was concerned, had just been incinerated by his deceptions. By murder. All she had to do was tell Mallan, and Khryton was as good as dead.

CHAPTER

THIRTY-TWO

Mallan

"Has she given you an answer yet?"

"Be patient, Mallan," Tamsin chided him. "I only presented the idea to her a day ago. Give her time to come to terms with letting him go. It's not an easy decision."

"You sound like you sympathize with her." Mallan grumbled.

"That's what you wanted, wasn't it? For me to be her friend. Congratulations, I am. That means I care. Unlike you, my heart is capable of feeling something real."

"You assume I don't truly care about her?" The dire warning rumbled in Mallan's chest, causing the witch to cower uncharacteristically .

Tamsin cleared her throat, "No. I'm sorry. I spoke out of turn. Of course you love her. How can one not? Just look at how your sister and Auren have taken to her despite Rhanda's control. How she's even won over her father and brother..."

"That's the problem, isn't' it?" Mallan cut Tamsin off with a wry, disbelieving chuckle. "She should forget them too, then."

"No, Mallan. Messing with Imara's memories that much can cause more damage than good."

"I didn't go into this just so she could become one big happy family with Khryton. You said she was the one, that this daughter of my enemy would be the one to guarantee his fall and determine the fate of Morrea. The years of planning everything down to the smallest detail; hiding her mother from him, ensuring she had nowhere to go, becoming her savior, and leading to the murder of that pathetic mortal husband of hers, Lorn. I even went as far as invading her dreams as the poor fool, for fuck's sake. All of it will go to waste if she doesn't turn against him and choose me. If she doesn't say the words. If she doesn't taste my blood and receive my venom."

"I understand, my Lord."

"Do you? I can't take out Khryton without Imara, Tamsin. Try something else. I need the bastard gone."

"Give her more time, Mallan. She will choose you, she's so close. Her feelings for you are strong enough that she questions herself. The crumb you had me lay for a way to ease her pain and guilt, I'm certain she will take it. Then she will be yours, your destiny fulfilled. She has no love for her father. Khryton will fall and Morrea will bow to you. The mortal world will be free for the taking, for you to enslave."

"She grows close to Lautrec. His influence could sway her the other way and give Khryton the upper hand. I fear she won't be able to resist familial influence."

"Don't worry about Lautrec," Tamsin demurred, her magenta eyes shifting. Mallan watched as she moved to the window overlooking the back courtyard and sat on the sill. "He's a tool, all beauty with no brains, and Imara's smart. She'll see that soon enough."

He smirked sardonically, "No, he's not." Mallan looked out over the courtyard and over the edge of the property to the vast sea beyond. The wheels in his head churned like the waves. Tamsin was wrong about Lautrec, he was far from being what she accused him to be. Khryton's line was ripe with under-handedness.

A flash of dark hair streaked across the courtyard toward the rookery. Imara. She moved with purpose, with a fury in her stride. Mallan sprung into action and bolted from his office, only to be stopped at the door. Imara's scent lingered at the threshold and what happened struck him like lightning. She'd overheard their conversation.

Tamsin appeared at his side, "What is it?"

"She was listening. Imara was here recently, and she heard our schemes." The witch needed no instruction from him and she took off with Imara's name on her lips. Mallan wasn't far behind her.

THIRTY-THREE

Imara

As soon as she made up her mind, Imara flew from her suite in search of Mallan. Her need to find Tamsin and make herself forget put firmly on hold with the message from her mother. Imara knew he was scheduled to meet with several high fae from the Under Court that had questions about the treaty he'd signed. He hadn't been looking forward to it, but he was ready to sway them into believing peace could exist between the courts. Imara knew he'd give that peace up happily as soon as she found him. He'd delight in it.

It didn't take long for Imara to descend the flights of stairs to the first floor of Shadowmire. The fire in her belly demanded swiftness, demanded justice.

"How she's even won over her father and brother..." Tamsin's voice drifted in the air as Imara approached his office.

"That's the problem, isn't it?" Mallan cut Tamsin off with a wry, disbelieving chuckle. Imara stopped at the door, which was cracked just enough to glimpse them. The pair were staring each other down. Whatever they'd been arguing about this time appeared serious. It was better to not interrupt, so Imara decided to return to her suite and send word through a maid that it was imperative she spoke with them.

What she heard next stopped her in her tracks. "She should forget them too, then."

"No, Mallan. Messing with Imara's memories that much can cause more damage than good."

"I didn't go into this just so she could become one big happy family with Khryton. You said she was the one, that this daughter of my enemy would be the one to guarantee his fall and determine the fate of Morrea. The years of planning everything down to the smallest detail; hiding her mother from him, ensuring she had nowhere to go, becoming her savior, and leading to the murder of that pathetic mortal husband of hers, Lorn. I even went as far as invading her dreams as the poor fool, for fuck's sake. All of it will go to waste if she doesn't turn against him and choose me. If she doesn't say the words. If she doesn't taste my blood and receive my venom."

"I understand, my Lord."

"Do you? I can't take out Khryton without Imara, Tamsin. Try something else. I need the bastard gone." Mallan's words were shocking, he'd orchestrated her whole life. Lorn's death, even though he swore he had no hand in it.

"Give her more time, Mallan. She will choose you, she's so close. Her feelings for you are strong enough that she questions herself. The crumb you had me lay for a way to ease her pain and guilt, I'm certain she will take it. Then she will be yours, your destiny fulfilled. She has no love for her father. Khryton will fall and Morrea will bow to you. The mortal world will be free for the taking, for you to enslave."

Silence rang for half a second before Mallan spoke again. "She grows close to Lautrec. His influence could sway her the other way and give Khryton the upper hand. I fear she won't be able to resist familial influence."

Imara couldn't believe what she was hearing. The truth, the whole truth, about why Mallan had taken her. How he had taken her, manipulated Imara's whole life until that moment. Manipulated almost every decision she made since coming to his home. Imara's world erupted as she learned she wasn't anything more than a tool, a weapon against her father. Against whomever she didn't choose.

She didn't want to choose either.

Khryton wanted to wipe out mortals, breed them away. Mallan wanted to subjugate them. Neither of those things could happen. Imara may not have had a home in Morrea to return to, but she didn't wish that world ill. Morrea was her mother's world, Lorn's family's world, and countless others that didn't deserve subjugation or to be used to wipe their race away.

Mallan lied. He lied about Lorn. It was the worst infraction of them all. Tamsin wanted to make her forget him. Everyone was using her. Against her.

She had to run.

Imara found herself headed toward the rookery, longing for a friendly face, even if it wasn't human or fae. She needed a silent comfort, an ear that wouldn't have an opinion. Corvus, her faithful bird friend, seemed the only creature that fit the bill.

The minute Imara neared the towering bird house an excited chittering filled the air, it wasn't too long after that Corvus's bright white feathers broke through the contrasting blue black of his murder and swooped down to greet her. He landed on her shoulder, his feathers fluffed and little face twitching side to side in study. Smart as he was, he sensed Imara's despair and inched closer to her face, nuzzling her cheek. She closed her eyes, taking in the sweet bird's affection.

"Imara!" her named called on the wind from above snapped her eyes back open. She was as good as found. Imara was caged in near the rookery, it had been a mistake to go there. Panic beat like a drum in her ears, she wasn't ready to confront them. The recent discoveries still played raw and discordant in her mind.

"Imara!" When her name pierced the air again, Corvus once again proved how wonderful a companion had chosen Imara. The bird hopped from her shoulder, gliding through the air until he neared the bushes that sat against the base of the rookery and landed. He squawked repeatedly, his little feet dancing about. Corvus wanted her to go to him.

"Shush," she whispered harshly to the bird, "they'll hear us." He listened and silenced his calls, only to dart in and out of the bush. "You want me to go in there?" Corvus flapped his wings, a silent yes, just before darting back in.

Imara's name came again, closer. If she didn't want to be found, she'd have to hide in the bush like the bird wanted her to. She couldn't believe she was taking advice from a raven, but desperate times called for desperate measures. Imara got down and crawled in.

Branches scratched against Imara's skin and caught in her hair as she pushed into the bush. She felt ridiculous. Surely she'd be found in no time in such a poor hiding place. There wasn't enough space for her to fully disappear into the foliage. Imara told herself she would have to have a serious discussion about size difference with Corvus, if she evaded detection. Not that the bird would understand.

The raven squawked again, urgently, as if calling Imara forward. "I can't fly!" she hissed, reminding him that unlike him and some fae, she did not have wings. The rookery, and therefore, the bush, sat at the edge of a cliff. There wasn't anything on the other side waiting for her except an unknown height to fall. Imara maneuvered enough to stick her head out the other side of the shrubbery.

On the other side, Corvus hopped happily to see his human. Behind him, Imara delighted in seeing there wasn't a sheer drop off, but what appeared to be the start of a path that led downward. After she struggled out of the confined space of the bush, Imara continued to crawl to where the slope began. There, she found a zig-zagging stone staircase that led down to a thin strip of beach.

"I could kiss you, Corvus." The raven had given her a path of escape.

With hurried feet, Imara flew down the steps, her loyal feathered companion keeping close in the air as she went. When her toes hit the sand, a sense of relief washed through Imara. She surveyed her surroundings. About a hundred feet to the right, the beach ended at a cliff wall that stretched out into the water. But, to her left, the beach stretched on, beyond sight where it hazed in the distance. The decision was made for her. Left it was.

Without hesitation, Imara took off down the thin strip of sand, allowing the surf to crash over her feet, with no plans to stop anytime soon. If she could, Imara would run all the way to the High Court. To Lautrec. She knew her brother would have her back. That was impossible, though. With so many unknown dangers between them, and that Khryton was bound to be where her brother was, there were limitations to what she could do.

As she ran, Imara realized she'd been so foolish to not attempt to run away sooner, but then again, she hadn't known the whole story.

The beach broadened as she traveled further from Shadowmire. Still, Imara kept close to the water in hopes it would wash away any traces that she'd been there. Imara would not make it easy for Mallan or Tamsin to find her. She never wanted them to. If they did, she didn't know what she would do or how she would react. All Imara knew was that it wouldn't be pretty. There was too much turmoil building for it to be anything else.

Suddenly, the wet sand beneath Imara's foot gave way to a gaping hole, sending her tumbling forward. The hole, likely formed by a geoduck buried deep beneath the surface, didn't relinquish its hold on her, causing her ankle to pop and twist with searing pain.

Imara desperately dug her foot free from the sand and got up, determined to keep moving. Her ankle, though, wasn't. The slightest amount of weight on it had Imara wincing back into the sand, her foot barking in pain.

"Fuck!" she screamed over the crashing waves. It wasn't fair. The accidental delay was going to cost her precious space and time she'd put between her and Shadowmire. She never wanted to see those halls or the traitors within them again. To be waylaid by something so random, so inconsequential, unleashed a new storm of despair. Soon her screams gave way to silent tears. Not even Corvus keeping her company made her feel any better.

The wind picked up, increasing with every passing second until it was howling over the water. The ferocity only kept increasing, becoming a full-fledged storm in seconds. A cyclone. There was something strange about the raging weather, Imara thought. It came from nowhere, and formed in conditions that shouldn't have been possible. Plus, it was small. The storm was confined to a radius of feet rather than miles. Even stranger, it appeared to be making a direct path towards her.

Imara scrambled, crab walking without putting too much pressure on her injured ankle, to move out of its path. Every inch of headway she made was erased when the bizarre cyclone changed its path to be in alignment with her. She knew then the storm wasn't ordinary. It was targeting her.

As far as she could recall, Mallan didn't have any power over water or weather. His realm was shadows and dreams. Neither did any of his close allies, though it was possible Tamsin could. She was a witch whose power was limited to her imagination and strength.

Imara's hands clawed frantically at the sand behind her. It would be useless, she understood that there was no outrunning the strange weather in her condition. She had to try, though. She wouldn't give up without a fight.

Corvus sensed the danger, too. He took off high into the air, where the storm couldn't touch him, and flew off. Imara watched him with an envious eye and wished she was like the lucky bird, that she could sprout wings of her own.

The storm surged the moment her raven disappeared, leaping at Imara. With a scream, Imara flung her arms protectively over herself to stave off the storm as it enveloped her.

Silence filled the air.

When Imara dared to unlock her eyes, what she found stole her words. Surrounding her on all sides were sloping walls of swirling water. She was in a bubble, and she wasn't alone. In front of Imara stood the very nixie that gave her the kelp bracelet in Brine Bay.

"Sister," she greeted in her half drowned voice. "It's very good to see you again."

"Why have you trapped me?" Imara demanded rather than return the pleasant greeting.

"I am protecting us the only way I know how. I've longed to speak with you privately since you gave us that song, and even now that I've found you here, there are outsiders listening. One of Lord Mallan's ravens in nearby."

The nixie meant Corvus. "He's not Mallan's," Imara bit. "Corvus is mine. Loyal to me."

"Either way, I can't risk the bird overhearing," she cocked her head, as though listening for signs of others outside of the watery bubble. "Tell me, Sister, what do I call you?"

"Imara," her voice wavered. She couldn't help but feel frightened after hearing the tales about the nixies.

"Sister, Imara," she bowed her head, "I am Balle. Representative of the nixies and everything Below. It is important we talk."

"Why do you keep calling me that? Sister?"

Balle motioned to the gold and gems embedded in Imara's arm that had once been the bracelet she gave her, "It changed." Imara had almost forgotten about it. The permanent piece of jewelry was something she barely noticed anymore, it was as much part of her as her own flesh. She'd gotten used to it.

Imara ran her fingers over the golden threads winding to her elbow. "What does that mean?" she seethed, her anger rising. Tamsin had yet to deliver answers about the transformation the bracelet went through. Imara was tired of not getting the answers she deserved. Tired of being toyed with.

Balle raised her hands in a non-threatening gesture, "It's okay, Imara. The bracelet did as it was supposed to, as I suspected it would. It connects you to us, to the Below. As you are meant to be."

"Can you stop being cryptic?"

"How about I show you while I tell the tale? You'll get a clearer picture."

Imara gave a curt nod of approval and Balle turned, stretching a webbed hand out to the water wall. A stream trickled between the two, gathering in an orb that floated inches above the nixie's palm. The orb grew to twice the size of a large melon before the stream stopped and she moved her hand to point to Imara, the orb following her path. Placing her other hand over the top of it, Balle turned the ball of water so her hands flanked its sides. The nixie flung her arms wide, and the orb transformed into a flat rectangle that floated between them.

"Long ago, a prophecy came to light, telling Queen Alette that she must leave her beloved Below and Sylphea in order to protect its future. To protect the future of the entire world, the lands of fae and mortal alike." The water screen danced to life as Balle spoke, a watery figure of a beautiful fae woman with flowing locks beneath a crown appeared. The woman paced back and forth, distressed. "She worried about obeying the prophecy, for her people she would leave behind that would be left to the whims of her sister queens. The brutality of their battles. She thought Sylphea would have a better chance if she stayed."

The water morphed into a new image. Queen Alette melded with the screen, the image of a baby in its place. "The seer convinced her to go with a detail of the prophesy, a child thrice blessed." Three figures appeared around the infant, each one passing a watery orb to the babe that melded with it. "Powers inherited from father. Powers inherited by mother. Powers given freely in fealty. A child that only her pure heart could bring about."

"Queen Alette made the hard decision to leave her people. If it was truly for the best, the sacrifice would be worth it in the end. She would leave for Morrea and live as a mortal." The lost fae queen formed on the screen again, her thin and lithe body slowly growing a belly heavy with child. "She drained her powers, save enough to disappear into the mortal world, to conceive a child through magic that would hold none of its own. The magic would lie dormant in the child and all of its descendants, as per the prophecy, until fae magic was once more introduced. A child conceived by mortal and fae."

The watery screen shifted from Queen Alette into figure after figure, each one growing and continuing the line. Finally, it settled on one figure, a girl. Slowly, that girl turned. "The child would return to Sylphea someday, where her magic would manifest, slowly and steadily, coming in full when she makes that all important decision." As Balle finished her tale, the water girl finish her turn.

The girl was Imara.

The screen splashed to the sand at their feet. All she could do was stare at Balle in disbelief. As the shock of seeing her own face before wore off, Imara began tracing the fine gold threads on her skin. "Are you saying that I'm..." she couldn't finish.

"Yes, Imara, Sister. You are the descendant of Queen Alette. It is you that decides who controls Sylphea, and therefore Morrea. It is a weighty decision, I pray you make the best one."

Images of her father and Mallan played through her head. Both had hurt Imara, betrayed her. Imara couldn't trust either. It was a matter of who was the lesser of two evils. But how did she choose? "Which one is the right one?" She asked, hoping Balle had some insight.

"I don't know. I have told you all I can. If I could guide you, I would. As it is, my time is up, I have been ashore too long already. I have to return below," Balle bowed, hand over heart, "Before I go, I will give you one last gift. Good luck, Imara. You're going to need it."

Balle turned and calmly walked out of the globe of water, leaving Imara behind. The surrounding sphere warbled and contracted until it was a cyclone before her in the sand. It spun in place, faster and faster, then was suddenly gone.

Imara stared out over the water, feeling lost and confused. Burdened with knowing what she had to decide. She had to decide not only who she would align with, but the fate of two lands.

"Imara?" a familiar voice she'd nearly forgotten whispered from near her feet. Imara looked down, head spinning and breath unsteady, falling to her knees when she saw the owner of that beautiful voice.

Lorn.

THIRTY-FOUR

Mallan

By the time Mallan reached the rookery, there was no sign of Imara anywhere. Corvus was missing, too. How had he missed her? There was no way from the rookery other than the path in. The gravel crunched under Mallan's feet as he spun to head back to the estate. The remaining flock sprung into the air with a cacophony of cries, but they weren't loud enough to drown the roar he set loose.

He'd been stupid. In his single-mindedness to guide Imara to the choices he needed her to make, he'd lost sight of being vigilant. He should have sensed her at the door, stopped the conversation with Tamsin. Instead, he may have driven his destiny straight into the arms of her father, his enemy.

Mallan raced to the house, desperate to find Imara there. She had to have somehow gotten past him and back into the estate without notice. He called for his goblins. "Search every inch of Shadowmire, the surrounding grounds," he ordered. "Imara couldn't have disappeared into thin air, she has to be here or nearby somewhere." The words barely left his mouth before he began his own search.

The first place he wanted to check was Imara's suite, pleading silently to the Mothers she was there, either packing or panicking. Both.

The suite doors were wide open when he got there, inside he could hear someone moving about. Mallan couldn't rely on his nose to tell if she was there or not, her scent lingered heavily everywhere in and around the room. With bated breath, he stepped inside, releasing the air from his lungs forcefully when he saw not Imara, but one of her maids.

"Lord Mallan," the maid's pale cerulean eyes widened, and she dropped the pillow she'd been handling. "What can I do for you?"

"Have you seen Imara?" Mallan rushed at the maid, stopping short of grabbing her shoulders and shaking her. "Have you?" He demanded again when she didn't answer immediately.

"No, Lord Mallan. Not since her visitor left."

Mallan's mind narrowed, flying directly to a visitor from Khryton's court. Someone sent to whisper in her ear. "Who visited her?" his frustration laced his word with aggression and the maid cowered.

"The Living Ghost. He had a message for her."

The relief that spread through him lasted only moments. He quickly came to realize why Samir would have a message for Imara. Tilly must have passed.

"Her mother?" Mallan whispered the question, his heart wrenching for his Starling. She'd been seeking him out for comfort with the news of her mother's demise, and found only betrayal.

"I don't know, Lord Mallan. They were alone when the message was given, but I saw her rush from the suite not long after he arrived. Her cheeks were stained with tears, though she seemed more furious than devastated."

"Thank you," he dismissed the maid with more politeness than he had ever spoken to a servant. "Before you go, have you noticed anything missing from the suite?"

The maid, still wide eyed and off kilter from Mallan's gratitude, surveyed the suite. Nothing appeared out of place at first glance. She opened her mouth to answer, only to be interrupted by an insistent tapping at the windows, drawing her master's attention away from her.

At the window, Mallan saw Corvus's white feathers beating desperately against the panes. Stunned by the raven's appearance, Mallan froze and the maid beat him to the window, opening it to let the bird in. Corvus flew right to Mallan, lighting on his shoulder. The bird's frenzied state didn't change, however. He continued to squawk and flap with intensity.

"What's wrong with it?" the maid asked with a tremble in her voice.

"I can only guess," Mallan growled, not at her fear but at what he took the bird's frantic state to mean. Something was wrong with Imara. He couldn't be sure, though, there was only one thing to do. Mallan sent a tendril of his shadows into the bird, Corvus's eyes glowed red as it settled in him. "Be my eyes, guide me," he ordered the raven, who took off without hesitation.

As Mallan watched the bird fly from the estate, the rest of the rookery took flight to join Corvus.

CHAPTER

THIRTY-FIVE

Lorn

L orn was shaken by being deposited on the beach, disoriented. His eyes locked on the sand that clung to his hands in disbelief. One minute he was tending to the kelp beds at the cottage, the next whisked away to wherever he'd landed.

He looked up, blinded by the sun in the distance, though when his vision adjusted, he couldn't believe what he was seeing. "Imara," he barely heard his own prayer-like voice. She didn't move or say anything in response.

"Imara?" He questioned again, louder this time.

"Lorn!" Imara flung herself on him, wrapping her arms around him tight to make sure what she saw was real as his arms wrapped around her to ensure the same of her. She was real. Her soft scent washed over him, sweet floral notes laced with petrichor; a scent so uniquely her. Having her in his arms after all this time made the world right. His midnight, her moonlight, inexcusably meant to be together. One couldn't exist without the other.

He pulled back, his hands reaching for Imara's face, "It's really you." His roughened fingers grazed her delicate skin, ran through her tangled hair. Imara's clear, tear lined blue eyes closed to worship the feeling of it. It had been too long, far too long, since they'd felt each other's hands. "Please don't close your eyes," he whispered. "I need to see your eyes."

A sob filled laugh escaped her lips as she listened to his plea, and her eyes met his again. Overwhelmed with happiness, Lorn's lips found hers in desperately reverent kisses, each one a thank you to the heavens for the miracle of being together again. Both of them cried happily, their salty tears seasoning their kisses and making them all that much sweeter.

"How are you here?" Imara pulled away and lay her head against his broad shoulder. "You died. I saw it, Mallan's goblins left you lifeless at General Price's cabin. How?" an amazed laugh came from her, a sound of pure joy.

"No. But came too close to death's door that had an angel not intervened, I would have."

"An angel?"

"So I thought, at first. I was barely clinging to life, angry I hadn't been able to stop the attack or protect you. I couldn't go after you. I felt like a failure, Imara."

Imara hugged Lorn a little tighter, "Never. You could never be a failure."

"You are too sweet, my wife," he planted a kiss on the top of her head before continuing, and Imara melted closer to him at that magical word. Wife. That was the word he'd longed to say to her all this time. "I lay there dying when the cabin filled with a bright light. At first I thought I succumbed to the wounds, that by some miracle I'd made it to heaven. A man appeared before me, tall and golden lit. The light faded, and he remained, became clear enough to make out features; broad shouldered, strong, with sharp cheeks, pointed ears, and unearthly blue eyes that stood out against his dark skin."

A kernel of anger flitted across Imara's face when he spoke about the golden man, and quickly calmed. "Who was it?"

"He called himself Aradus, and instructed me to be still. Soon a woman joined him, she shared his blue eyes, though hers were larger. Stranger. She had no pupils, no whites, just globes of blue almost too large for her delicate face. Her eyes weren't the only thing strange about her. She had pale green hair, and her skin was brindled with the same color stripes. Aradus introduced her as his sister, Caprice." Lorn felt guilty omitting what else he knew about the pair, that they were her half siblings. Lying is something they swore never to do to each other. He wasn't sure how much about herself she'd learned, and didn't want to overwhelm her with too much.

His words didn't surprise Imara, rather she nodded as she listened as though she were putting pieces together. As if she recognized who he spoke of. If not who, but what the creatures he spoke of were.

"It was only when the pair lifted me I realized I wasn't in the cabin any longer," Lorn's story moved forward. "I was somewhere else, another cottage somewhere. Caprice healed me and nursed me back to health over the following weeks. Aradus came and went as he pleased, bringing supplies every time he appeared."

"My strength grew, and I became eager to leave and try to find you. They wouldn't let me leave, insisting I needed more rest."

"I tried escaping one night, with no idea where to go or how to find you. I was simply determined to do it. The moment I stepped outside, I knew the odds were against me. Mountains hugged the back of the cottage, the sea surrounded the front.

Still, I tried leaving. Nothing would deter me, except I couldn't leave. There was some sort of barrier keeping me there. I pounded on it all night."

"Aradus found me the next morning, curled next to that invisible wall. It was then he explained what had happened, who they were, where I was. Every part of their story was more unbelievable than the next. I've been there since, living with Caprice, helping her. Helping Aradus when he came. All the while, they promised when the time was right, that I could leave, and they would help me find you. Now, here I am. Unexpectedly and happily. Though, I could have used some warning from them about how I ended up here, on this beach."

"They didn't tell you?"

"No, I was minding the kelp bed at the edge of the barrier when a tornado of water crashed through it, swooping me up and transporting me here."

"A good surprise?"

"The best," he gathered her hands in his and his lips found Imara's again. "One I'll never let go of again."

A squawk broke the calm around the pair, their attention pulled towards it. High in the sky a murder crested the horizon, a white raven with black wings heading the group.

"Oh, no." Imara's face fell, and the bliss they'd wrapped themselves in crashing with it.

"What's wrong?"

"It's Corvus, my raven. He must have thought I was in danger and went for help from the only one he knew could."

"Who?"

"His name is Lord Mallan. He rules the Under Court of Sylphea and is set on having me as his. We need to run," Imara ordered, ignoring the pain in her ankle, scrambling to her feet, and pulling Lorn with her.

The moment they were both on their feet, an all too familiar black cloud enveloped them. Lorn's body tensed. The last time he'd encountered such black clouds, he'd nearly died. There would be no third chance at life, and no way he'd let the approaching foe best him again. Imara belonged to no one but herself. Her love was a gift he'd always be grateful for.

Imara

The cloud spit Lorn and Imara out in the middle of the courtyard, still adorned with flowers from the party. Their beauty faded from time, and knowledge that left a sour taste in her mouth. Immediately, Mallan's steadfast goblin grunts surrounded the pair, each one training their weapons on them.

"Stay back," Imara seethed, hobbling in front of Lorn to protect him. They wouldn't dare hurt her to get to him. Mallan would eliminate them all. Not that he would have a chance to, "I won't hesitate to strike each of you down if you even try to touch him."

"That, I'd like to see very much, Starling. But how do you propose to do that without a weapon?" The sound of Mallan's voice behind her sent ice through Imara's veins. The goblins she could handle, him not so much.

"Call them off, Mallan," Imara turned to face the dark fae lord.

"Anything you ask," he plied before giving the command.

"At ease." The goblin assembly pulled their weapons to rest and stepped back to make room for their lord, yet none tensed any less. They were ready to strike at the command she knew had to be coming.

Slow and methodical, Mallan circled them, his hands clasped behind his back and a glint in his eye Imara had never seen before. He enjoyed this power, this calm terror. "Lorn," he drawled, "I'd like to say how good it is to see you again, but I'd be lying. I'm not a fan of lies." Imara bristled. He lied, he was deception incarnate.

"Again? I've never met you before."

Mallan chuckled behind them, "Sure you have." When he came back into view, he had donned his human glamor. He stopped, arms spread wide and a sneering grin plastered on his face.

"Gio," Lorn spat. Their captor only chuckled again. He moved to lunge at the fae before him, his amber eyes flashing darkly. Imara grabbed onto her husband's wrist, stopping him from attacking. They didn't stand a chance of leaving if he did.

Mallan shifted back into his true form, turning his attention to his horde. "I'm just curious how you survived, how my goblins failed in what they're trained to do so well. It's very disappointing."

"You manipulative son of a bitch," it was Imara's turn to lunge for Mallan. She didn't fear his wrath, his hurting her. He wouldn't. She was too valuable to his plans.

"Hmmm, true. You have met my mother."

His attempt at joking enraged Imara even more. Without thinking, she charged forward, shoving Mallan with all her might.

"You lied! You said you never ordered Lorn's supposed death!"

"I never ordered my goblins to kill him. That was no lie. My orders were to obtain you, by whatever means necessary," he reached out, catching her chin with his fingers and gazing down at her with a heated stare.

"I hate you," Imara yanked out of his grasp, stepping backwards to Lorn and taking his hand in hers.

Mallan's eyes flashed on their entwined hands and his lip curled as he took in a deep breath. A moment later, his demeanor changed. His head tipped to the side, and he licked his lips. Those dark eyes of his once again heated and raked over Imara. The gap between him, Lorn, and Imara closed in an instant. "I really don't think you do, Starling," he crooned in a low, husky tone. "In fact, I know just how much you don't. How much you crave me," he looked Lorn straight in the eye with those words.

Imara let her hand slip from Lorn's and wrapped her arms tightly around herself. Every passionate moment between her and Mallan played in her mind, causing Imara's eyes to cast down to the courtyard's ground.

"Let us go," Lorn seethed, avoiding Mallan's insinuation, though his jaw clenched, the muscles there taught and ticking.

"I can't do that, Lorn. Imara and I are destined for each other, and you are just a stone in the road."

"You're wrong. Imara could never love someone like you."

Mallan's eyes lit, as though he'd been waiting for an opening to taunt Lorn again. "Oh, but she does, just look at her." Imara could feel Lorn's eyes on her, questioning her. She couldn't look back at him, see the hurt in his beautiful golden specked eyes. There was nowhere for her to hide from the shame that she felt at that moment.

Gentle, rough fingers stroked Imara's cheek, gliding down to cup her chin. With equal tenderness, Lorn guided her face until their eyes met. There wasn't anything except love in them, not even an ounce of the disgust she expected to see. "She thought I was dead, she wouldn't have been seduced otherwise, or easily."

"That's where you're wrong, Lorn. So very wrong," their attention snapped to Mallan. One look at the triumphant glee on his face, and Imara knew exactly how he was about to betray her. "You were supposedly in your grave a mere few weeks before her desire for me bloomed."

"I don't care. You manipulated my wife into it." Lorn's refusal to break snapped Mallan out of reminiscing.

"Tell me then, Lorn, how it feels to know that only a few nights ago that she begged me to take her. She panted and ground against me, her creamy thighs wrapped around me as I tasted her flesh. Our hearts thundering in synchronization as she clawed her fingers into my hair, needing to be closer." He paused a moment, rolling his head in relishing the memory.

Lorn broke, a feral scream tearing from his throat as he lunged at Mallan. This time there was no stopping him, he was lost to the rage. Before he could strike, Mallan's goblins took action. "Don't hurt them," Mallan ordered as he watched.

Doom filled Imara, she knew there was no way this would end well. All of her anger and fear gushed to the surface, unleashing a torrent of desperate tears as her own screams joined the chaos.

Two large goblins tackled Lorn to the ground, binding his hands. Imara tried to run to him, to help, but a pair of scaly hands grabbed her, wrapped her in a tight embrace. No matter how hard she struggled, how much Imara clawed and stomped, he didn't let go. All she could do was make desperate, sobbing pleas.

As the melee died down and the goblins dragged Lorn to his feet, Mallan descended upon him in his smoke, coming out of it with the dagger Samir had gifted Imara. Grabbing a handful of Lorn's hair, he touched the blade to her husband's neck, a small tendril of smoke drifted into the air on contact, the aroma of burning flesh came with it. "You are nothing! An insect easily crushed beneath my heel."

Lorn struggled against the goblins. "I'll kill you," he defied.

Mallan dug his dagger deeper into Lorn's skin, piercing the flesh just enough to release a thready rivulet of blood. He would kill him just to take what Imara loved from her. To cement her as his own without a rival. Imara's insides shrank at the thought. A world without Lorn was not one worth living in. He didn't deserve to die for loving her. Lorn deserved life, even if it meant she wasn't part of it.

Through the sobs that choked her voice, Imara did the most painful thing she could think of. She gave him up, "No! Don't kill him. Spare Lorn and I'll be yours." The words felt heavy on her tongue. Unwanted and foreign. After all, it was less than a year ago that she swore her love and devotion for Lorn before God. She was his, if only for a fleeting moment before he was taken from her.

The words had power. Mallan loosened his grip on Lorn's hair, whose head fell slack against his chest. "You would spare this wretch with your fealty, Starling?"

"I would," Imara replied with a curt nod. "Only you must swear to spare him." She shifted, moving her steady gaze from Mallan to Lorn. Lorn struggled to lift his head, his pained eyes locking onto mine. "I would do anything so that he may live." Imara would let the world burn to keep Lorn safe. Mallan gave the silent order for his goblin to release her.

"No, Imara. Don't do this," though his voice came out weakened, Lorn's plea held strength. Imara's resolution cracked, threatened to tumble to dust. She knew she couldn't obey her husband, not then. There was a time she'd have done anything he asked of her, but things were different. Imara had to make this one sacrifice. Her heart for his life. He'd have done the same for her.

A single tear slipped from her eyes as Imara ignored the crumbling will inside of her. "Yes. Spare Lorn, and I will be yours, Mallan."

Mallan's lips lifted in a victorious smirk. Eyes shining with malicious glee, he lifted his blade to his wrist and sliced through his flesh; an ecstatic, gasping laugh escaping him with the action. His blood flowed, rich and crimson, against his otherworldly paleness, as he commanded, "Swear it, and drink." He held the wound out for Imara.

Her steps echoed over the stones as Imara stepped forward. She'd never felt more sure of anything in her life, not even when she stood at the altar with Lorn to become his wife. Imara's hands clasped Mallan's arm. With one last loving look at Lorn, her husband, her forever, she mouthed her goodbye. *I love you.*

"I am yours, Mallan."

"Swear it, Starling. Swear you give yourself over to me, body and soul. You'll enter willingly into a bond to be sealed in ceremony for all time, rejecting your humanity and embracing your fae lineage. Willingly, you'll take my venom and shed your mortal life to be fae."

"I swear it." Imara's mouth clamped over the wound on Mallan's arm, allowing his iron sweet blood to wash over her tongue. She shivered as the warmth of it seeped down her throat and she felt his evil infecting her. Imara couldn't get enough of it. Tendrils of darkness snaked their way through her body, preparing her body for the transformation to come from the inside out. Imara's grief gave way to tides of anger and hate.

Imara belonged to Mallan.

To Be Continued...

PLAYLIST

No Time to Die - Billie Eilish
Dark Side - Bishop Briggs
Wicked Game - Chris Isaak
Always Remember Us This Way - Lady Gaga
High Water - Bishop Briggs
I Hate the Way - Sofia Carson
Roads - Portishead
Dead Man's Arms - Bishop Briggs
Gloomy Sunday - Sarah Brightman
I Hate Everything About You - Three Days Grace
Is This Real - LisaHall
Infinity - Jaymes Young
Bed of Roses - Bon Jovi
Bad Dreams-Stripped - Faouzia

ACKNOWLEDGMENTS

Land of Smoke and Nightmares came to me on the road, the music playing on the radio painting a picture in my mind that had to come alive. Little did I know when I first started, the story would become a therapeutic way for me to process a loss, a way for me to find a new path without someone I once held dear. I came out stronger on the other end of it.

I would like to thank my family; my supportive husband and three children. They are among my greatest cheerleaders, along with the rest of my family and my friends. Without their encouragement my works wouldn't be the same.

To the incredible Juliann Whicker and Veronique Manfredini, thank you for your input when my head hit creative walls. And to my beta readers, as always your input was invaluable to making Imara and Mallan come to life on the page in the best way.

To my readers, thank you for your continued support.

I love you all.

About the Author

Dawn J. Braithwaite is an author from the glorious Pacific Northwest, relishing in the rain and weirdness found there in abundance. A mild mannered geek with a dark sense of humor, Dawn thrives on nerd and pop culture, and the written word. She lives with her three children, husband, and small menagerie of furry and scaled animals.

"I am too small to contain the worlds within me."
Dawn J. Braithwaite

ALSO BY DAWN J BRAITHWAITE

Of Secrets and Crowns

Like the Moon: A Portal Worlds Novel

Stones of Blood